Penguin Books
A Damsel in Distress

Pelham Grenville Wodehou[illegible]
the son of a civil servant, and educated [illegible]
spent a brief period working for the Hong Kong an[illegible]
Bank before abandoning finance for writing, earning a living [illegible]
journalism and selling stories to magazines.

An enormously popular and prolific writer, he produced about a hundred books. Probably best known for Jeeves, the ever resourceful 'gentleman's personal gentleman', and the good-hearted young blunderer Bertie Wooster, Wodehouse created many other comic figures, notably Lord Emsworth, the Hon. Galahad Threepwood, Psmith and the numerous members of the Drones Club. He was part-author and writer of fifteen straight plays and of 250 lyrics for some thirty musical comedies. *The Times* hailed him as a 'comic genius recognized in his lifetime as a classic and an old master of farce'.

P. G. Wodehouse said, 'I believe there are two ways of writing novels. One is mine, making a sort of musical comedy without music and ignoring real life altogether; the other is going right deep down into life and not caring a damn.'

Wodehouse married in 1914 and took American citizenship in 1955. He was created a Knight of the British Empire in the 1975 New Year's Honours List. In a BBC interview he said that he had no ambitions left now that he had been knighted and there was a waxwork of him in Madame Tussaud's. He died on St Valentine's Day, 1975, at the age of ninety-three.

P. G. Wodehouse published and forthcoming in Penguin

Jeeves and Wooster
Aunts Aren't Gentlemen
Carry on, Jeeves
Code of the Woosters
The Inimitable Jeeves
Jeeves and the Feudal Spirit
Jeeves in the Offing
Joy in the Morning
The Mating Season
Much Obliged, Jeeves
Right Ho, Jeeves
Ring for Jeeves
Stiff Upper Lip, Jeeves
Thank you, Jeeves
Very Good, Jeeves

and the omnibus
Jeeves and Wooster

Life at Blandings
Blandings Castle
Full Moon
Galahad at Blandings
Heavy Weather
Lord Emsworth Acts for the Best
Lord Emsworth and Others
A Pelican at Blandings
Pigs Have Wings
Service with a Smile
Something Fresh
Summer Lightning
Sunset at Blandings
Uncle Dynamite
Uncle Fred in the Springtime

and the omnibuses
Imperial Blandings
Life at Blandings
Uncle Fred

On Golf
The Clicking of Cuthbert
The Heart of a Goof

Mike and Psmith
Leave it to Psmith
Mike and Psmith
Psmith in the City
Psmith, Journalist

and the omnibus
The World of Psmith

Also
The Adventures of Sally
Bachelors Anonymous
Big Money
Cocktail Time
A Damsel in Distress
Do Butlers Burgle Banks?
Eggs, Beans and Crumpets
French Leave
The Girl in Blue
Hot Water
If I Were You
The Indiscretions of Archie
Laughing Gas
The Luck of the Bodkins
The Man with Two Left Feet
Money for Nothing
Money in the Bank
Pearls, Girls and Monty Bodkin
Piccadilly Jim
The Pothunters and Other Stories
Sam the Sudden
The Small Bachelor
Summer Moonshine
Ukridge
Uneasy Money
Young Men in Spats

and the omnibus
The World of Mr Mulliner

P. G. Wodehouse

A Damsel in Distress

P.G. Wodehouse

A Damsel in Distress

PENGUIN BOOKS

PENGUIN BOOKS

Published by the Penguin Group
Penguin Books Ltd, 80 Strand, London WC2R 0RL, England
Penguin Putnam Inc., 375 Hudson Street, New York, New York 10014, USA
Penguin Books Australia Ltd, Ringwood, Victoria, Australia
Penguin Books Canada Ltd, 10 Alcorn Avenue, Toronto, Ontario, Canada M4V 3B2
Penguin Books India (P) Ltd, 11 Community Centre, Panchsheel Park, New Delhi – 110 017, India
Penguin Books (NZ) Ltd, Cnr Rosedale and Airborne Roads, Albany, Auckland, New Zealand
Penguin Books (South Africa) (Pty) Ltd, 24 Sturdee Avenue, Rosebank 2196 South Africa

Penguin Books Ltd, Registered Offices: 80 Strand, London WC2R 0RL, England

www.penguin.com

First published by Herbert Jenkins 1919
Published in Penguin Books 1961
16

Set in Trump Mediaeval
Phototypeset by Intype London Ltd
Printed in England by Clays Ltd, St Ives plc

I

Inasmuch as the scene of this story is that historic pile Belpher Castle, in the county of Hampshire, it would be an agreeable task to open it with a leisurely description of the place, followed by some notes on the history of the Earls of Marshmoreton, who have owned it since the fifteenth century. Unfortunately, in these days of rush and hurry, a novelist works at a disadvantage. He must leap into the middle of his tale with as little delay as he would employ in boarding a moving tramcar. He must get off the mark with the smooth swiftness of a jack-rabbit surprised while lunching. Otherwise, people throw him aside and go out to picture palaces.

I may briefly remark that the present Lord Marshmoreton is a widower of some forty-eight years: that he has two children – a son, Percy Wilbraham Marsh, Lord Belpher, who is on the brink of his twenty-first birthday, and a daughter, Lady Patricia Maud Marsh, who is just twenty: that the châtelaine of the castle is Lady Caroline Byng, Lord Marshmoreton's sister, who married the very wealthy colliery owner, Clifford Byng, a few years before his death (which unkind people say she hastened): and that she has a stepson, Reginald. Give me time to mention these few facts and I am done. On the glorious past of the Marshmoretons I will not even touch.

Luckily, the loss to literature is not irreparable. Lord Marshmoreton himself is engaged upon a history of the family, which will doubtless be on every bookshelf as soon as his lordship gets it finished. And, as for the castle and its surroundings, including the model dairy and the amber drawing-room, you may see them for yourself any Thursday, when Belpher is thrown open to the public on payment of a fee of one shilling a head. The money is collected by Keggs the butler, and goes to a worthy local charity. At least, that is the idea. But the voice of calumny is never silent, and there exists a school of thought, headed by Albert, the page-boy, which holds that Keggs sticks to these shillings like glue, and adds them to his already considerable savings in the Farmers' and Merchants' Bank, on the left side of the High Street in Belpher village, next door to the Oddfellows' Hall.

With regard to this, one can only say that Keggs looks far too much like a particularly saintly bishop to indulge in any such practices. On the other hand, Albert knows Keggs. We must leave the matter open.

Of course, appearances are deceptive. Anyone, for instance, who had been standing outside the front entrance of the castle at eleven o'clock on a certain June morning might easily have made a mistake. Such a person would probably have jumped to the conclusion that the middle-aged lady of a determined cast of countenance who was standing near the rose-garden, talking to the gardener and watching the young couple strolling on the terrace below, was the mother of the pretty girl, and that she was smiling because the latter had recently become engaged to the tall, pleasant-faced youth at her side.

Sherlock Holmes himself might have been misled. One can hear him explaining the thing to Watson in one of those lightning flashes of inductive reasoning of his. 'It is the only explanation, my dear Watson. If the lady were merely complimenting the gardener on his rose-garden, and if her smile were merely caused by the excellent appearance of that rose-garden, there would be an answering smile on the face of the gardener. But, as you see, he looks morose and gloomy.'

As a matter of fact, the gardener – that is to say, the

stocky, brown-faced man in shirt sleeves and corduroy trousers who was frowning into a can of whale-oil solution – was the Earl of Marshmoreton, and there were two reasons for his gloom. He hated to be interrupted while working, and, furthermore, Lady Caroline Byng always got on his nerves, and never more so than when, as now, she speculated on the possibility of a romance between her stepson Reggie and his lordship's daughter Maud.

Only his intimates would have recognized in this curious corduroy-trousered figure the seventh Earl of Marshmoreton. The Lord Marshmoreton who made intermittent appearances in London, who lunched among bishops at the Athenaeum Club without exciting remark, was a correctly dressed gentleman whom no one would have suspected of covering his sturdy legs in anything but the finest cloth. But if you will glance at your copy of *Who's Who*, and turn up the 'M's', you will find in the space allotted to the Earl the words '*Hobby – Gardening*'. To which, in a burst of modest pride, his lordship has added 'Awarded first prize for Hybrid Teas, Temple Flower Show, 1911'. The words tell their own story.

Lord Marshmoreton was the most enthusiastic amateur gardener in a land of enthusiastic amateur gardeners. He lived for his garden. The love which other men expend on their nearest and dearest Lord Marshmoreton lavished on seeds, roses, and loamy soil. The hatred which some of his order feel for Socialists and Demagogues Lord Marshmoreton kept for rose-slugs, rose-beetles, and the small, yellowish-white insect which is so depraved and sinister a character that it goes through life with an alias – being sometimes called a rose-hopper and sometimes a thrips. A simple soul, Lord Marshmoreton – mild and pleasant. Yet put him among the thrips, and he became a dealer-out of death and slaughter, a destroyer in the class of Attila the Hun and Genghis Khan. Thrips feed on the underside of rose leaves, sucking their juice and causing them to turn yellow; and Lord Marshmoreton's views on these things were so rigid that he would have poured whale-oil solution on his grandmother if he had found her on the underside of one of his rose leaves sucking its juice.

The only time in the day when he ceased to be the horny-handed toiler and became the aristocrat was in the evening after dinner, when, egged on by Lady Caroline, who gave him no rest in the matter – he would retire to his private study and work on his History of the Family, assisted by his able secretary, Alice Faraday. His progress on that massive work was, however, slow. Ten hours in the open air made a man drowsy, and too often Lord Marshmoreton would fall asleep in mid-sentence to the annoyance of Miss Faraday, who was a conscientious girl and liked to earn her salary.

The couple on the terrace had turned. Reggie Byng's face, as he bent over Maud, was earnest and animated, and even from a distance it was possible to see how the girl's eyes lit up at what he was saying. She was hanging on his words. Lady Caroline's smile became more and more benevolent.

'They make a charming pair,' she murmured. 'I wonder what dear Reggie is saying. Perhaps at this very moment—'

She broke off with a sigh of content. She had had her troubles over this affair. Dear Reggie, usually so plastic in her hands, had displayed an unaccountable reluctance to offer his agreeable self to Maud – in spite of the fact that never, not even on the public platform which she adorned so well, had his stepmother reasoned more clearly than she did when pointing out to him the advantages of the match. It was not that Reggie disliked Maud. He admitted that she was a 'topper', on several occasions going so far as to describe her as ' absolutely priceless'. But he seemed reluctant to ask her to marry him. How could Lady Caroline know that Reggie's entire world – or such of it as was not occupied by racing cars and golf – was filled by Alice Faraday? Reggie had never told her. He had not even told Miss Faraday.

'Perhaps at this very moment,' went on Lady Caroline, 'the dear boy is proposing to her.'

Lord Marshmoreton grunted, and continued to peer with a questioning eye in the awesome brew which he had prepared for the thrips.

'One thing is very satisfactory,' said Lady Caroline. 'I mean that Maud seems entirely to have got over that ridiculous infatuation of hers for that man she met in Wales last summer. She could not be so cheerful if she were still brooding on that. I hope you will admit now, John, that I was right in keeping her practically a prisoner here and never allowing her a chance of meeting the man again either by accident or design. They say absence makes the heart grow fonder. Stuff! A girl of Maud's age falls in and out of love half a dozen times a year. I feel sure she has almost forgotten the man by now.'

'Eh?' said Lord Marshmoreton. His mind had been far away, dealing with green-flies.

'I was speaking about that man Maud met when she was staying with Brenda in Wales.'

'Oh, yes!'

'Oh, yes!' echoed Lady Caroline annoyed. 'Is that the only comment you can find to make? Your only daughter becomes infatuated with a perfect stranger – a man we have never seen – of whom we know nothing, not even his name – nothing except that he is an American and hasn't a penny – Maud admitted that. And all you say is "Oh, yes"!'

'But it's all over now, isn't it? I understood the dashed affair was all over.'

'We hope so. But I should feel safer if Maud were engaged to Reggie. I do think you might take the trouble to speak to Maud.'

'Speak to her? I do speak to her.' Lord Marshmoreton's brain moved slowly when he was preoccupied with his roses. 'We're on excellent terms.'

Lady Caroline frowned impatiently. Hers was an alert, vigorous mind, bright and strong like a steel trap, and her brother's vagueness and growing habit of inattention irritated her.

'I mean to speak to her about becoming engaged to Reggie. You are her father. Surely you can at least try to persuade her.'

'Can't coerce a girl.'

'I never suggested that you should coerce her, as you put it. I merely meant that you could point out to her, as a father, where her duty and happiness lie.'

'Drink this!' cried his lordship with sudden fury, spraying his can over the nearest bush, and addressing his remark to the invisible thrips. He had forgotten Lady Caroline completely. 'Don't stint yourselves! There's lots more!'

A girl came down the steps of the castle and made her way towards them. She was a good-looking girl, with an air of quiet efficiency about her. Her eyes were grey and whimsical. Her head was uncovered, and the breeze stirred her dark hair. She made a graceful picture in the morning sunshine, and Reggie Byng, sighting her from the terrace, wobbled in his tracks, turned pink, and lost the thread of his remarks.

The sudden appearance of Alice Faraday always affected him like that.

'I have copied out the notes you made last night, Lord Marshmoreton. I typed two copies.'

Alice Faraday spoke in a quiet, respectful, yet subtly authoritative voice. She was a girl of great character. Previous employers of her services as secretary had found her a jewel. To Lord Marshmoreton she was rapidly becoming a perfect incubus. Their views on the relative importance of gardening and family histories did not coincide. To him the history of the Marshmoreton family was the occupation of the idle hour: she seemed to think that he ought to regard it as a life-work. She was always coming and digging him out of the garden and dragging him back to what should have been a purely after-dinner task. It was Lord Marshmoreton's habit, when he awoke after one of his naps too late to resume work, to throw out some vague promise of 'attending to it tomorrow'; but, he reflected bitterly, the girl ought to have the tact and sense to understand that this was only polite persiflage, and not to be taken literally.

'They are very rough,' continued Alice, addressing her conversation to the seat of his lordship's corduroy trousers. Lord Marshmoreton always assumed a stooping attitude when he saw Miss Faraday approaching with papers in her hand; for he laboured under a pathetic delusion, of which no amount of failures could rid him, that if she did not see his face she would withdraw. 'You remember last night you promised you would attend to them this morning.' She paused long enough to receive a non-committal grunt by way of answer. 'Of course, if you're busy – ' she said placidly, with a half-glance at Lady Caroline. That masterful woman could always be counted on as an ally in these little encounters.

'Nothing of the kind!' said Lady Caroline crisply. She was still ruffled by the lack of attention which her recent utterances had received, and welcomed the chance of administering discipline. 'Get up at once, John, and go in and work.'

'I am working,' pleaded Lord Marshmoreton.

Despite his forty-eight years his sister Caroline still had the power at times to make him feel like a small boy. She had been a great martinet in the days of their mutual nursery.

'The Family History is more important than grubbing about in the dirt. I cannot understand why you do not leave this sort of thing to MacPherson. Why you should pay him liberal wages and then do his work for him, I cannot see. You know the publishers are waiting for the History. Go and attend to these notes at once.'

'You promised you would attend to them this morning, Lord Marshmoreton,' said Alice invitingly.

Lord Marshmoreton clung to his can of whale-oil solution with the clutch of a drowning man. None knew better than he that these interviews, especially when Caroline was present to lend the weight of her dominating personality, always ended in the same way.

'Yes, yes, yes!' he said. 'Tonight, perhaps. After dinner, eh? Yes, after dinner. That will be capital.'

'I think you ought to attend to them this morning,' said Alice, gently persistent. It really perturbed this girl to feel that she was not doing work enough to merit her generous salary. And on the subject of the history of the Marshmoreton family she was an enthusiast. It had a glamour for her.

Lord Marshmoreton's fingers relaxed their hold. Throughout the rose-garden hundreds of spared thrips went on with their morning meal, unwitting of doom averted.

'Oh, all right, all right, all right! Come into the library.'

'Very well, Lord Marshmoreton.' Miss Faraday turned to Lady Caroline. 'I have been looking up the trains, Lady Caroline. The best is the twelve-fifteen. It has a dining-car, and stops at Belpher if signalled.'

'Are you going away, Caroline?' inquired Lord Marshmoreton hopefully.

'I am giving a short talk to the Social Progress League at Lewisham. I shall return tomorrow.'

'Oh!' said Marshmoreton, hope fading from his voice.

'Thank you, Miss Faraday,' said Lady Caroline. 'The twelve-fifteen.'

'The motor will be round at a quarter to twelve.'

'Thank you. Oh, by the way, Miss Faraday, will you

call to Reggie as you pass, and tell him I wish to speak to him.'

Maud had left Reggie by the time Alice Faraday reached him, and that ardent youth was sitting on a stone seat, smoking a cigarette and entertaining himself with meditations in which thoughts of Alice competed for precedence with graver reflections connected with the subject of the correct stance for his approach shots. Reggie's was a troubled spirit these days. He was in love, and he had developed a bad slice with his mid-iron. He was practically a soul in torment.

'Lady Caroline asked me to tell you that she wishes to speak to you, Mr Byng.'

Reggie leaped from his seat.

'Hullo-ullo-ullo! *There* you are! I mean to say, what?'

He was conscious, as was his custom in her presence, of a warm, prickly sensation in the small of the back. Some kind of elephantiasis seemed to have attacked his hands and feet, swelling them to enormous proportions. He wished profoundly that he could get rid of his habit of yelping with nervous laughter whenever he encountered the girl of his dreams. It was calculated to give her a wrong impression of a chap – make her think him a fearful chump and what not!

'Lady Caroline is leaving by the twelve-fifteen.'

'That's good! What I mean to say is – oh, she is, is she? I see what you mean.' The absolute necessity of saying something at least moderately coherent gripped him. He rallied his forces. 'You wouldn't care to come for a stroll, after I've seen the mater, or a row on the lake, or any rot like that, would you?'

'Thank you very much, but I must go in and help Lord Marshmoreton with his book.'

'What a rotten – I mean, what a dam' shame!'

The pity of it tore at Reggie's heart strings. He burned with generous wrath against Lord Marshmoreton, that modern Simon Legree, who used his capitalistic power to make a slave of this girl and keep her toiling indoors when all the world was sunshine.

'Shall I go and ask him if you can't put it off till after dinner?'

'Oh, no, thanks very much. I'm sure Lord Marshmoreton wouldn't dream of it.'

She passed on with a pleasant smile. When he had recovered from the effect of this Reggie proceeded slowly to the upper level to meet his stepmother.

'Hullo, mater. Pretty fit and so forth? What did you want to see me about?'

'Well, Reggie, what is the news?'

'Eh? What? News? Didn't you get hold of a paper at breakfast? Nothing much in it. Tam Duggan beat Alec Fraser three up and two to play at Prestwick. I didn't notice anything else much. There's a new musical comedy at the Regal. Opened last night, and seems to be just like mother makes. The *Morning Post* gave it a topping notice. I must trickle up to town and see it some time this week.'

Lady Caroline frowned. This slowness in the uptake, coming so soon after her brother's inattention, displeased her.

'No, no, no. I mean you and Maud have been talking to each other for quite a long time, and she seemed very interested in what you were saying. I hoped you might have some good news for me.'

Reggie's face brightened. He caught her drift.

'Oh, ah, yes, I see what you mean. No, there wasn't anything of that sort or shape or order.'

'What were you saying to her, then, that interested her so much?'

'I was explaining how I landed dead on the pin with my spoon out of a sand-trap at the eleventh hole yesterday. It certainly was a pretty ripe shot, considering. I'd sliced into this bally bunker, don't you know; I simply can't keep 'em straight with the iron nowadays – and there the pill was, grinning up at me from the sand. Of course, strictly speaking, I ought to have used a niblick, but – '

'Do you mean to say, Reggie, that, with such an excellent opportunity, you did *not* ask Maud to marry you?'

'I see what you mean. Well, as a matter of absolute fact, I, as it were, didn't.'

Lady Caroline uttered a wordless sound.

'By the way, mater,' said Reggie, 'I forgot to tell you about that. It's all off.'

'What!'

'Absolutely. You see, it appears there's a chappie unknown for whom Maud has an absolute pash. It seems she met this sportsman up in Wales last summer. She was caught in the rain, and he happened to be passing and rallied round with his raincoat, and one thing led to another. Always raining in Wales, what! Good fishing, though, here and there. Well, what I mean is, this cove was so deucedly civil, and all that, that now she won't look at anybody else. He's the blue-eyed boy, and everybody else is an also-ran, with about as much chance as a blind man with one arm trying to get out of a bunker with a tooth-pick.'

'What perfect nonsense! I know all about that affair. It was just a passing fancy that never meant anything. Maud has got over that long ago.'

'She didn't seem to think so.'

'Now, Reggie,' said Lady Caroline tensely, 'please listen to me. You know that the castle will be full of people in a day or two for Percy's coming-of-age, and this next few days may be your last chance of having a real, long, private talk with Maud. I shall be seriously annoyed if you neglect this opportunity. There is no excuse for the way you are behaving. Maud is a charming girl – '

'Oh, absolutely! One of the best.'

'Very well, then!'

'But, mater, what I mean to say is – '

'I don't want any more temporizing, Reggie!'

'No, no! Absolutely not!' said Reggie dutifully, wishing he knew what the word meant, and wishing also that life had not become so frightfully complex.

'Now, this afternoon, why should you not take Maud for a long ride in your car?'

Reggie grew more cheerful. At least he had an answer for that.

'Can't be done, I'm afraid. I've got to motor into town to meet Percy. He's arriving from Oxford this morning. I promised to meet him in town and tool him back in the car.'

'I see. Well, then, why couldn't you – ?'

'I say, mater, dear old soul,' said Reggie hastily, 'I think you'd better tear yourself away and what not. If you're catching the twelve-fifteen, you ought to be staggering round to see you haven't forgotten anything. There's the car coming round now.'

'I wish now I had decided to go by a later train.'

'No, no, mustn't miss the twelve-fifteen. Good, fruity train. Everybody speaks well of it. Well, see you anon, mater. I think you'd better run like a hare.'

'You will remember what I said?'

'Oh, absolutely!'

'Good-bye, then. I shall be back tomorrow.'

Reggie returned slowly to his stone seat. He breathed a little heavily as he felt for his cigarette case. He felt like a hunted fawn.

Maud came out of the house as the car disappeared down the long avenue of elms. She crossed the terrace to where Reggie sat brooding on life and its problems.

'Reggie!'

Reggie turned.

'Hullo, Maud, dear old thing. Take a seat.'

Maud sat down beside him. There was a flush on her

pretty face, and when she spoke her voice quivered with suppressed excitement.

'Reggie,' she said, laying a small hand on his arm. 'We're friends, aren't we?'

Reggie patted her back paternally. There were few people he liked better than Maud.

'Always have been since the dear old days of childhood, what!'

'I can trust you, can't I?'

'Absolutely!'

'There's something I want you to do for me, Reggie. You'll have to keep it a dead secret of course.'

'The strong, silent man. That's me. What is it?'

'You're driving into town in your car this afternoon, aren't you, to meet Percy?'

'That was the idea.'

'Could you go this morning instead – and take me?'

'Of course.'

Maud shook her head.

'You don't know what you are letting yourself in for, Reggie, or I'm sure you wouldn't agree so lightly. I'm not allowed to leave the castle, you know, because of what I was telling you about.'

'The chappie?'

'Yes. So there would be terrible scenes if anybody found out.'

'Never mind, dear old soul. I'll risk it. None shall learn your secret from these lips.'

'You're a darling, Reggie.'

'But what's the idea? Why do you want to go today particularly?'

Maud looked over her shoulder.

'Because – ' She lowered her voice, though there was no one near. 'Because *he* is back in London! He's a sort of secretary, you know, Reggie, to his uncle, and I saw in the paper this morning that the uncle returned yesterday after a long voyage in his yacht. So – he must have come back, too. He has to go everywhere his uncle goes.'

'And everywhere the uncle went, the chappie was sure to go!' murmured Reggie. 'Sorry. Didn't mean to interrupt.'

'I *must* see him. I haven't seen him since last summer – nearly a whole year! And he hasn't written to me, and I haven't dared to write to him, for fear of the letter going wrong. So, you see, I must go. Today's my only chance. Aunt Caroline has gone away. Father will be busy in the garden, and won't notice whether I'm here or not. And, besides, tomorrow it will be too late, because Percy will be here. He was more furious about the thing than anyone.'

'Rather the proud aristocrat, Percy,' agreed Reggie. 'I understand absolutely. Tell me just what you want me to do.'

'I want you to pick me up in the car about half a mile down the road. You can drop me somewhere in Piccadilly. That will be near enough to where I want to go. But the most important thing is about Percy. You must persuade him to stay and dine in town and come back here after dinner. Then I shall be able to get back by an afternoon train, and no one will know I've been gone.'

'That's simple enough, what? Consider it done. When do you want to start?'

'At once.'

'I'll toddle round to the garage and fetch the car.' Reggie chuckled amusedly. 'Rum thing! The mater's just been telling me I ought to take you for a drive.'

'You *are* a darling, Reggie, really!'

Reggie gave her back another paternal pat.

'I know what it means to be in love, dear old soul. I say, Maud, old thing, do you find love puts you off your stroke? What I mean is, does it make you slice your approach-shots?'

Maud laughed.

'No. It hasn't had any effect on my game so far. I went round in eighty-six the other day.'

Reggie sighed enviously.

'Women are wonderful!' he said. 'Well, I'll be legging it and fetching the car. When you're ready, stroll along down the road and wait for me.'

When he had gone Maud pulled a small newspaper clipping from her pocket. She had extracted it from yesterday's copy of the *Morning Post's* society column. It contained only a few words:

> Mr Wilbur Raymond has returned to his residence at No 11a Belgrave Square from a prolonged voyage in his yatch, the *Siren*.

Maud did not know Mr Wilbur Raymond, and yet that paragraph had sent the blood tingling through every vein in her body. For as she had indicated to Reggie, when the Wilbur Raymonds of this world return to their town residences, they bring with them their nephew and secretary. Geoffrey Raymond. And Geoffrey Raymond was the man Maud had loved ever since the day when she had met him in Wales.

2

The sun that had shone so brightly on Belpher Castle at noon, when Maud and Reggie Byng set out on their journey, shone on the West-End of London with equal pleasantness at two o'clock. In Little Gooch Street all the children of all the small shopkeepers who support life in that backwater by selling each other vegetables and singing canaries were out and about playing curious games of their own invention. Cats washed themselves on doorsteps, preparatory to looking in for lunch at one of the numerous garbage cans which dotted the sidewalk. Waiters peered austerely from the windows of the two Italian restaurants which carry on the Lucretia Borgia tradition by means of one shilling and sixpenny table d'hôte luncheons. The proprietor of the grocery store on the corner was bidding a silent farewell to a tomato which even he, though a dauntless optimist, had been compelled to recognize as having outlived its utility. On all these things the sun shone with a genial smile. Round the corner, in Shaftesbury Avenue, an east wind was doing its best to pierce the hardened hides of the citizenry; but it did not penetrate into Little Gooch Street, which, facing south and being narrow and sheltered, was enabled practically to bask.

Mac, the stout guardian of the stage door of the Regal Theatre, whose gilded front entrance is on the Avenue, emerged from the little glass case in which the management kept him, and came out to observe life and its phenomena with an indulgent eye. Mac was feeling happy this morning. His job was a permanent one, not influenced by the success or failure of the productions which followed one another at the theatre throughout the year; but he felt, nevertheless, a sort of proprietary interest in these ventures, and was pleased when they secured the approval of the public. Last night's opening, a musical piece by an American author and composer, had undoubtedly made a big hit, and Mac was glad, because he liked what he had seen of the company, and, in the brief time in which he had known him, had come to entertain a warm regard for George Bevan, the composer, who had travelled over from New York to help with the London production.

George Bevan turned the corner now, walking slowly, and, it seemed to Mac, gloomily towards the stage door. He was a young man of about twenty-seven, tall and well-knit, with an agreeable, clean-cut face, of which a pair of good and honest eyes were the most noticeable feature. His sensitive mouth was drawn down a little at the corners, and he looked tired.

'Morning, Mac.'

'Good morning, sir.'

'Anything for me?'

'Yes, sir. Some telegrams. I'll get 'em. Oh, I'll *get* 'em,' said Mac, as if reassuring some doubting friend and supporter as to his ability to carry through a labour of Hercules.

He disappeared into his glass case. George Bevan remained outside in the street surveying the frisking children with a sombre glance. They seemed to him very noisy, very dirty, and very young. Disgustingly young. Theirs was joyous, exuberant youth which made a fellow feel at least sixty. Something was wrong with George today, for normally he was fond of children. Indeed, normally he was fond of most things. He was a good-natured and cheerful young man, who liked life and the great majority of those who lived it contemporaneously with himself. He had no enemies and many friends.

But today he had noticed from the moment he had got

out of bed that something was amiss with the world. Either he was in the grip of some divine discontent due to the highly developed condition of his soul, or else he had a grouch. One of the two. Or it might have been the reaction from the emotions of the previous night. On the morning after an opening your sensitive artist is always apt to feel as if he had been dried over a barrel.

Besides, last night there had been a supper party after the performance at the flat which the comedian of the troupe had rented in Jermyn Street, a forced, rowdy supper party where a number of tired people with over-strained nerves had seemed to feel it a duty to be artificially vivacious. It had lasted till four o'clock when the morning papers with the notices arrived, and George had not got to bed till four-thirty. These things colour the mental outlook.

Mac reappeared.

'Here you are, sir.'

'Thanks.'

George put the telegrams in his pocket. A cat, on its way back from lunch, paused beside him in order to use his leg as a serviette. George tickled it under the ear abstractedly. He was always courteous to cats, but today he went through the movements perfunctorily and without enthusiasm.

The cat moved on. Mac became conversational.

'They tell me the piece was a hit last night, sir.'

'It seemed to go very well.'

'My Missus saw it from the gallery, and all the first-nighters was speaking very 'ighly of it. There's a regular click, you know, sir, over here in London, that goes to all the first nights in the gallery. 'Ighly critical they are always. Specially if it's an American piece like this one. If they don't like it, they precious soon let you know. My Missus ses they was all speakin' very 'ighly of it. My missus says she ain't seen a livelier show for a long time, and she's a great theatregoer. My missus says they was all specially pleased with the music.'

'That's good.'

'The *Morning Leader* give it a fine write-up. How was the rest of the papers?'

'Splendid, all of them. I haven't seen the evening papers yet. I came out to get them.'

Mac looked down the street.

'There'll be a rehearsal this afternoon, I suppose, sir? Here's Miss Dore coming along.'

George followed his glance. A tall girl in a tailor-made suit of blue was coming towards them. Even at a distance one caught the genial personality of the new arrival. It seemed to go before her like a heartening breeze. She picked her way carefully through the children crawling on the sidewalk. She stopped for a moment and said something to one of them. The child grinned. Even the proprietor of the grocery store appeared to brighten up at the sight of her, as at the sight of some old friend.

'How's business, Bill?' she called to him as she passed the spot where he stood brooding on the mortality of tomatoes. And, though he replied 'Rotten', a faint, grim smile did nevertheless flicker across his tragic mask.

Billie Dore, who was one of the chorus of George Bevan's musical comedy, had an attractive face, a mouth that laughed readily, rather bright golden hair (which, she was fond of insisting with perfect truth, was genuine though appearances were against it), and steady blue eyes. The latter were frequently employed by her in quelling admirers who were encouraged by the former to become too ardent. Billie's views on the opposite sex who forgot themselves were as rigid as those of Lord Marshmoreton concerning thrips. She liked men, and she would signify this liking in a practical manner by lunching and dining with them, but she was entirely self-supporting, and when men overlooked that fact she reminded them of it in no uncertain voice; for she was a girl of ready speech and direct.

''Morning, George. 'Morning, Mac. Any mail?'

'I'll see, miss.'

'How did your better four-fifths like the show, Mac?'

'I was just telling Mr Bevan, miss, that the missus said she 'adn't seen a livelier show for a long time.'

'Fine. I knew I'd be a hit. Well, George, how's the boy this bright afternoon?'

'Limp and pessimistic.'

'That comes of sitting up till four in the morning with festive hams.'

'You were up as late as I was, and you look like Little Eva after a night of sweet, childish slumber.'

'Yes, but I drank ginger ale, and didn't smoke eighteen cigars. And yet, I don't know. I think I must be getting old, George. All-night parties seem to have lost their charm. I was ready to quit at one o'clock, but it didn't seem matey. I think I'll marry a farmer and settle down.'

George was amazed. He had not expected to find his present view of life shared in this quarter.

'I was just thinking myself,' he said, feeling not for the first time how different Billie was from the majority of those with whom his profession brought him in contact, 'how flat it all was. The show business I mean, and these darned first nights, and the party after the show which you can't sidestep. Something tells me I'm about through.'

Billie Dore nodded.

'Anybody with any sense is always about through with the show business. I know I am. If you think I'm wedded to my art, let me tell you I'm going to get a divorce the first chance that comes along. It's funny about the show business. The way one drifts into it and sticks, I mean. Take me, for example. Nature had it all doped out for me to be the Belle of Hicks Corners. What I ought to have done was to buy a gingham bonnet and milk cows. But

I would come to the great city and help brighten up the tired business man.'

'I didn't know you were fond of the country, Billie.'

'Me? I wrote the words and music. Didn't you know I was a country kid? My dad ran a Bide a Wee Home for flowers, and I used to know them all by their middle names. He was a nursery gardener out in Indiana. I tell you, when I see a rose nowadays, I shake its hand and say: "Well, well, Cyril, how's everything with *you*? And how are Joe and Jack and Jimmy and all the rest of the boys at home?" Do you know how I used to put in my time the first few nights I was over here in London? I used to hang around Covent Garden with my head back, sniffing. The boys that mess about with the flowers there used to stub their toes on me so often that they got to look on me as part of the scenery.'

'That's where we ought to have been last night.'

'We'd have had a better time. Say, George, did you see the awful mistake on Nature's part that Babe Sinclair showed up with towards the middle of the proceedings? You must have noticed him, because he took up more room than any one man was entitled to. His name was Spenser Gray.'

George recalled having been introduced to a fat man of his own age who answered to that name.

'It's a darned shame,' said Billie indignantly. 'Babe is only a kid. This is the first show she's been in. And I happen to know there's an awfully nice boy over in New York crazy to marry her. And I'm certain this gink is giving her a raw deal. He tried to get hold of me about a week ago, but I turned him down hard; and I suppose he thinks Babe is easier. And it's no good talking to her; she thinks he's wonderful. That's another kick I have against the show business. It seems to make girls such darned chumps. Well, I wonder how much longer Mr Arbuckle is going to be retrieving my mail. What ho, within there Fatty!'

Mac came out, apologetic, carrying letters.

'Sorry, miss. By an oversight I put you among the G's.'

'All's well that ends well. "Put me among the G's." There's a good title for a song for you, George. Excuse me while I grapple with the correspondence. I'll bet half of these are mash notes. I got three between the first and second acts last night. Why the nobility and gentry of this burg should think that I'm their affinity just because I've got golden hair – which is perfectly genuine, Mac; I can show you the pedigree – and because I earn an honest living singing off the key, is more than I can understand.'

Mac leaned his massive shoulders comfortably against the building, and resumed his chat.

'I expect you're feeling very 'appy today, sir?'

George pondered. He was certainly feeling better since he had seen Billie Dore, but he was far from being himself.

'I ought to be, I suppose. But I'm not.'

'Ah, you're getting blarzy, sir, that's what it is. You've 'ad too much of the fat, *you* 'ave. This piece was a big 'it in America, wasn't it?'

'Yes. It ran over a year in New York, and there are three companies of it out now.'

'That's 'ow it is, you see. You've gone and got blarzy. Too big a 'elping of success, you've 'ad.' Mac wagged a head like a harvest moon. 'You aren't a married man, are you, sir?'

Billie Dore finished skimming through her mail, and crumpled the letters up into a large ball, which she handed to Mac.

'Here's something for you to read in your spare moments, Mac. Glance through them any time you have a suspicion you may be a chump, and you'll have the comfort of knowing that there are others. What were you saying about being married?'

'Mr Bevan and I was 'aving a talk about 'im being blarzy, miss.'

'Are you blarzy, George?'

'So Mac says.'

'And *why* is he blarzy, miss?' demanded Mac rhetorically.

'Don't ask *me*,' said Billie. 'It's not my fault.'

'It's because, as I was saying, 'e's 'ad too big a 'elping of success, and because 'e ain't a married man. You did say you wasn't a married man, didn't you, sir?'

'I didn't. But I'm not.'

'That's 'ow it is, you see. You pretty soon gets sick of pulling off good things, if you ain't got nobody to pat you on the back for doing of it. Why, when I was single, if I got 'old of a sure thing for the three o'clock race and picked up a couple of quid, the thrill of it didn't seem to linger somehow. But now, if some of the gentlemen that come 'ere put me on to something safe and I make a bit, 'arf the fascination of it is taking the stuff 'ome and rolling it on to the kitchen table and 'aving 'er pat me on the back.'

'How about when you lose?'

'I don't tell 'er,' said Mac simply.

'You seem to understand the art of being happy, Mac.'

'It ain't an art, sir. It's just gettin' 'old of the right little woman, and 'aving a nice little 'ome of your own to go back to at night.'

'Mac,' said Billie admiringly, 'you talk like a Tin Pan Alley song hit, except that you've left out the scent of honeysuckle and Old Mister Moon climbing up over the trees. Well, you're quite right. I'm all for the simple and domestic myself. If I could find the right man, and he didn't see me coming and duck, I'd become one of the Mendelssohn's March Daughters right away. Are you going, George? There's a rehearsal at two-thirty for cuts.'

'I want to get the evening papers and send off a cable or two. See you later.'

'We shall meet at Philippi.'

Mac eyed George's retreating back till he had turned the corner.

'A nice pleasant gentleman, Mr Bevan,' he said. 'Too bad 'e's got the pip the way 'e 'as, just after 'avin' a big success like this 'ere. Comes of bein' a artist, I suppose.'

Miss Dore dived into her vanity case and produced a puff with which she proceeded to powder her nose.

'All composers are nuts, Mac. I was in a show once where the manager was panning the composer because there wasn't a number in the score that had a tune to it. The poor geek admitted they weren't very tuney, but said the thing about his music was that it had such a wonderful aroma. They all get that way. The jazz seems to go to their heads. George is all right, though, and don't let anyone tell you different.'

'Have you known him long, miss?'

'About five years. I was a stenographer in the house that published his songs when I first met him. And there's another thing you've got to hand it to George for. He hasn't let success give him a swelled head. The money that boy makes is sinful, Mac. He wears thousand dollar bills next to his skin winter and summer. But he's just the same as he was when I first knew him, when he was just hanging around Broadway, looking out for a chance to be allowed to slip a couple of interpolated numbers into any old show that came along. Yes. Put it in your diary, Mac, and write it on your cuff, George Bevan's all right. He's an ace.'

Unconscious of these eulogies, which, coming from one whose judgement he respected, might have cheered him up, George wandered down Shaftesbury Avenue feeling more depressed than ever. The sun had gone in for the time being, and the east wind was frolicking round him like a playful puppy, patting him with a cold paw, nuzzling his ankles, bounding away and bounding back again, and behaving generally as east winds do when they discover a victim who has come out without his spring overcoat. It was plain to George now that the sun and the wind were a couple of confidence tricksters working together as a team. The sun had disarmed him with specious promises and an air of cheery goodfellowship, and had delivered him into the hands of the wind, which was now going through him with the swift thoroughness of the professional hold-up artist. He quickened his steps, and began to wonder if he was so sunk in senile decay as to have acquired a liver.

He discarded the theory as repellent. And yet there must be a reason for his depression. Today of all days, as Mac had pointed out, he had everything to make him happy. Popular as he was in America, this was the first piece of his to be produced in London, and there was no doubt that it was a success of unusual dimensions. And yet he felt no elation.

He reached Piccadilly and turned westwards. And then, as he passed the gates of the In and Out Club, he had a moment of clear vision and understood everything. He was depressed because he was bored, and he was bored because he was lonely. Mac, that solid thinker, had been right. The solution of the problem of life was to get hold of the right girl and have a home to go back to at night. He was mildly surprised that he had tried in any other direction for an explanation of his gloom. It was all the more inexplicable in that fully eighty per cent of the lyrics which he had set in the course of his musical comedy career had had that thought at the back of them.

George gave himself up to an orgy of sentimentality. He seemed to be alone in the world which had paired itself off into a sort of seething welter of happy couples. Taxicabs full of happy couples rolled by every minute. Passing omnibuses creaked beneath the weight of happy couples. The very policeman across the street had just grinned at a flitting shop girl, and she had smiled back at him. The only female in London who did not appear to be attached was a girl in brown who was coming along the sidewalk at a leisurely pace, looking about her in a manner that suggested that she found Piccadilly a new and stimulating spectacle.

As far as George could see she was an extremely pretty girl, small and dainty, with a proud little tilt to her head and the jaunty walk that spoke of perfect health. She was, in fact, precisely the sort of girl that George felt he could love with all the stored-up devotion of an old buffer of twenty-seven who had squandered none of his rich nature in foolish flirtations. He had just begun to weave a rose-tinted romance about their two selves, when a cold reaction set in. Even as he paused to watch the girl threading her way through the crowd, the east wind jabbed an icy finger down the back of his neck, and the chill of it sobered him. After all, he reflected bitterly, this girl was only alone because she was on her way somewhere to meet some confounded man. Besides there was no earthly chance of getting to know her. You can't rush up to pretty girls in the street and tell them you are lonely. At least, you can, but it doesn't get you anywhere except the police station. George's gloom deepened – a thing he would not have believed possible a moment before. He felt that he had been born too late. The restraints of modern civilization irked him. It was not, he told himself, like this in the good old days.

In the Middle Ages, for example, this girl would have been a Damsel; and in that happy time practically everybody whose technical rating was that of Damsel was in distress and only too willing to waive the formalities in return for services rendered by the casual passer-by. But the twentieth century is a prosaic age, when girls are merely girls and have no troubles at all. Were he to stop this girl in brown and assure her that his aid and comfort were at her disposal, she would undoubtedly call that large policeman from across the way, and the romance would begin and end within the space of thirty seconds, or, if the policeman were a quick mover, rather less.

Better to dismiss dreams and return to the practical side of life by buying the evening papers from the shabby individual beside him, who had just thrust an early edition in his face. After all notices are notices, even when the heart is aching. George felt in his pocket for the necessary money, found emptiness, and remembered that he had left all his ready funds at his hotel. It was just one of the things he might have expected on a day like this.

The man with the papers had the air of one whose business is conducted on purely cash principles. There was only one thing to be done, return to the hotel, retrieve his money, and try to forget the weight of the world and its cares in lunch. And from the hotel he could dispatch the two or three cables which he wanted to send to New York.

The girl in brown was quite close now, and George was enabled to get a clearer glimpse of her. She more than fulfilled the promise she had given at a distance. Had she been constructed to his own specifications, she would not have been more acceptable in George's sight. And now she was going out of his life for ever. With an overwhelming sense of pathos, for there is no pathos more bitter than that of parting from someone we have never met, George hailed a taxicab which crawled at the side of the road; and, with all the refrains of all the sentimental song hits he had ever composed ringing in his ears, he got in and passed away.

'A rotten world,' he mused, as the cab, after proceeding a couple of yards, came to a standstill in a block of the traffic. 'A dull, flat bore of a world, in which nothing happens or ever will happen. Even when you take a cab it just sticks and doesn't move.'

At this point the door of the cab opened, and the girl in brown jumped in.

'I'm so sorry,' she said breathlessly, 'but would you mind hiding me, please.'

3

George hid her. He did it, too, without wasting precious time by asking questions. In a situation which might well have thrown the quickest-witted of men off his balance, he acted with promptitude, intelligence, and despatch. The fact is, George had for years been an assiduous golfer; and there is no finer school for teaching concentration and a strict attention to the matter in hand. Few crises, however unexpected, have the power to disturb a man who has so conquered the weakness of the flesh as to have trained himself to bend his left knee, raise his left heel, swing his arms well out from the body, twist himself into the shape of a corkscrew, and use the muscle of the wrist, at the same time keeping his head still and his eye on the ball. It is estimated that there are twenty-three important points to be borne in mind simultaneously while making a drive at golf; and to the man who has mastered the art of remembering them all the task of hiding girls in taxicabs is mere child's play. To pull down the blinds on the side of the vehicle nearest the kerb was with George the work of a moment. Then he leaned out of the centre window in such a manner as completely to screen the interior of the cab from public view.

'Thank you so much,' murmured a voice behind him. It seemed to come from the floor.

'Not at all,' said George, trying a sort of vocal chip-shot out of the corner of his mouth, designed to lift his voice backwards and lay it dead inside the cab.

He gazed upon Piccadilly with eyes from which the

scales had fallen. Reason told him that he was still in Piccadilly. Otherwise it would have seemed incredible to him that this could be the same street which a moment before he had passed judgement upon and found flat and uninteresting. True, in its salient features it had altered little. The same number of stodgy-looking people moved up and down. The buildings retained their air of not having had a bath since the days of the Tudors. The east wind still blew. But, though superficially the same, in reality Piccadilly had altered completely. Before it had been just Piccadilly. Now it was a golden street in the City of Romance, a main thoroughfare of Baghdad, one of the principal arteries of the capital of Fairyland. A rose-coloured mist swam before George's eyes. His spirits, so low but a few moments back, soared like a good niblick shot out of the bunker of Gloom. The years fell away from him till, in an instant, from being a rather poorly preserved, liverish greybeard of sixty-five or so, he became a sprightly lad of twenty-one in a world of springtime and flowers and laughing brooks. In other words, taking it by and large, George felt pretty good. The impossible had happened; Heaven had sent him an adventure, and he didn't care if it snowed.

It was possibly the rose-coloured mist before his eyes that prevented him from observing the hurried approach of a faultlessly attired young man, aged about twenty-one, who during George's preparations for ensuring privacy in his cab had been galloping in pursuit in a resolute manner that suggested a well-dressed bloodhound somewhat overfed and out of condition. Only when this person stopped and began to pant within a few inches of his face did he become aware of his existence.

'You, sir!' said the bloodhound, removing a gleaming silk hat, mopping a pink forehead, and replacing the luminous superstructure once more in position. 'You, sir!'

Whatever may be said of the possibility of love at first sight, in which theory George was now a confirmed believer, there can be no doubt that an exactly opposite phenomenon is of frequent occurrence. After one look at some people even friendship is impossible. Such a one, in George's opinion, was this gurgling excrescence underneath the silk hat. He comprised in his single person practically all the qualities which George disliked most. He was, for a young man, extraordinarily obese. Already a second edition of his chin had been published, and the perfectly cut morning coat which encased his upper section bulged out in an opulent semi-circle. He wore a little moustache, which to George's prejudiced eye seemed more a complaint than a moustache. His face was red, his manner dictatorial, and he was touched in the wind. Take him for all in all he looked like a bit of bad news.

George had been educated at Lawrenceville and Harvard, and had subsequently had the privilege of mixing socially with many of New York's most prominent theatrical managers; so he knew how to behave himself. No Vere de Vere could have exhibited greater respose of manner.

'And what,' he inquired suavely, leaning a little further out of the cab, 'is eating *you*, Bill?'

A messenger boy, two shabby men engaged in non-essential industries, and a shop girl paused to observe the scene. Time was not of the essence to these confirmed sightseers. The shop girl was late already, so it didn't matter if she was any later; the messenger boy had nothing on hand except a message marked 'Important: Rush'; and as for the two shabby men, their only immediate plans consisted of a vague intention of getting to some public house and leaning against the wall; so George's time was their time. One of the pair put his head on one side and said: 'What ho!'; the other picked up a cigar stub from the gutter and began to smoke.

'A young lady just got into your cab,' said the stout young man.

'Surely not?' said George.

'What the devil do you mean – surely not?'

'I've been in the cab all the time, and I should have noticed it.'

At this juncture the block in the traffic was relieved, and the cab bowled smartly on for some fifty yards when it was again halted. George, protruding from the window like a snail, was entertained by the spectacle of the pursuit. The hunt was up. Short of throwing his head up and baying, the stout young man behaved exactly as a bloodhound in similar circumstances would have conducted itself. He broke into a jerky gallop, attended by his self-appointed associates; and, considering that the young man was so stout, that the messenger boy considered it unprofessional to hurry, that the shop girl had doubts as to whether sprinting was quite ladylike, and that the two Bohemians were moving at a quicker gait than a shuffle for the first occasion in eleven years, the cavalcade made good time. The cab was still stationary when they arrived in a body.

'Here he is, guv'nor,' said the messenger boy, removing a bead of perspiration with the rush message.

'Here he is, guv'nor,' said the non-smoking Bohemian. 'What oh!'

'Here I am!' agreed George affably. 'And what can I do for you?'

The smoker spat appreciatively at a passing dog. The point seemed to him well taken. Not for many a day had he so enjoyed himself. In an arid world containing too few goes of gin and too many policemen, a world in which the poor were oppressed and could seldom even enjoy a quiet cigar without having their fingers trodden upon, he found himself for the moment contented, happy, and expectant. This looked like a row between toffs, and of all things which most intrigued him a row between toffs ranked highest.

'R!' he said approvingly. 'Now you're torkin'!'

The shop girl had espied an acquaintance in the crowd. She gave tongue.

'Mordee! Cummere! Cummere quick! Sumfin' hap' nin'!'

Maudie, accompanied by perhaps a dozen more of London's millions, added herself to the audience. These all belonged to the class which will gather round and watch silently while a motorist mends a tyre. They are not impatient. They do not call for rapid and continuous action. A mere hole in the ground, which of all sights is perhaps the least vivid and dramatic, is enough to grip their attention for hours at a time. They stared at George and George's cab with unblinking gaze. They did not know what would happen or when it would happen, but they intended to wait till something did happen. It might be for years or it might be for ever, but they meant to be there when things began to occur.

Speculations became audible.

'Wot is it? 'Naccident?'

'Nah! Gent 'ad 'is pocket picked!'

'Two toffs 'ad a scrap!'

'Feller bilked the cabman!'

A sceptic made a cynical suggestion.

'They're doin' of it for the pictures.'

The idea gained instant popularity.

''Jear that? It's a fillum!'

'Wot o', Charlie!'

'The kemerer's 'idden in the keb.'

'Wot'll they be up to next!'

A red-nosed spectator with a tray of collar-studs harnessed to his stomach started another school of thought. He spoke with decision as one having authority.

'Nothin' of the blinkin' kind! The fat 'un's bin 'avin'

one or two around the corner, and it's gorn and got into 'is 'ead!'

The driver of the cab, who till now had been ostentatiously unaware that there was any sort of disturbance among the lower orders, suddenly became humanely inquisitive.

'What's it all about?' he asked, swinging around and addressing George's head.

'Exactly what I want to know,' said George. He indicated the collar-stud merchant. 'The gentleman over there with the portable Woolworth-bargain-counter seems to me to have the best theory.'

The stout young man, whose peculiar behaviour had drawn all this flattering attention from the many-headed and who appeared considerably ruffled by the publicity, had been puffing noisily during the foregoing conversation. Now, having recovered sufficient breath to resume the attack, he addressed himself to George once more.

'Damn you, sir, will you let me look inside that cab?'

'Leave me,' said George, 'I would be alone.'

'There is a young lady in that cab. I saw her get in, and I have been watching ever since, and she has not got out, so she is there now.'

George nodded approval of this close reasoning.

'Your argument seems to be without a flaw. But what then? We applaud the Man of Logic, but what of the Man of Action? What are you going to do about it?'

'Get out of my way!'

'I won't.'

'Then I'll force my way in!'

'If you try it, I shall infallibly bust you one on the jaw.'

The stout young man drew back a pace.

'You can't do that sort of thing, you know.'

'I know I can't,' said George, 'but I shall. In this life, my dear sir, we must be prepared for every emergency. We must distinguish between the unusual and the impossible. It would be unusual for a comparative stranger to lean out of a cab window and sock you one, but you appear to have laid your plans on the assumption that it would be impossible. Let this be a lesson to you!'

'I tell you what it is – '

'The advice I give to every young man starting life is "Never confuse the unusual with the impossible!" Take the present case, for instance. If you had only realized the possibility of somebody some day busting you on the jaw when you tried to get into a cab, you might have thought out dozens of crafty schemes for dealing with the matter. As it is, you are unprepared. The thing comes on you as a surprise. The whisper flies around the clubs: "Poor old What's-his-name has been taken unawares. He cannot cope with the situation!"'

The man with the collar-studs made another diagnosis. He was seeing clearer and clearer into the thing every minute.

'Looney!' he decided. 'This 'ere one's bin moppin' of it up, and the one in the keb's orf 'is bloomin' onion. That's why 'e 's standin' up instead of settin'. 'E won't set down 'cept you bring 'im a bit o' toast, 'cos he thinks 'e 's a poached egg.'

George beamed upon the intelligent fellow.

'Your reasoning is admirable, but – '

He broke off here, not because he had no more to say, but for the reason that the stout young man, now in quite a berserk frame of mind, made a sudden spring at the cab door and clutched the handle, which he was about to wrench when George acted with all the promptitude and decision which had marked his behaviour from the start.

It was a situation which called for the nicest judgement. To allow the assailant free play with the handle or even to wrestle with him for its possession entailed the risk that the door might open and reveal the girl. To bust the young man on the jaw, as promised, on the other hand, was not in George's eyes a practical policy. Excellent a deterrent as the threat of such a proceeding might be, its actual accomplishment was not to be thought of. Gaols yawn and actions for assault lie in wait for those who go about the place busting their fellows on the jaw. No. Something swift, something decided and immediate was indicated, but something that stopped short of technical battery.

George brought his hand round with a sweep and knocked the stout young man's silk hat off.

The effect was magical. We all of us have our Achilles' heel, and – paradoxically enough – in the case of the stout young man that heel was his hat. Superbly built by the only hatter in London who can construct a silk hat that is a silk hat, and freshly ironed by loving hands but a brief hour before at the only shaving-parlour in London where ironing is ironing and not a brutal attack, it was his pride and joy. To lose it was like losing his trousers. It made him feel insufficiently clad. With a passionate cry like that of some wild creature deprived of its young, the erstwhile Berserk released the handle and sprang in pursuit. At the same moment the traffic moved on again.

The last George saw was a group scene with the stout young man in the middle of it. The hat had been popped up into the infield, where it had been caught by the messenger boy. The stout young man was bending over it and stroking it with soothing fingers. It was too far off for anything to be audible, but he seemed to George to be murmuring words of endearment to it. Then, placing it on his head, he darted out into the road and George saw him no more. The audience remained motionless, staring at the spot where the incident had happened. They would continue to do this till the next policeman came along and moved them on.

With a pleasant wave of farewell, in case any of them might be glancing in his direction, George drew in his body and sat down.

The girl in brown had risen from the floor, if she had ever been there, and was now seated composedly at the further end of the cab.

4

'Well, that's that!' said George.

'I'm so much obliged,' said the girl.

'It was a pleasure,' said George.

He was enabled now to get a closer, more leisurely and much more satisfactory view of this distressed damsel than had been his good fortune up to the present. Small details which, when he had first caught sight of her, distance had hidden from his view, now presented themselves. Her eyes, he discovered, which he had supposed brown, were only brown in their general colour-scheme. They were shot with attractive little flecks of gold, matching perfectly the little streaks of gold which the sun, coming out again on one of his flying visits and now shining benignantly once more on the world, revealed in her hair. Her chin was square and determined, but its resoluteness was contradicted by a dimple and by the pleasant good-humour of the mouth; and a further softening of the face was effected by the nose, which seemed to have started out with the intention of being dignified and aristocratic but had defeated its purpose by tilting very slightly at the tip. This was a girl who would take chances, but would take them with a smile and a laugh when she lost.

George was but an amateur physiognomist, but he could read what was obvious in the faces he encountered; and the more he looked at this girl, the less he was able to understand the scene which had just occurred. The thing mystified him completely. For all her good-humour, there was an air, a manner, a something capable and defensive, about this girl with which he could not imagine any man venturing to take liberties. The gold-brown eyes, as they met his now, were friendly and smiling, but he could imagine them freezing into a stare baleful enough and haughty enough to quell such a person as the silk-hatted young man with a single glance. Why, then, had that super-fatted individual been able to demoralize her to the extent of flying to the shelter of strange cabs? She was composed enough now, it was true, but it had been quite plain that at the moment when she entered the taxi her nerve had momentarily forsaken her. There were mysteries here, beyond George.

The girl looked steadily at George and George looked steadily at her for the space of perhaps ten seconds. She seemed to George to be summing him up, weighing him. That the inspection proved satisfactory was shown by the fact that at the end of this period she smiled. Then she laughed, a clear pealing laugh which to George was far more musical than the most popular song-hit he had ever written.

'I suppose you are wondering what it's all about?' she said.

This was precisely what George was wondering most consumedly.

'No, no,' he said. 'Not at all. It's not my business.'

'And of course you're much too well bred to be inquisitive about other people's business?'

'Of course I am. What *was* it all about?'

'I'm afraid I can't tell you.'

'But what am I to say to the cabman?'

'I don't know. What do men usually say to cabmen?'

'I mean he will feel very hurt if I don't give him a full explanation of all this. He stooped from his pedestal to make inquiries just now. Condescension like that deserves some recognition.'

'Give him a nice big tip.'

George was reminded of his reason for being in the cab.

'I ought to have asked before,' he said. 'Where can I drive you?'

'Oh, I mustn't steal your cab. Where were you going?'

'I was going back to my hotel. I came out without any money, so I shall have to go there first to get some.'

The girl started.

'What's the matter?' asked George.

'I've lost my purse!'

'Good Lord! Had it much in it?'

'Not very much. But enough to buy a ticket home.'

'Any use asking where that is?'

'None, I'm afraid.'

'I wasn't going to, of course.'

'Of course not. That's what I admire so much in you. You aren't inquisitive.'

George reflected.

'There's only one thing to be done. You will have to wait in the cab at the hotel, while I go and get some money. Then, if you'll let me, I can lend you what you require.'

'It's much too kind of you. Could you manage eleven shillings?'

'Easily. I've just had a legacy.'

'Of course, if you think I ought to be economical, I'll go third-class. That would only be five shillings. Ten-and-six is the first-class fare. So you see the place I want to get to is two hours from London.'

'Well, that's something to know.'

'But not much, is it?'

'I think I had better lend you a sovereign. Then you'll be able to buy a lunch-basket.'

'You think of everything. And you're perfectly right. I shall be starving. But how do you know you will get the money back?'

'I'll risk it.'

'Well, then, I shall have to be inquisitive and ask your

name. Otherwise I shan't know where to send the money.'

'Oh, there's no mystery about me. I'm an open book.'

'You needn't be horrid about it. I can't help being mysterious.'

'I didn't mean that.'

'It sounded as if you did. Well, who is my benefactor?'

'My name is George Bevan. I am staying at the Carlton at present.'

'I'll remember.'

The taxi moved slowly down the Haymarket. The girl laughed.

'Yes?' said George.

'I was only thinking of back there. You know, I haven't thanked you nearly enough for all you did. You were wonderful.'

'I'm very glad I was able to be of any help.'

'What *did* happen? You must remember I couldn't see a thing except your back, and I could only hear indistinctively.'

'Well, it started by a man galloping up and insisting that you had got into the cab. He was a fellow with the appearance of a before-using advertisement of an anti-fat medicine and the manners of a ring-tailed chimpanzee.'

The girl nodded.

'Then it was Percy! I knew I wasn't mistaken.'

'Percy?'

'That is his name.'

'It would be! I could have betted on it.'

'What happened then?'

'I reasoned with the man, but didn't seem to soothe him, and finally he made a grab for the door-handle, so I knocked off his hat, and while he was retrieving it we moved on and escaped.'

The girl gave another silver peal of laughter.

'Oh, what a shame I couldn't see it. But how resourceful of you! How did you happen to think of it?'

'It just came to me,' said George modestly.

A serious look came into the girl's face. The smile died out of her eyes. She shivered.

'When I think how some men might have behaved in your place!'

'Oh, no. Any man would have done just what I did. Surely, knocking off Percy's hat was an act of simple courtesy which anyone would have performed automatically!'

'You might have been some awful bounder. Or, what would have been almost worse, a slow-witted idiot who would have stopped to ask questions before doing anything. To think I should have had the luck to pick you out of all London!'

'I've been looking on it as a piece of luck – but entirely from my viewpoint.'

She put a small hand on his arm, and spoke earnestly.

'Mr Bevan, you mustn't think that, because I've been laughing a good deal and have seemed to treat all this as a joke, you haven't saved me from real trouble. If you hadn't been there and hadn't acted with such presence of mind, it would have been terrible!'

'But surely, if that fellow was annoying you, you could have called a policeman?'

'Oh, it wasn't anything like that. It was much, much worse. But I mustn't go on like this. It isn't fair on you.' Her eyes lit up again with the old shining smile. 'I know you have no curiosity about me, but there's no knowing whether I might not arouse some if I went on piling up the mystery. And the silly part is that really there's no mystery at all. It's just that I can't tell anyone about it.'

'That very fact seems to me to constitute the makings of a pretty fair mystery.'

'Well, what I mean is, I'm not a princess in disguise trying to escape from anarchists, or anything like those things you read about in books. I'm just in a perfectly simple piece of trouble. You would be bored to death if I told you about it.'

'Try me.'

She shook her head.

'No. Besides, here we are.' The cab had stopped at the hotel, and a commissionaire was already opening the door. 'Now, if you haven't repented of your rash offer and really are going to be so awfully kind as to let me have that money, would you mind rushing off and getting it, because I must hurry. I can just catch a good train, and it's hours to the next.'

'Will you wait here? I'll be back in a moment.'

'Very well.'

The last George saw of her was another of those exhilarating smiles of hers. It was literally the last he saw of her, for, when he returned not more than two minutes later, the cab had gone, the girl had gone, and the world was empty.

To him, gaping at this wholly unforeseen calamity the commissionaire vouchsafed information.

'The young lady took the cab on, sir.'

'Took the cab on?'

'Almost immediately after you had gone, sir, she got in again and told the man to drive to Waterloo.'

George could make nothing of it. He stood there in silent perplexity, and might have continued to stand indefinitely, had not his mind been distracted by a dictatorial voice at his elbow.

'You, sir! Dammit!'

A second taxi-cab had pulled up, and from it a stout, scarlet-faced young man had sprung. One glance told George all. The hunt was up once more. The bloodhound had picked up the trail. Percy was in again!

For the first time since he had become aware of her flight, George was thankful that the girl had disappeared. He perceived that he had too quickly eliminated Percy from the list of the Things That Matter. Engrossed with his own affairs, and having regarded their late skirmish as a decisive battle from which there would be no rallying, he had overlooked the possibility of this annoying and unnecessary person following them in another cab – a task which, in the congested, slow-moving traffic, must have been a perfectly simple one. Well, here he was, his soul manifestly all stirred up and his blood-pressure at a far higher figure than his doctor would have approved of, and the matter would have to be opened all over again.

'Now then!' said the stout young man.

George regarded him with a critical and unfriendly eye. He disliked this fatty degeneration excessively. Looking him up and down, he could find no point about him that gave him the least pleasure, with the single exception of the state of his hat, in the side of which he was rejoiced to perceive there was a large and unshapely dent.

'You thought you had shaken me off! You thought you'd given me the slip! Well, you're wrong!'

George eyed him coldly.

'I know what's the matter with *you*,' he said. 'Someone's been feeding you meat.'

The young man bubbled with fury. His face turned a deeper scarlet. He gesticulated.

'You blackguard! Where's my sister?'

At this extraordinary remark the world rocked about George dizzily. The words upset his entire diagnosis of the situation. Until that moment he had looked upon this man as a Lothario, a pursuer of damsels. That the other could possibly have any right on his side had never occurred to him. He felt unmanned by the shock. It seemed to cut the ground from under his feet.

'Your sister!'

'You heard what I said. Where is she?'

George was still endeavouring to adjust his scattered faculties. He felt foolish and apologetic. He had imagined himself unassailably in the right, and it now appeared that he was in the wrong.

For a moment he was about to become conciliatory. Then the recollection of the girl's panic and her hints at some trouble which threatened her – presumably through the medium of this man, brother or no brother – checked him. He did not know what it was all about, but the one thing that did stand out clearly in the welter of confused happenings was the girl's need for his assistance. Whatever might be the rights of the case, he was her accomplice, and must behave as such.

'I don't know what you're talking about,' he said.

The young man shook a large, gloved fist in his face.

'You blackguard!'

A rich, deep, soft, soothing voice slid into the heated scene like the Holy Grail sliding athwart a sunbeam.

'What's all this?'

A vast policeman had materialized from nowhere. He stood beside them, a living statue of Vigilant Authority. One thumb rested easily on his broad belt. The fingers of the other hand caressed lightly a moustache that had caused more heart-burnings among the gentler sex than any other two moustaches in the C-division. The eyes above the moustache were stern and questioning.

'What's all this?'

George liked policemen. He knew the way to treat them. His voice, when he replied, had precisely the correct note of respectful deference which the Force likes to hear.

'I really couldn't say, officer,' he said, with just that air of having in a time of trouble found a kind elder brother to help him out of his difficulties which made the constable his ally on the spot. 'I was standing here, when this man suddenly made his extraordinary attack on me. I wish you would ask him to go away.'

The policeman tapped the stout young man on the shoulder.

'This won't do, you know!' he said austerely. 'This sort o' thing won't do 'ere, you know!'

'Take your hands off me!' snorted Percy.

A frown appeared on the Olympian brow. Jove reached for his thunderbolts.

''Ullo! 'Ullo! 'Ullo!' he said in a shocked voice, as of a god defied by a mortal. ''Ullo! 'Ullo! 'Ul-*lo*!'

His fingers fell on Percy's shoulder again, but this time not in a mere warning tap. They rested where they fell – in an iron clutch.

'It won't do, you know,' he said. 'This sort o' thing won't *do*!'

Madness came upon the stout young man. Common prudence and the lessons of a carefully taught youth fell from him like a garment. With an incoherent howl he wriggled round and punched the policeman smartly in the stomach.

'Ho!' quoth the outraged officer, suddenly becoming human. His left hand removed itself from the belt, and he got a business-like grip on his adversary's collar. 'Will you come along with me!'

It was amazing. The thing had happened in such an incredibly brief space of time. One moment, it seemed to George, he was the centre of a nasty row in one of the most public spots in London; the next, the focus had shifted; he had ceased to matter; and the entire attention of the metropolis was focused on his late assailant, as, urged by the arm of the Law, he made that journey to Vine Street Police Station which so many a better man than he had trod.

George watched the pair as they moved up the Haymarket, followed by a growing and increasingly absorbed crowd; then he turned into the hotel.

'This', he said to himself, 'is the middle of a perfect day! And I thought London dull!'

5

George awoke next morning with a misty sense that somehow the world had changed. As the last remnants of sleep left him, he was aware of a vague excitement. Then he sat up in bed with a jerk. He had remembered that he was in love.

There was no doubt about it. A curious happiness pervaded his entire being. He felt young and active. Everything was emphatically for the best in this best of all possible worlds. The sun was shining. Even the sound of someone in the street below whistling one of his old compositions, of which he had heartily sickened twelve months before, was pleasant to his ears, and this in spite of the fact that the unseen whistler only touched the key in odd spots and had a poor memory for tunes. George sprang lightly out of bed, and turned on the cold tap in the bathroom. While he lathered his face for its morning shave he beamed at himself in the mirror.

It had come at last. The Real Thing.

George had never been in love before. Not really in love. True, from the age of fifteen, he had been in varying degrees of intensity attracted sentimentally by the opposite sex. Indeed, at that period of life of which Mr Booth Tarkington has written so searchingly – the age of seventeen – he had been in love with practically every female he met and with dozens whom he had only seen in the distance; but ripening years had mellowed his taste and robbed him of that fine romantic catholicity. During the last five years women had found him more or less cold. It was the nature of his profession that had largely brought about this cooling of the emotions. To a man who, like George, has worked year in and year out at the composition of musical comedies, woman comes to lose many of those attractive qualities which ensnare the ordinary male. To George, of late years, it had begun to seem that the salient feature of woman as a sex was her disposition to kick. For five years he had been wandering in a world of women, many of them beautiful, all of them superficially attractive, who had left no other impress on his memory except the vigour and frequency with which they had kicked. Some had kicked about their musical numbers, some about their love-scenes; some had grumbled about their exit lines, others about the lines of their second-act frocks. They had kicked in a myriad differing ways – wrathfully, sweetly, noisily, softly, smilingly, tearfully, pathetically, and patronizingly; but they had all kicked; with the result that woman had now become to George not so much a flaming inspiration or a tender goddess as something to be dodged – tactfully, if possible; but, if not possible, by open flight. For years he had dreaded to be left alone with a woman, and had developed a habit of gliding swiftly away when he saw one bearing down on him.

The psychological effect of such a state of things is not difficult to realize. Take a man of naturally quixotic temperament, a man of chivalrous instincts and a feeling for romance, and cut him off for five years from the exercise of those qualities, and you get an accumulated store of foolishness only comparable to an escape of gas in a sealed room or a cellarful of dynamite. A flicker of a match, and there is an explosion.

This girl's tempestuous irruption into his life had supplied flame for George. Her bright eyes, looking into his, had touched off the spiritual trinitrotoluol which he had been storing up for so long. Up in the air in a million pieces had gone the prudence and self-restraint of a lifetime. And here he was, as desperately in love as any troubadour of the Middle Ages.

It was not till he had finished shaving and was testing the temperature of his bath with a shrinking toe that the realization came over him in a wave that, though he might be in love, the fairway of love was dotted with more bunkers than any golf course he had ever played on in his life. In the first place, he did not know the girl's name. In the second place, it seemed practically impossible that he would ever see her again. Even in the midst of his optimism George could not deny that these facts might reasonably be considered in the nature of obstacles. He went back into his bedroom, and sat on the bed. This thing wanted thinking over.

He was not depressed – only a little thoughtful. His faith in his luck sustained him. He was, he realized, in the position of a man who has made a supreme drive from the tee, and finds his ball near the green but in a cuppy lie. He had gained much; it now remained for him to push his success to the happy conclusion. The driver of Luck must be replaced by the spoon – or, possibly, the niblick – of Ingenuity. To fail now, to allow this girl to pass out of his life merely because he did not know who she was or where she was, would stamp him a feeble adventurer. A fellow could not expect Luck to do everything for him. He must supplement its assistance with his own efforts.

What had he to go on? Well nothing much, if it came to that, except the knowledge that she lived some two hours by train out of London, and that her journey started from Waterloo Station. What would Sherlock Holmes have done? Concentrated thought supplied no answer to the question; and it was at this point that the cheery optimism with which he had begun the day left George and gave place to a grey gloom. A dreadful phrase, haunting in its pathos, crept into his mind. 'Ships that pass in the night!' It might easily turn out that way. Indeed, thinking over the affair in all its aspects as he dried himself after his tub, George could not see how it could possibly turn out any other way.

He dressed moodily, and left the room to go down to breakfast. Breakfast would at least alleviate this sinking feeling which was unmanning him. And he could think more briskly after a cup or two of coffee.

He opened the door. On a mat outside lay a letter.

The handwriting was feminine. It was also in pencil, and strange to him. He opened the envelope.

'Dear Mr Bevan' (it began).

With a sudden leap of the heart he looked at the signature.

The letter was signed 'The Girl in the Cab'.

Dear Mr Bevan,

I hope you won't think me very rude, running off without waiting to say good-bye. I had to. I saw Percy driving up in a cab and knew that he must have followed us. He did not see me, so I got away all right. I managed splendidly about the money for I remembered that I was wearing a nice brooch, and stopped on the way to the station to pawn it.

Thank you ever so much again for all your wonderful kindness.

Yours,

'The Girl in the Cab'.

George read the note twice on the way down to the breakfast room, and three times more during the meal; then, having committed its contents to memory down to the last comma, he gave himself up to glowing thoughts.

What a girl! He had never in his life before met a woman who could write a letter without a postscript, and this was but the smallest of her unusual gifts. The resource of her, to think of pawning that brooch! The sweetness of her to bother to send him a note! More than ever before was he convinced that he had met his ideal, and more than ever before was he determined that a triviality like being unaware of her name and address should not keep him from her. It was not as if he had no clue to go upon. He knew that she lived two hours from London and started home from Waterloo. It narrowed the thing down absurdly. There were only about three counties in which she could possibly live; and a man must be a poor fellow who is incapable of searching through a few small counties for the girl he loves. Especially a man with luck like his.

Luck is a goddess not to be coerced and forcibly wooed by those who seek her favours. From such masterful spirits she turns away. But it happens sometimes that, if we put our hand in hers with the humble trust of a little child, she will have pity on us, and not fail us in our hour of need. On George, hopefully watching for something to turn up, she smiled almost immediately.

It was George's practice, when he lunched alone, to relieve the tedium of the meal with the assistance of reading matter in the shape of one or more of the evening papers. Today, sitting down to a solitary repast at the Piccadilly grill-room, he had brought with him an early edition of the *Evening News*. And one of the first items which met his eye was the following, embodied in a column on one of the inner pages devoted to humorous comments in prose and verse on the happenings of the day. This particular happening the writer had apparently considered worthy of being dignified by rhyme. It was headed:

THE PEER AND THE POLICEMAN

Outside the Carlton, 'tis averred, these stirring happenings occurred. The hour, 'tis said (and no one doubts) was half past two, or thereabouts. The day was fair, the sky was blue, and everything was peaceful too, when suddenly a well-dressed gent engaged in heated argument and roundly to abuse began another well-dressed gentleman. His suède-gloved fist he raised on high to dot the other in the eye. Who knows what horrors might have been, had there not come upon the scene old London city's favourite son, Policeman C231. 'What means this conduct? Prithee stop!' exclaimed that admirable slop. With which he placed a warning hand upon the brawler's collarband. We simply hate to tell the rest. No subject here for flippant jest. The mere remembrance of the tale has made our ink turn deadly pale. Let us be brief. Some demon sent stark madness on the well-dressed gent. He gave the constable a punch just where the latter kept his lunch. The constable said 'Well! Well! Well!' and marched him to a dungeon cell. At Vine Street Station out it came – Lord Belpher was the culprit's name. But British Justice is severe alike on pauper and on peer; with even hand she holds the scale; a thumping fine, in lieu of gaol, induced Lord B to feel remorse and learn he mustn't punch the Force.

George's mutton chop congealed on the plate, untouched. The French fried potatoes cooled off, unnoticed. This was no time for food. Rightly indeed had he relied upon his luck. It had stood by him nobly. With this clue, all was over except getting to the nearest Free Library and consulting *Burke's Peerage*. He paid his bill and left the restaurant.

Ten minutes later he was drinking in the pregnant information that Belpher was the family name of the Earl of Marshmoreton, and that the present earl had one son, Percy Wilbraham Marsh, *educ.* Eton and Christ Church, Oxford, and what the book with its customary curtness called 'one *d.*' – Patricia Maud. The family seat, said Burke, was Belpher Castle, Belpher, Hants.

Some hours later, seated in a first-class compartment of a train that moved slowly out of Waterloo Station, George watched London vanish behind him. In the pocket closest to his throbbing heart was a single ticket to Belpher.

6

At about the time that George Bevan's train was leaving Waterloo, a grey racing car drew up with a grinding of brakes and a sputter of gravel in front of the main entrance of Belpher Castle. The slim and elegant young man at the wheel removed his goggles, pulled out a watch, and addressed the stout young man at his side.

'Two hours and eighteen minutes from Hyde Park Corner, Boots. Not so dusty, what?'

His companion made no reply. He appeared to be plunged in thought. He, too, removed his goggles, revealing a florid and gloomy face, equipped, in addition to the usual features, with a small moustache and an extra chin. He scowled forbiddingly at the charming scene which the goggles had hidden from him.

Before him, a symmetrical mass of grey stone and green ivy, Belpher Castle towered against a light blue sky. On either side rolling park land spread as far as the eye could see, carpeted here and there with violets, dotted with great oaks and ashes and Spanish chestnuts, orderly, peaceful, and English. Nearer, on his left, were rose-gardens, in the centre of which, tilted at a sharp angle, appeared the seat of a pair of corduroy trousers, whose wearer seemed to be engaged in hunting for snails. Thrushes sang in the green shrubberies; rooks cawed in the elms. Somewhere in the distance sounded the tinkle of sheep bells and the lowing of cows. It was, in fact, a scene which, lit by the evening sun of a perfect spring day and fanned by a gentle westerly wind, should have brought balm and soothing meditations to one who was the sole heir to all this Paradise.

But Percy, Lord Belpher, remained uncomforted by the notable cooperation of Man and Nature, and drew no solace from the reflection that all these pleasant things would one day be his own. His mind was occupied at the moment, to the exclusion of all other thoughts, by the recollection of that painful scene in Bow Street Police Court. The magistrate's remarks, which had been tactless and unsympathetic, still echoed in his ears. And that infernal night in Vine Street Police Station . . . The darkness . . . The hard bed . . . The discordant vocalizing of the drunk and disorderly in the next cell . . . Time might soften these memories, might lessen the sharp agony of them; but nothing could remove them altogether.

Percy had been shaken to the core of his being. Physically, he was still stiff and sore from the plank bed. Mentally, he was a volcano. He had been marched up the Haymarket in the full sight of all London by a bounder of a policeman. He had been talked to like an erring child by a magistrate whom nothing could convince that he had not been under the influence of alcohol at the moment of his arrest. (The man had said things about his liver, kindly be-warned-in-time-and-pull-up-before-it-is-too-late things, which would have seemed to Percy indecently frank if spoken by his medical adviser in the privacy of the sick chamber.) It is perhaps not to be wondered at that Belpher Castle, for all its beauty of scenery and architecture, should have left Lord Belpher a little cold. He was seething with a fury which the conversation of Reggie Byng had done nothing to allay in the course of the journey from London. Reggie was the last person he would willingly have chosen as a companion in his hour of darkness. Reggie was not soothing. He would insist on addressing him by his old Eton nickname of Boots which Percy detested. And all the way down he had been breaking out at intervals into ribald comments on the recent unfortunate occurrence which were very hard to bear.

He resumed this vein as they alighted and rang the bell.

'This', said Reggie, 'is rather like a bit out of a melodrama. Convict son totters up the steps of the old home and punches the bell. What awaits him beyond? Forgiveness? Or the raspberry? True, the white-haired butler who knew him as a child will sob on his neck, but what of the old dad? How will dad take the blot on the family escutcheon?'

Lord Belpher's scowl deepened.

'It's not a joking matter,' he said coldly.

'Great Heavens, I'm not joking. How could I have the heart to joke at a moment like this, when the friend of my youth has suddenly become a social leper?'

'I wish to goodness you would stop.'

'Do you think it is any pleasure to me to be seen about with a man who is now known in criminal circles as Percy, the Piccadilly Policeman-Puncher? I keep a brave face before the world, but inwardly I burn with shame and agony and what not.'

The great door of the castle swung open, revealing Keggs, the butler. He was a man of reverend years, portly and dignified, with a respectfully benevolent face that beamed gravely on the young master and Mr Byng, as if their coming had filled his cup of pleasure. His light, slightly protruding eyes expressed reverential goodwill. He gave just that touch of cosy humanity to the scene which the hall with its half-lights and massive furniture needed to make it perfect to the returned wanderer. He seemed to be intimating that this was a moment to which he had looked forward long, and that from now on quiet happiness would reign supreme. It is distressing to have to reveal the jarring fact that, in his hours of privacy when off duty, this apparently ideal servitor was so far from being a respecter of persons that he was accustomed to speak of Lord Belpher as 'Percy', and even as 'His Nibs'. It was, indeed, an open secret among the upper servants at the castle, and a fact hinted at with awe among the lower, that Keggs was at heart a Socialist.

'Good evening, your lordship. Good evening, sir.'

Lord Belpher acknowledged the salutation with a grunt, but Reggie was more affable.

'How are you, Keggs? Now's your time, if you're going to do it.' He stepped a little to one side and indicated Lord Belpher's crimson neck with an inviting gesture.

'I beg your pardon, sir?'

'Ah. You'd rather wait till you can do it a little more privately. Perhaps you're right.'

The butler smiled indulgently. He did not understand what Reggie was talking about, but that did not worry him. He had long since come to the conclusion that Reggie was slightly mad, a theory supported by the latter's valet, who was of the same opinion. Keggs did not dislike Reggie, but intellectually he considered him negligible.

'Send something to drink into the library, Keggs,' said Lord Belpher.

'Very good, your lordship.'

'A topping idea,' said Reggie. 'I'll just take the old car round to the garage, and then I'll be with you.'

He climbed to the steering wheel, and started the engine. Lord Belpher proceeded to the library, while Keggs melted away through the green baize door at the end of the hall which divided the servants' quarters from the rest of the house.

Reggie had hardly driven a dozen yards when he perceived his stepmother and Lord Marshmoreton coming towards him from the direction of the rose-garden. He drew up to greet them.

'Hullo, mater. What ho, uncle! Back again at the old homestead, what?'

Beneath Lady Caroline's aristocratic front agitation seemed to lurk.

'Reggie, where is Percy?'

'Old Boots? I think he's gone to the library. I just decanted him out of the car.'

Lady Caroline turned to her brother.

'Let us go to the library, John.'

'All right. All right. All right,' said Lord Marshmoreton irritably. Something appeared to have ruffled his calm.

Reggie drove on. As he was strolling back after putting the car away he met Maud.

'Hullo, Maud, dear old thing.'

'Why, hullo, Reggie. I was expecting you back last night.'

'Couldn't get back last night. Had to stick in town and rally round old Boots. Couldn't desert the old boy in his hour of trial.' Reggie chuckled amusedly. '"Hour of trial", is rather good, what? What I mean to say is, that's just what it was, don't you know.'

'Why, what happened to Percy?'

'Do you mean to say you haven't heard? Of course not. It wouldn't have been in the morning papers. Why, Percy punched a policeman.'

'Percy did *what*?'

'Slugged a slop. Most dramatic thing. Sloshed him in the midriff. Absolutely. The cross marks the spot where the tragedy occurred.'

Maud caught her breath. Somehow, though she could not trace the connexion, she felt that this extraordinary happening must be linked up with her escapade. Then her sense of humour got the better of apprehension. Her eyes twinkled delightedly.

'You don't mean to say *Percy* did that?'

'Absolutely. The human tiger, and what not. Menace to Society and all that sort of thing. No holding him. For some unexplained reason the generous blood of the Belphers boiled over, and then – *zing*. They jerked him off to Vine Street. Like the poem, don't you know. "And poor old Percy walked between with gyves upon his wrists." And this morning, bright and early, the beak parted him from ten quid. You know, Maud, old thing, our duty stares us plainly in the eyeball. We've got to train old Boots down to a reasonable weight and spring him on the National Sporting Club. We've been letting a champion middleweight blush unseen under our very roof tree.'

Maud hesitated a moment.

'I suppose you don't know', she asked carelessly, 'why he did it? I mean, did he tell you anything?'

'Couldn't get a word out of him. Oysters garrulous and tombs chatty in comparison. Absolutely. All I know is that he popped one into the officer's waistband. What led up to it is more than I can tell you. How would it be to stagger to the library and join the *post-mortem*?'

'The *post-mortem*?'

'Well, I met the mater and his lordship on their way to the library, and it looked to me very much as if the mater must have got hold of an evening paper on her journey from town! When did she arrive?'

'Only a short while ago.'

'Then that's what's happened. She would have bought an evening paper to read in the train. By jove, I wonder if she got hold of the one that had the poem about it. One chappie was so carried away by the beauty of the episode that he treated it in verse. I think we ought to look in and see what's happening.'

Maud hesitated again. But she was a girl of spirit. And she had an intuition that her best defence would be attack. Bluff was what was needed. Wide-eyed, innocent wonder . . . After all, Percy couldn't be certain he had seen her in Piccadilly.

'All right.'

'By the way, dear old girl,' inquired Reggie, 'did your little business come out satisfactorily? I forgot to ask.'

'Not very. But it was awfully sweet of you to take me into town.'

'How would it be,' said Reggie nervously, 'not to dwell

too much on that part of it? What I mean to say is, for heaven's sake don't let the mater know I rallied round.'

'Don't worry,' said Maud with a laugh. 'I'm not going to talk about the thing at all.'

Lord Belpher, meanwhile, in the library, had begun with the aid of a whisky and soda to feel a little better. There was something about the library with its sombre half-tones that soothed his bruised spirit. The room held something of the peace of a deserted city. The world, with its violent adventures and tall policemen, did not enter here. There was balm in those rows and rows of books which nobody ever read, those vast writing tables at which nobody ever wrote. From the broad mantelpiece the bust of some unnamed ancient looked down almost sympathetically. Something remotely resembling peace had begun to steal into Percy's soul, when it was expelled by the abrupt opening of the door and the entry of Lady Caroline Byng and his father. One glance at the face of the former was enough to tell Lord Belpher that she knew all.

He rose defensively.

'Let me explain.'

Lady Caroline quivered with repressed emotion. This masterly woman had not lost control of herself, but her aristocratic calm had seldom been so severely tested. As Reggie had surmised, she had read the report of the proceedings in the evening paper in the train, and her world had been reeling ever since. Caesar, stabbed by Brutus, could scarcely have experienced a greater shock. The other members of her family had disappointed her often. She had become inured to the spectacle of her brother working in the garden in corduroy trousers and in other ways behaving in a manner beneath the dignity of an Earl of Marshmoreton. She had resigned herself to the innate flaw in the character of Maud which had allowed her to fall in love with a nobody whom she had met without an introduction. Even Reggie had exhibited at times democratic traits of which she thoroughly disapproved. But of her nephew Percy she had always been sure. He was solid rock. He, at least, she had always felt, would never do anything to injure the family prestige. And now, so to speak, 'Lo, Ben Adhem's name led all the rest.' In other words, Percy was the worst of the lot. Whatever indiscretions the rest had committed, at least they had never got the family into the comic columns of the evening papers. Lord Marshmoreton might wear corduroy trousers and refuse to entertain the County at garden parties and go to bed with a book when it was his duty to act as host at a formal ball; Maud might give her heart to an impossible person whom nobody had ever heard of; and Reggie might be seen at fashionable restaurants with pugilists; but at any rate evening paper poets had never written facetious verses about their exploits. This crowning degradation had been reserved for the hitherto blameless Percy, who, of all the young men of Lady Caroline's acquaintance, had till now appeared to have the most scrupulous sense of his position, the most rigid regard for the dignity of his great name. Yet, here he was, if the carefully considered reports in the daily press were to be believed, spending his time in the very springtide of his life running about London like a frenzied Hottentot, brutally assaulting the police. Lady Caroline felt as a bishop might feel if he suddenly discovered that some favourite curate had gone over to the worship of Mumbo Jumbo.

'Explain?' she cried. 'How can you explain? *You – my* nephew, the heir to the title, behaving like a common rowdy in the streets of London . . . your name in the papers . . .'

'If you knew the circumstances.'

'The circumstances? They are in the evening paper. They are in print.'

'In verse,' added Lord Marshmoreton. He chuckled amiably at the recollection. He was an easily amused man. 'You ought to read it, my boy. Some of it was capital . . .'

'John!'

'But deplorable, of course,' added Lord Marshmoreton hastily. 'Very deplorable.' He endeavoured to regain his sister's esteem by a show of righteous indignation. 'What do you mean by it, damn it? You're my only son. I have watched you grow from child to boy, from boy to man, with tender solicitude. I have wanted to be proud of you. And all the time, dash it, you are prowling about London like a lion, seeking whom you may devour, terrorizing the metropolis, putting harmless policemen in fear of their lives . . .'

'Will you listen to me for a moment?' shouted Percy. He began to speak rapidly, as one conscious of the necessity of saying his say while the saying was good. 'The facts are these. I was walking along Piccadilly on my way to lunch at the club, when, near Burlington Arcade, I was amazed to see Maud.'

Lady Caroline uttered an exclamation.

'Maud? But Maud was here.'

'I can't understand it,' went on Lord Marshmoreton, pursuing his remarks. Righteous indignation had, he felt, gone well. It might be judicious to continue in that vein, though privately he held the opinion that nothing in Percy's life so became him as this assault on the Force. Lord Marshmoreton, who in his time had committed all the follies of youth, had come to look on his blameless son as scarcely human. 'It's not as if you were wild. You've never got into any scrapes at Oxford. You've spent your time collecting old china and prayer rugs. You wear flannel next your skin . . .'

'Will you please be quiet,' said Lady Caroline impatiently. 'Go on, Percy.'

'Oh, very well,' said Lord Marshmoreton. 'I only spoke. I merely made a remark.'

'You say you saw Maud in Piccadilly, Percy?'

'Precisely. I was on the point of putting it down to an extraordinary resemblance, when suddenly she got into a cab. Then I knew.'

Lord Marshmoreton could not permit this to pass in silence. He was a fair-minded man.

'Why shouldn't the girl have got into a cab? Why must a girl walking along Piccadilly be my daughter Maud just because she got into a cab. London,' he proceeded, warming to the argument and thrilled by the clearness and coherence of his reasoning, 'is full of girls who take cabs.'

'She didn't take a cab.'

'You just said she did,' said Lord Marshmoreton cleverly.

'I said she got into a cab. There was somebody else already in the cab. A man. Aunt Caroline, it was *the* man.'

'Good gracious,' ejaculated Lady Caroline, falling into a chair as if she had been hamstrung.

'I am absolutely convinced of it,' proceeded Lord Belpher solemnly. 'His behaviour was enough to confirm my suspicions. The cab had stopped in a block of the traffic, and I went up and requested him in a perfectly civil manner to allow me to look at the lady who had just got in. He denied that there was a lady in the cab. And I had seen her jump in with my own eyes. Throughout the conversation he was leaning out of the window with the obvious intention of screening whoever was inside from my view. I followed him along Piccadilly in another cab, and tracked him to the Carlton. When I arrived there he was standing on the pavement outside. There were no signs of Maud. I demanded that he tell me her whereabouts . . .'

'That reminds me,' said Lord Marshmoreton cheerfully, 'of a story I read in one of the papers. I daresay it's old. Stop me if you've heard it. A woman says to the maid: "Do you know anything of my husband's whereabouts?" And the maid replies – '

'Do be quiet,' snapped Lady Caroline. 'I should have thought that you would be interested in a matter affecting the vital welfare of your only daughter.'

'I am. I am,' said Lord Marshmoreton hastily. 'The maid replied: "They're at the wash." Of course I am. Go on, Percy. Good God, boy, don't take all day telling us your story.'

'At that moment the fool of a policeman came up and wanted to know what the matter was. I lost my head. I admit it freely. The policeman grasped my shoulder, and I struck him.'

'Where?' asked Lord Marshmoreton, a stickler for detail.

'What *does* that matter?' demanded Lady Caroline. 'You did quite right, Percy. These insolent jacks in office ought not to be allowed to manhandle people. Tell me, what this man was like?'

'Extremely ordinary-looking. In fact, all I can remember about him was that he was clean-shaven. I cannot understand how Maud could have come to lose her head over such a man. He seemed to me to have no attraction whatever,' said Lord Belpher, a little unreasonably, for Apollo himself would hardly appear attractive when knocking one's best hat off.

'It must have been the same man.'

'Precisely. If we wanted further proof, he was an American. You recollect that we heard that the man in Wales was American.'

There was a portentous silence. Percy stared at the floor. Lady Caroline breathed deeply. Lord Marshmoreton, feeling that something was expected of him, said 'Good Gad!' and gazed seriously at a stuffed owl on a bracket. Maud and Reggie Byng came in.

'What ho, what ho, what ho!' said Reggie breezily. He always believed in starting a conversation well, and putting people at their ease. 'What ho! What ho!'

Maud braced herself for the encounter.

'Hullo, Percy, dear,' she said, meeting her brother's accusing eye with the perfect composure that comes only from a thoroughly guilty conscience. 'What's all this I hear about your being the Scourge of London? Reggie says that policemen dive down manholes when they see you coming.'

The chill in the air would have daunted a less courageous girl. Lady Caroline had risen, and was staring sternly. Percy was puffing the puffs of an overwrought soul. Lord Marshmoreton, whose thoughts had wandered off to the rose-garden, pulled himself together and tried to look menacing. Maud went on without waiting for a reply. She was all bubbling gaiety and insouciance, a charming picture of young English girlhood that nearly made her brother foam at the mouth.

'Father dear,' she said, attaching herself affectionately to his buttonhole, 'I went round the links in eighty-three this morning. I did the long hole in four. One under par, a thing I've never done before in my life.' ('Bless my soul,' said Lord Marshmoreton weakly, as, with an apprehensive eye on his sister, he patted his daughter's shoulder.) 'First, I sent a screecher of a drive right down the middle of the fairway. Then I took my brassy and put the ball just on the edge of the green. A hundred and eighty yards if it was an inch. My approach putt – '

Lady Caroline, who was no devotee of the royal and ancient game, interrupted the recital.

'Never mind what you did this morning. What did you do yesterday afternoon?'

'Yes,' said Lord Belpher. 'Where were you yesterday afternoon?'

Maud's gaze was the gaze of a young child who has never even attempted to put anything over in all its little life.

'Whatever do you mean?'

'What were you doing in Piccadilly yesterday afternoon?' said Lady Caroline.

'Piccadilly? The place where Percy fights policemen? I don't understand.'

Lady Caroline was no sportsman. She put one of those direct questions, capable of being answered only by 'Yes' or 'No', which ought not to be allowed in controversy. They are the verbal equivalent of shooting a sitting bird.

'Did you or did you not go to London yesterday Maud?'

The monstrous unfairness of this method of attack pained Maud. From childhood up she had held the customary feminine views upon the Lie Direct. As long as it was a question of suppression of the true or suggestion of the false she had no scruples. But she had a distaste for deliberate falsehood. Faced now with a choice between two evils, she chose the one which would at least leave her self-respect.

'Yes, I did.'

Lady Caroline looked at Lord Belpher. Lord Belpher looked at Lady Caroline.

'You went to meet that American of yours?'

'Yes.'

Reggie Byng slid softly from the room. He felt that he would be happier elsewhere. He had been an acutely embarrassed spectator of this distressing scene, and had been passing the time by shuffling his feet, playing with his coat buttons, and perspiring.

'Don't go, Reggie,' said Lord Belpher.

'Well, what I mean to say is – family row and what not – if you see what I mean – I've one or two things I ought to do – '

He vanished. Lord Belpher frowned a sombre frown.

'Then it *was* that man who knocked my hat off?'

'What do you mean?' said Lady Caroline. 'Knocked your hat off? You never told me he knocked your hat off.'

'It was when I was asking him to let me look inside

the cab. I had grasped the handle of the door, when he suddenly struck my hat, causing it to fly off. And, while I was picking it up, he drove away.'

'C'k,' exploded Lord Marshmoreton. 'C'k, c'k, c'k.' He twisted his face by a supreme exertion of will power into a mask of indignation. 'You ought to have had the scoundrel arrested,' he said vehemently. 'It was a technical assault.'

'The man who knocked your hat off, Percy,' said Maud, 'was not . . . He was a different man altogether. A stranger.'

'As if you would be in a cab with a stranger,' said Lady Caroline caustically. 'There are limits, I hope, to even your indiscretions.'

Lord Marshmoreton cleared his throat. He was sorry for Maud, whom he loved.

'Now, looking at the matter broadly – '

'Be quiet,' said Lady Caroline.

Lord Marshmoreton subsided.

'I wanted to avoid you,' said Maud, 'so I jumped into the first cab I saw.'

'I don't believe it,' said Percy.

'It's the truth.'

'You are simply trying to put us off the scent.'

Lady Caroline turned to Maud. Her manner was plaintive. She looked like a martyr at the stake who deprecatingly lodges a timid complaint, fearful the while lest she may be hurting the feelings of her persecutors by appearing even for a moment out of sympathy with their activities.

'My dear child, why will you not be reasonable in this matter? Why will you not let yourself be guided by those who are older and wiser than you?'

'Exactly,' said Lord Belpher.

'The whole thing is too absurd.'

'Precisely,' said Lord Belpher.

Lady Caroline turned on him irritably.

'Please do not interrupt, Percy. Now, you've made me forget what I was going to say.'

'To my mind,' said Lord Marshmoreton, coming to the surface once more, 'the proper attitude to adopt on occasions like the present – '

'Please,' said Lady Caroline.

Lord Marshmoreton stopped, and resumed his silent communion with the stuffed bird.

'You can't stop yourself being in love, Aunt Caroline,' said Maud.

'You can *be* stopped if you've somebody with a level head looking after you.'

Lord Marshmoreton tore himself away from the bird.

'Why, when I was at Oxford in the year '87,' he said chattily, 'I fancied myself in love with the female assistant at a tobacconist shop. Desperately in love, dammit. Wanted to marry her. I recollect my poor father took me away from Oxford and kept me here at Belpher under lock and key. Lock *and* key, dammit. I was deucedly upset at the time, I remember.' His mind wandered off into the glorious past. 'I wonder what that girl's name was. Odd one can't remember names. She had chestnut hair and a mole on the side of her chin. I used to kiss it, I recollect – '

Lady Caroline, usually such an advocate of her brother's researches into the family history, cut the reminiscences short.

'Never mind that now.'

'I don't. I got over it. That's the moral.'

'Well,' said Lady Caroline, 'at any rate poor father acted with great good sense on that occasion. There seems nothing to do but to treat Maud in just the same way. You shall not stir a step from the castle till you have got over this dreadful infatuation. You will be watched.'

'*I* shall watch you,' said Lord Belpher solemnly, 'I shall watch your every movement.'

A dreamy look came into Maud's brown eyes.

'Stone walls do not a prison make nor iron bars a cage,' she said softly.

'That wasn't *your* experience, Percy, my boy,' said Lord Marshmoreton.

'They make a very good imitation,' said Lady Caroline coldly, ignoring the interruption.

Maud faced her defiantly. She looked like a princess in captivity facing her gaolers.

'I don't care. I love him, and I always shall love him, and nothing is ever going to stop me loving him – because I love him,' she concluded a little lamely.

'Nonsense,' said Lady Caroline. 'In a year from now you will have forgotten his name. Don't you agree with me, Percy?'

'Quite,' said Lord Belpher.

'I shan't.'

'Deuced hard things to remember, names,' said Lord Marshmoreton. 'If I've tried once to remember that tobacconist girl's name, I've tried a hundred times. I have an idea it began with an "L". Muriel or Hilda or something.'

'Within a year,' said Lady Caroline, 'you will be wondering how you ever came to be so foolish. Don't you think so, Percy?'

'Quite,' said Lord Belpher.

Lord Marshmoreton turned on him irritably.

'Good God, boy, can't you answer a simple question with a plain affirmative? What do you mean – quite? If somebody came to me and pointed you out and said, "Is that your son?" do you suppose I should say "Quite"? I wish the devil you didn't collect prayer rugs. It's sapped your brain.'

'They say prison life often weakens the intellect, father,' said Maud. She moved towards the door and turned the handle. Albert, the page-boy, who had been courting earache by listening at the keyhole, straightened his small body and scuttled away. 'Well, is that all, Aunt Caroline? May I go now?'

'Certainly. I have said all I wished to say.'

'Very well. I'm sorry to disobey you, but I can't help it.'

'You'll find you can help it after you've been cooped up here for a few more months,' said Percy.

A gentle smile played over Maud's face.

'Love laughs at locksmiths,' she murmured softly, and passed from the room.

'What did she say?' asked Lord Marshmoreton, interested. 'Something about somebody laughing at a locksmith? I don't understand. Why should anyone laugh at locksmiths? Most respectable men. Had one up here only the day before yesterday, forcing open the drawer of my desk. Watched him do it. Most interesting. He smelt rather strongly of a damned bad brand of tobacco. Fellow must have a throat of leather to be able to smoke the stuff. But he didn't strike me as an object of derision. From first to last, I was never tempted to laugh once.'

Lord Belpher wandered moodily to the window and looked out into the gathering darkness.

'And this has to happen', he said bitterly, 'on the eve of my twenty-first birthday.'

7

The first requisite of an invading army is a base. George, having entered Belpher village and thus accomplished the first stage in his forward movement on the castle, selected as his base the Marshmoreton Arms. Selected is perhaps hardly the right word, as it implies choice, and in George's case there was no choice. There are two inns at Belpher, but the Marshmoreton Arms is the only one that offers accommodation for man and beast, assuming – that is to say – that the man and beast desire to spend the night. The other house, the Blue Boar, is a mere beerhouse, where the lower strata of Belpher society gather of a night to quench their thirst and to tell one another interminable stories without any point whatsoever. But the Marshmoreton Arms is a comfortable, respectable hostelry, catering for the village plutocrats. There of an evening you will find the local veterinary surgeon smoking a pipe with the grocer, the baker, and the butcher, with perhaps a sprinkling of neighbouring farmers to help the conversation along. On Saturdays there is a 'shilling ordinary' – which is rural English for a cut off the joint and a boiled potato, followed by hunks of the sort of cheese which believes that it pays to advertise, and this is usually well attended. On the other days of the week, until late in the evening, however, the visitor to the Marshmoreton Arms has the place almost entirely to himself.

It is to be questioned whether in the whole length and breadth of the world there is a more admirable spot for a man in love to pass a day or two than the typical English village. The Rocky Mountains, that traditional stamping-ground for the heart-broken, may be well enough in their way; but a lover has to be cast in a pretty stern mould to be able to be introspective when at any moment he may meet an annoyed cinnamon bear. In the English village there are no such obstacles to meditation. It combines the comforts of civilization with the restfulness of solitude in a manner equalled by no other spot except the New York Public Library. Here your lover may wander to and fro unmolested, speaking to nobody, by nobody addressed, and have the satisfaction at the end of the day of sitting down to a capitally cooked chop and chips, lubricated by golden English ale.

Belpher, in addition to all the advantages of the usual village, has a quiet charm all its own, due to the fact that it has seen better days. In a sense, it is a ruin, and ruins are always soothing to the bruised soul. Ten years before, Belpher had been a flourishing centre of the South of England oyster trade. It is situated by the shore, where Hayling Island, lying athwart the mouth of the bay, forms the waters into a sort of brackish lagoon, in much the same way as Fire Island shuts off the Great South Bay of Long Island from the waves of the Atlantic. The water of Belpher Creek is shallow even at high tide, and when the tide runs out it leaves glistening mud flats, which it is the peculiar taste of the oyster to prefer to any other habitation. For years Belpher oysters had been the mainstay of gay supper parties at the Savoy, the Carlton, and Romano's. Dukes doted on them; chorus girls wept if they were not on the bill of fare. And then, in an evil hour, somebody discovered that what made the Belpher Oyster so particularly plump and succulent was the fact that it breakfasted, lunched, and dined almost entirely on the local sewage. There is but a thin line ever between popular homage and execration. We see it in the case of politicians, generals, and prize-fighters; and oysters are no exception to the rule. There was a typhoid scare –

quite a passing and unjustified scare, but strong enough to do its deadly work; and almost overnight Belpher passed from a place of flourishing industry to the sleepy, by-the-world-forgotten spot which it was when George Bevan discovered it. The shallow water is still there; the mud is still there; even the oyster-beds are still there; but not the oysters nor the little world of activity which had sprung up around them. The glory of Belpher is dead; and over its gates Ichabod is written. But, if it has lost in importance, it has gained in charm; and George, for one, had no regrets. To him, in his present state of mental upheaval, Belpher was the ideal spot.

It was not at first that George roused himself to the point of asking why he was here and what – now that he was here – he proposed to do. For two languorous days he loafed, sufficiently occupied with his thoughts. He smoked long, peaceful pipes in the stable-yard, watching the ostlers as they groomed the horses; he played with the Inn puppy, bestowed respectful caresses on the Inn cat. He walked down the quaint cobbled street to the harbour, sauntered along the shore, and lay on his back on the little beach at the other side of the lagoon, from where he could see the red roofs of the village, while the imitation waves splashed busily on the stones, trying to conceal with bustle and energy the fact that the water even two hundred yards from the shore was only eighteen inches deep. For it is the abiding hope of Belpher Creek that it may be able to deceive the occasional visitor into mistaking it for the open sea.

And presently the tide would ebb. The waste of waters became a sea of mud, cheerfully covered as to much of its surface with green grasses. The evening sun struck rainbow colours from the moist softness. Birds sang in the thickets. And George, heaving himself up, walked back to the friendly cosiness of the Marshmoreton Arms. And the remarkable part of it was that everything seemed perfectly natural and sensible to him, nor had he any particular feeling that in falling in love with Lady Maud Marsh and pursuing her to Belpher he had set himself anything in the nature of a hopeless task. Like one kissed by a goddess in a dream, he walked on air; and, while one is walking on air, it is easy to overlook the boulders in the path.

Consider his position, you faint-hearted and self-pitying young men who think you have a tough row to hoe just because, when you pay your evening visit with the pound box of candy under your arm, you see the handsome sophomore from Yale sitting beside her on the porch, playing the ukulele. If ever the world has turned black to you in such a situation and the moon gone in behind a cloud, think of George Bevan and what he was up against. You are at least on the spot. You can at least put up a fight. If there are ukuleles in the world, there are also guitars, and tomorrow it may be you and not he who sits on the moonlit porch; it may be he and not you who arrives late. Who knows? Tomorrow he may not show up till you have finished the Bedouin's Love Song and are annoying the local birds, roosting in the trees, with Poor Butterfly.

What I mean to say is, you are on the map. You have a sporting chance. Whereas George . . . Well, just go over to England and try wooing an earl's daughter whom you have only met once – and then without an introduction; whose brother's hat you have smashed beyond repair; whose family wishes her to marry some other man: who wants to marry some other man herself – and not the same other man, but another other man; who is closely immured in a medieval castle . . . Well, all I say is – try it. And then go back to your porch with a chastened spirit and admit that you might be a whole lot worse off.

George, as I say, had not envisaged the peculiar difficulties of his position. Nor did he until the evening of his second day at the Marshmoreton Arms. Until then, as I have indicated, he roamed in a golden mist of dreamy meditation among the soothing by-ways of the village of Belpher. But after lunch on the second day it came upon him that all this sort of thing was pleasant but not practical. Action was what was needed. Action.

The first, the obvious move was to locate the castle. Inquiries at the Marshmoreton Arms elicited the fact that it was 'a step' up the road that ran past the front door of the inn. But this wasn't the day of the week when the general public was admitted. The sightseer could invade Belpher Castle on Thursdays only, between the hours of two and four. On other days of the week all he could do was to stand like Moses on Pisgah and take in the general effect from a distance. As this was all that George had hoped to be able to do, he set forth.

It speedily became evident to George that 'a step' was a euphemism. Five miles did he tramp before, trudging wearily up a winding lane, he came out on a breeze-swept hill-top, and saw below him, nestling in its trees, what was now for him the centre of the world. He sat on a stone wall and lit a pipe. Belpher Castle. Maud's home. There it was. And now what?

The first thought that came to him was practical, even prosaic – the thought that he couldn't possibly do this five-miles-there and-five-miles-back walk, every time he wanted to see the place. He must shift his base nearer the scene of operations. One of those trim, thatched cottages down there in the valley would be just the thing, if he could arrange to take possession of it. They sat there all round the castle, singly and in groups, like small dogs round their master. They looked as if they had been there for centuries. Probably they had, as they were made of stone as solid as that of the castle. There must have been a time, thought George, when the castle was the central rallying-point for all those scattered homes; when rumour of danger from marauders had sent all that little community scuttling for safety to the sheltering walls.

For the first time since he had set out on his expedition,

a certain chill, a discomforting sinking of the heart, afflicted George as he gazed down at the grim grey fortress which he had undertaken to storm. So must have felt those marauders of old when they climbed to the top of this very hill to spy out the land. And George's case was even worse than theirs. They could at least hope that a strong arm and a stout heart would carry them past those solid walls; they had not to think of social etiquette. Whereas George was so situated that an unsympathetic butler could put him to rout by refusing him admittance.

The evening was drawing in. Already, in the brief time he had spent on the hill-top, the sky had turned from blue to saffron and from saffron to grey. The plaintive voices of homing cows floated up to him from the valley below. A bat had left its shelter and was wheeling around him, a sinister blot against the sky. A sickle moon gleamed over the trees. George felt cold. He turned. The shadows of night wrapped him round, and little things in the hedgerows chirped and chittered mockery at him as he stumbled down the lane.

George's request for a lonely furnished cottage somewhere in the neighbourhood of the castle did not, as he had feared, strike the Belpher house-agent as the demand of a lunatic. Every well-dressed stranger who comes to Belpher is automatically set down by the natives as an artist, for the picturesqueness of the place has caused it to be much infested by the brothers and sisters of the brush. In asking for a cottage, indeed, George did precisely as Belpher society expected him to do; and the agent was reaching for his list almost before the words were out of his mouth. In less than half an hour George was out in the street again, the owner for the season of what the agent described as a 'gem' and the employer of a farmer's wife who lived near-by and would, as was her custom with artists, come in the morning and evening to 'do' for him. The interview would have taken but a few minutes, had it not been prolonged by the chattiness of the agent on the subject of the occupants of the castle, to which George listened attentively. He was not greatly encouraged by what he heard of Lord Marshmoreton. The earl had made himself notably unpopular in the village recently by his firm – the house-agent said 'pig-headed' – attitude in respect to a certain dispute about a right-of-way. It was Lady Caroline, and not the easy-going peer, who was really to blame in the matter; but the impression that George got from the house-agent's description of Lord Marshmoreton was that the latter was a sort of Nero, possessing, in addition to the qualities of a Roman tyrant, many of the least lovable traits of the ghila monster of Arizona. Hearing this about her father, and having already had the privilege of meeting her brother and studying him at first hand, his heart bled for Maud. It seemed to him that existence at the castle in such society must be little short of torture.

'I must do something,' he muttered. 'I must do something quick.'

'Beg pardon,' said the house-agent.

'Nothing,' said George. 'Well, I'll take that cottage. I'd better write you a cheque for the first month's rent now.'

So George took up his abode, full of strenuous – if vague – purpose, in the plainly furnished but not uncomfortable cottage known locally as 'the one down by Platt's'. He might have found a worse billet. It was a two-storied building of stained red brick, not one of the thatched nests on which he had looked down from the hill. Those were not for rent, being occupied by families whose ancestors had occupied them for generations back. The one down by Platt's was a more modern structure – a speculation, in fact, of the farmer whose wife came to 'do' for George, and designed especially to accommodate the stranger who had the desire and the money to rent it. It so departed from type that it possessed a small but undeniable bath-room. Besides this miracle, there was a cosy sitting-room, a larger bedroom on the floor above, and next to this an empty room facing north, which had evidently served artist occupants as a studio. The remainder of the ground floor was taken up by kitchen and scullery. The furniture had been constructed by somebody who would probably have done very well if he had taken up some other line of industry; but it was mitigated by a very fine and comfortable wicker easy chair, left there by one of last year's artists; and other artists had helped along the good work by relieving the plainness of the walls with a landscape or two. In fact, when George had removed from the room two antimacassars, three group photographs of the farmer's relations, an illuminated text, and a china statuette of the Infant Samuel, and stacked them in a corner of the empty studio, the place became almost a home from home.

Solitude can be very unsolitary if a man is in love. George never even began to be bored. The only thing that in any way troubled his peace was the thought that he was not accomplishing a great deal in the matter of helping Maud out of whatever trouble it was that had befallen her. The most he could do was to prowl about roads near the castle in the hope of an accidental meeting. And such was his good fortune that, on the fourth day of his vigil, the accidental meeting occurred.

Taking his morning prowl along the lanes, he was rewarded by the sight of a grey racing-car at the side of the road. It was empty, but from underneath it protruded a pair of long legs, while beside it stood a girl, at the sight of whom George's heart began to thump so violently that the long-legged one might have been pardoned had he supposed that his engine had started again of its own volition.

Until he spoke the soft grass had kept her from hearing his approach. He stopped close behind her, and cleared his throat. She started and turned, and their eyes met.

For a moment hers were empty of any recognition.

Then they lit up. She caught her breath quickly, and a faint flush came into her face.

'Can I help you?' asked George.

The long legs wriggled out into the road followed by a long body. The young man under the car sat up, turning a grease-streaked and pleasant face to George.

'Eh, what?'

'Can I help you? I know how to fix a car.'

The young man beamed in friendly fashion.

'It's awfully good of you, old chap, but so do I. It's the only thing I can do well. Thanks very much and so forth all the same.'

George fastened his eyes on the girl's. She had not spoken.

'If there is anything in the world I can possibly do for you,' he said slowly, 'I hope you will let me know. I should like above all things to help you.'

The girl spoke.

'Thank you,' she said in a low voice almost inaudible.

George walked away. The grease-streaked young man followed him with his gaze.

'Civil cove, that,' he said. 'Rather gushing though, what? American, wasn't he?'

'Yes. I think he was.'

'Americans are the civillest coves I ever struck. I remember asking the way of a chappie at Baltimore a couple of years ago when I was there in my yacht, and he followed me for miles, shrieking advice and encouragement. I thought it deuced civil of him.'

'I wish you would hurry up and get the car right, Reggie. We shall be awfully late for lunch.'

Reggie Byng began to slide backwards under the car.

'All right, dear heart. Rely on me. It's something quite simple.'

'Well, do be quick.'

'Imitation of greased lightning – very difficult,' said Reggie encouragingly. 'Be patient. Try and amuse yourself somehow. Ask yourself a riddle. Tell yourself a few anecdotes. I'll be with you in a moment. I say, I wonder what the cove is doing at Belpher? Deuced civil cove,' said Reggie approvingly. 'I liked him. And now, business of repairing breakdown.'

His smiling face vanished under the car like the Cheshire cat. Maud stood looking thoughtfully down the road in the direction in which George had disappeared.

8

The following day was a Thursday and on Thursdays, as has been stated, Belpher Castle was thrown open to the general public between the hours of two and four. It was a tradition of long standing, this periodical lowering of the barriers, and had always been faithfully observed by Lord Marshmoreton ever since his accession to the title. By the permanent occupants of the castle the day was regarded with mixed feelings. Lord Belpher, while approving of it in theory, as he did of all the family traditions – for he was a great supporter of all things feudal, and took his position as one of the hereditary aristocracy of Great Britain extremely seriously – heartily disliked it in practice. More than once he had been obliged to exit hastily by a further door in order to keep from being discovered sitting by a drove of tourists intent on inspecting the library or the great drawing-room; and now it was his custom to retire to his bedroom immediately after lunch and not to emerge until the tide of invasion had ebbed away.

Keggs, the butler, always looked forward to Thursdays with pleasurable anticipation. He enjoyed the sense of added authority which it gave him to herd these poor outcasts to and fro among the surroundings which were an every-day commonplace to himself. Also he liked hearing the sound of his own voice as it lectured in rolling periods on the objects of interest by the wayside. But even to Keggs there was a bitter mixed with the sweet. No one was better aware than himself that the nobility of his manner, excellent as a means of impressing the mob, worked against him when it came to a question of tips. Again and again had he been harrowed by the spectacle of tourists, huddled together like sheep, debating among themselves in nervous whispers as to whether they could offer this personage anything so contemptible as a half-crown for himself, and deciding that such an insult was out of the question. It was his constant endeavour, especially towards the end of the proceedings, to cultivate a manner blending a dignity fitting his position with a sunny geniality which would allay the timid doubts of the tourist and indicate to him that, bizarre as the idea might seem, there was nothing to prevent him placing his poor silver in more worthy hands.

Possibly the only member of the castle community who was absolutely indifferent to these public visits was Lord Marshmoreton. He made no difference between Thursday and any other day. Precisely as usual he donned his stained corduroys and pottered about his beloved garden; and when, as happened on an average once a quarter, some visitor, strayed from the main herd, came upon him as he worked and mistook him for one of the gardeners, he accepted the error without any attempt at explanation, sometimes going so far as to encourage it by adopting a rustic accent in keeping with his appearance. This sort of thing tickled the simple-minded peer.

George joined the procession punctually at two o'clock, just as Keggs was clearing his throat preparatory to saying, 'We are now in the main 'all, and before going any further I would like to call your attention to Sir Peter Lely's portrait of – ' It was his custom to begin his Thursday lectures with this remark, but today it was postponed; for, no sooner had George appeared, than a breezy voice on the outskirts of the throng spoke in a tone that made competition impossible.

'For goodness' sake, George.'

And Billie Dore detached herself from the group, a

trim vision in blue. She wore a dust-coat and a motor veil, and her eyes and cheeks were glowing from the fresh air.

'For goodness' sake, George, what are you doing here?'

'I was just going to ask you the same thing.'

'Oh, I motored down with a boy I know. We had a breakdown just outside the gates. We were on our way to Brighton for lunch. He suggested I should pass the time seeing the sights while he fixed up the sprockets or the differential gear or whatever it was. He's coming to pick me up when he's through. But, on the level, George, how do you get this way? You sneak out of town and leave the show flat, and nobody has a notion where you are. Why, we were thinking of advertising for you, or going to the police or something. For all anybody knew, you might have been sandbagged or dropped in the river.'

This aspect of the matter had not occurred to George till now. His sudden descent on Belpher had seemed to him the only natural course to pursue. He had not realized that he would be missed, and that his absence might have caused grave inconvenience to a large number of people.

'I never thought of that. I – well, I just happened to come here.'

'You aren't *living* in this old castle?'

'Not quite. I've a cottage down the road. I wanted a few days in the country so I rented it.'

'But what made you choose this place?'

Keggs, who had been regarding these disturbers of the peace with dignified disapproval, coughed.

'If you would not mind, madam. We are waiting.'

'Eh? How's that?' Miss Dore looked up with a bright smile. 'I'm sorry. Come along, George. Get in the game.' She nodded cheerfully to the butler. 'All right. All set now. You may fire when ready, Gridley.'

Keggs bowed austerely, and cleared his throat again.

'We are now in the main 'all, and before going any

further I would like to call your attention to Sir Peter Lely's portrait of the fifth countess. Said by experts to be in his best manner.'

There was an almost soundless murmur from the mob, expressive of wonder and awe, like a gentle breeze rustling leaves. Billie Dore resumed her conversation in a whisper.

'Yes, there was an awful lot of excitement when they found that you had disappeared. They were phoning the Carlton every ten minutes trying to get you. You see, the summertime number flopped on the second night, and they hadn't anything to put in its place. But it's all right. They took it out and sewed up the wound, and now you'd never know there had been anything wrong. The show was ten minutes too long, anyway.'

'How's the show going?'

'It's a riot. They think it will run two years in London. As far as I can make it out you don't call it a success in London unless you can take your grandchildren to see the thousandth night.'

'That's splendid. And how is everybody? All right?'

'Fine. That fellow Gray is still hanging round Babe. It beats me what she sees in him. Anybody but an infant could see the man wasn't on the level. Well, I don't blame you for quitting London, George. This sort of thing is worth fifty Londons.'

The procession had reached one of the upper rooms, and they were looking down from a window that commanded a sweep of miles of the countryside, rolling and green and wooded. Far away beyond the last covert Belpher Bay gleamed like a streak of silver. Billie Dore gave a little sigh.

'There's nothing like this in the world. I'd like to stand here for the rest of my life, just lapping it up.'

'I will call your attention,' boomed Keggs at their elbow, 'to this window, known in the fem'ly tredition as Leonard's Leap. It was in the year seventeen 'undred and eighty-seven that Lord Leonard Forth, eldest son of 'Is Grace the Dook of Lochlane, 'urled 'imself out of this window in order to avoid compromising the beautiful Countess of Marshmoreton, with oom 'e is related to 'ave 'ad a ninnocent romance. Surprised at an advanced hour by 'is lordship the earl in 'er ladyship's boudoir, as this room then was, 'e leaped through the open window into the boughs of the cedar tree which stands below, and was fortunate enough to escape with a few 'armless contusions.'

A murmur of admiration greeted the recital of the ready tact of this eighteenth-century Steve Brodie.

'There,' said Billie enthusiastically, 'that's exactly what I mean about this country. It's just a mass of Leonard's Leaps and things. I'd like to settle down in this sort of place and spend the rest of my life milking cows and taking forkfuls of soup to the deserving villagers.'

'We will now,' said Keggs, herding the mob with a gesture, 'proceed to the Amber Drawing-Room, containing some Gobelin Tapestries 'ighly spoken of by connoozers.'

The obedient mob began to drift out in his wake.

'What do you say, George,' asked Billie in an undertone, 'if we side-step the Amber Drawing-Room? I'm wild to get into that garden. There's a man working among those roses. Maybe he would show us round.'

George followed her pointing finger. Just below them a sturdy, brown-faced man in corduroys was pausing to light a stubby pipe.

'Just as you like.'

They made their way down the great staircase. The voice of Keggs, saying complimentary things about the Gobelin Tapestry, came to their ears like the roll of distant drums. They wandered out towards the rose-garden. The man in corduroys had lit his pipe and was bending once more to his task.

'Well, dadda,' said Billie amiably, 'how are the crops?'

The man straightened himself. He was a nice-looking man of middle age, with the kind eyes of a friendly dog. He smiled genially, and started to put his pipe away.

Billie stopped him.

'Don't stop smoking on my account,' she said. 'I like it. Well, you've got the right sort of a job, haven't you! If I was a man, there's nothing I'd like better than to put my eight hours in a rose-garden.' She looked about her. 'And this,' she said with approval, 'is just what a rose-garden ought to be.'

'Are you fond of roses – missy?'

'You bet I am! You must have every kind here that was ever invented. All the fifty-seven varieties.'

'There are nearly three thousand varieties,' said the man in corduroys tolerantly.

'I was speaking colloquially, dadda. You can't teach *me* anything about roses. I'm the guy that invented them. Got any Ayrshires?'

The man in corduroys seemed to have come to the conclusion that Billie was the only thing on earth that mattered. This revelation of a kindred spirit had captured him completely. George was merely among those present.

'Those – them – over there are Ayrshires, missy.'

'We don't get Ayrshires in America. At least, I never ran across them. I suppose they do have them.'

'You want the right soil.'

'Clay and lots of rain.'

'You're right.'

There was an earnest expression on Billie Dore's face that George had never seen there before.

'Say, listen, dadda, in this matter of rose-beetles, what would you do if – '

George moved away. The conversation was becoming too technical for him, and he had an idea that he would not be missed. There had come to him, moreover, in a flash one of those sudden inspirations which great generals get. He had visited the castle this afternoon without any settled plan other than a vague hope that he might somehow see Maud. He now perceived that there was no chance of doing this. Evidently, on Thursdays, the family went to earth and remained hidden until the sightseers had gone. But there was another avenue of communication open to him. This gardener seemed an exceptionally intelligent man. He could be trusted to deliver a note to Maud.

In his late rambles about Belpher Castle in the company of Keggs and his followers, George had been privileged to inspect the library. It was an easily accessible room, opening off the main hall. He left Billie and her new friend deep in a discussion of slugs and plant-lice, and walked quickly back to the house. The library was unoccupied.

George was a thorough young man. He believed in leaving nothing to chance. The gardener had seemed a trustworthy soul, but you never knew. It was possible that he drank. He might forget or lose the precious note. So, with a wary eye on the door, George hastily scribbled it in duplicate. This took him but a few minutes. He went out into the garden again to find Billie Dore on the point of stepping into a blue automobile.

'Oh, there you are, George. I wondered where you had got to. Say, I made quite a hit with dadda. I've given him my address, and he's promised to send me a whole lot of roses. By the way, shake hands with Mr Forsyth. This is George Bevan, Freddie, who wrote the music of our show.'

The solemn youth at the wheel extended a hand.

'Topping show. Topping music. Topping all round.'

'Well, good-bye, George. See you soon, I suppose?'

'Oh, yes. Give my love to everybody.'

'All right. Let her rip, Freddie. Good-bye.'

'Good-bye.'

The blue car gathered speed and vanished down the

drive. George returned to the man in corduroys, who had bent himself double in pursuit of a slug.

'Just a minute,' said George hurriedly. He pulled out the first of the notes. 'Give this to Lady Maud the first chance you get. It's important. Here's a sovereign for your trouble.'

He hastened away. He noticed that gratification had turned the other nearly purple in the face, and was anxious to leave him. He was a modest young man, and effusive thanks always embarrassed him.

There now remained the disposal of the duplicate note. It was hardly worth while, perhaps, taking such a precaution, but George knew that victories are won by those who take no chances. He had wandered perhaps a hundred yards from the rose-garden when he encountered a small boy in the many-buttoned uniform of a page. The boy had appeared from behind a big cedar, where, as a matter of fact, he had been smoking a stolen cigarette.

'Do you want to earn a half-crown?' asked George.

The market value of messengers had slumped.

The stripling held his hand out.

'Give this note to Lady Maud.'

'Right ho!'

'See that it reaches her at once.'

George walked off with the consciousness of a good day's work done. Albert the page, having bitten his half-crown, placed it in his pocket. Then he hurried away, a look of excitement and gratification in his deep blue eyes.

9

While George and Billie Dore wandered to the rose-garden to interview the man in corduroys, Maud had been seated not a hundred yards away – in a very special haunt of her own, a cracked stucco temple set up in the days of the Regency on the shores of a little lily-covered pond. She was reading poetry to Albert the page.

Albert the page was a recent addition to Maud's inner circle. She had interested herself in him some two months back in much the same spirit as the prisoner in his dungeon cell tames and pets the conventional mouse. To educate Albert, to raise him above his groove in life, and develop his soul, appealed to her romantic nature as a worthy task, and as a good way of filling in the time. It is an exceedingly moot point – and one which his associates of the servants' hall would have combated hotly – whether Albert possessed a soul. The most one could say for certain is that he looked as if he possessed one. To one who saw his deep blue eyes and their sweet, pensive expression as they searched the middle distance he seemed like a young angel. How was the watcher to know that the thought behind that far-off gaze was simply a speculation as to whether the bird on the cedar tree was or was not within range of his catapult? Certainly Maud had no such suspicion. She worked hopefully day by day to rouse Albert to an appreciation of the nobler things of life.

Not but what it was tough going. Even she admitted that. Albert's soul did not soar readily. It refused to leap from the earth. His reception of the poem she was reading could scarcely have been called encouraging. Maud finished it in a hushed voice, and looked pensively across the dappled water of the pool. A gentle breeze stirred the water-lilies, so that they seemed to sigh.

'Isn't that beautiful, Albert?' she said.

Albert's blue eyes lit up. His lips parted eagerly.

'That's the first hornet I seen this year,' he said pointing.

Maud felt a little damped.

'Haven't you been listening, Albert?'

'Oh, yes, m'lady! Ain't he a wopper, too?'

'Never mind the hornet, Albert.'

'Very good, m'lady.'

'I wish you wouldn't say "Very good, m'lady". It's like – like – ' She paused. She had been about to say that it was like a butler, but, she reflected regretfully, it was probably Albert's dearest ambition to be like a butler. 'It doesn't sound right. Just say "Yes".'

'Yes, m'lady.'

Maud was not enthusiastic about the 'M'lady', but she let it go. After all, she had not quite settled in her own mind what exactly she wished Albert's attitude towards herself to be. Broadly speaking, she wanted him to be as like as he could to a medieval page, one of those silk-and-satined little treasures she had read about in the Ingoldsby Legends. And, of course, they presumably said 'my lady'. And yet – she felt – not for the first time – that it is not easy, to revive the Middle Ages in these curious days. Pages, like other things, seem to have changed since then.

'That poem was written by a very clever man who married one of my ancestresses. He ran away with her from this very castle in the seventeenth century.'

'Lor,' said Albert as a concession, but he was still interested in the hornet.

'He was far below her in the eyes of the world, but she knew what a wonderful man he was, so she didn't mind what people said about her marrying beneath her.'

'Like Susan when she married the pleeceman.'

'Who was Susan?'

'Red-'eaded gel that used to be cook 'ere. Mr Keggs says to 'er, 'e says, "You're marrying beneath you, Susan," 'e says. I 'eard 'im. I was listenin' at the door. And she says to 'im, she says, "Oh, go and boil your fat 'ead," she says.'

This translation of a favourite romance into terms of the servants' hall chilled Maud like a cold shower. She recoiled from it.

'Wouldn't you like to get a good education, Albert,' she said perseveringly, 'and become a great poet and write wonderful poems?'

Albert considered the point, and shook his head.

'No, m'lady.'

It was discouraging. But Maud was a girl of pluck. You cannot leap into strange cabs in Piccadilly unless you have pluck. She picked up another book from the stone seat.

'Read me some of this,' she said, 'and then tell me if it doesn't make you feel you want to do big things.'

Albert took the book cautiously. He was getting a little fed up with all this sort of thing. True, 'er ladyship gave him chocolates to eat during these sessions, but for all that it was too much like school for his taste. He regarded the open page with disfavour.

'Go on,' said Maud, closing her eyes. 'It's very beautiful.'

Albert began. He had a husky voice, due, it is to be feared, to precocious cigarette smoking, and his enunciation was not as good as it might have been.

'Wiv' blekest morss the flower-ports
    Was – I mean were – crusted one and orl;
Ther rusted niles fell from the knorts
    That 'eld the pear to the garden-worll.
Ther broken sheds looked sed and stringe;
    Unlifted was the clinking latch;

Weeded and worn their ancient thatch
Er-pon ther lownely moated gringe,
She only said "Me life is dreary,
'E cometh nort," she said.'

Albert rather liked this part. He was never happy in narrative unless it could be sprinkled with a plentiful supply of 'he said's' and 'she said's'. He finished with some gusto.

'She said "I am aweary, aweary,
I would that I was dead."'

Maud had listened to this rendition of one of her most adored poems with much the same feeling which a composer with an over-sensitive ear would suffer on hearing his pet opus assassinated by a schoolgirl. Albert, who was a willing lad and prepared, if such should be her desire, to plough his way through the entire seven stanzas, began the second verse, but Maud gently took the book away from him. Enough was sufficient.

'Now, wouldn't you like to be able to write a wonderful thing like that, Albert?'

'Not me, m'lady.'

'You wouldn't like to be a poet when you grow up?'

Albert shook his golden head.

'I want to be a butcher when I grow up, m'lady.'

Maud uttered a little cry.

'A butcher?'

'Yus, m'lady. Butchers earn good money,' he said, a light of enthusiasm in his blue eyes, for he was now on his favourite subject. 'You've got to 'ave meat, yer see, m'lady. It ain't like poetry, m'lady, which no one wants.'

'But, Albert,' cried Maud faintly. 'Killing poor animals. Surely you wouldn't like that?'

Albert's eyes glowed softly, as might an acolyte's at the sight of the censer.

'Mr Widgeon down at the 'ome farm,' he murmured reverently, 'he says, if I'm a good boy, 'e'll let me watch 'im kill a pig Toosday.'

He gazed out over the water-lilies, his thoughts far away. Maud shuddered. She wondered if medieval pages were ever quite as earthy as this.

'Perhaps you had better go now, Albert. They may be needing you in the house.'

'Very good, m'lady.'

Albert rose, not unwilling to call it a day. He was conscious of the need for a quiet cigarette. He was fond of Maud, but a man can't spend all his time with the women.

'Pigs squeal like billy-o, m'lady!' he observed by way of adding a parting treasure to Maud's stock of general knowledge. 'Oo! 'Ear 'em a mile orf, you can!'

Maud remained where she was, thinking, a wistful figure. Tennyson's *Mariana* always made her wistful even when rendered by Albert. In the occasional moods of sentimental depression which came to vary her normal cheerfulness, it seemed to her that the poem might have been written with a prophetic eye to her special case, so nearly did it crystallize in magic words her own story.

With blackest moss the flower-pots
Were thickly crusted, one and all.

Well, no, not that particular part, perhaps. If he had found so much as one flower-pot of his even thinly crusted with any foreign substance, Lord Marshmoreton would have gone through the place like an east wind, dismissing gardeners and under-gardeners with every breath. But –

She only said 'My life is dreary,
He cometh not,' she said.

She said 'I am aweary, aweary,
I would that I were dead!'

How exactly – at these moments when she was not out on the links picking them off the turf with a midiron or engaged in one of those other healthful sports which tend to take the mind off its troubles – those words summed up her case.

Why didn't Geoffrey come? Or at least write? She could not write to him. Letters from the castle left only by way of the castle post-bag, which Rogers, the chauffeur, took down to the village every evening. Impossible to entrust the kind of letter she wished to write to any mode of delivery so public – especially now, when her movements were watched. To open and read another's letters is a low and dastardly act, but she believed that Lady Caroline would do it like a shot. She longed to pour out her heart to Geoffrey in a long, intimate letter, but she did not dare to take the risk of writing for a wider public. Things were bad enough as it was, after that disastrous sortie to London.

At this point a soothing vision came to her – the vision of George Bevan knocking off her brother Percy's hat. It was the only pleasant thing that had happened almost as far back as she could remember. And then, for the first time, her mind condescended to dwell for a moment on the author of that act, George Bevan, the friend in need, whom she had met only the day before in the lane. What was George doing at Belpher? His presence there was significant, and his words even more so. He had stated explicitly that he wished to help her.

She found herself oppressed by the irony of things. A knight had come to the rescue – but the wrong knight. Why could it not have been Geoffrey who waited in ambush outside the castle, and not a pleasant but negligible stranger? Whether, deep down in her consciousness, she was aware of a fleeting sense of disappointment in Geoffrey, a swiftly passing thought that he had failed her, she could hardly have said, so quickly did she crush it down.

She pondered on the arrival of George. What was the use of his being somewhere in the neighbourhood if she had no means of knowing where she could find him? Situated as she was, she could not wander at will about the countryside, looking for him. And, even if she found him, what then? There was not much that any stranger, however pleasant, could do.

She flushed at a sudden thought. Of course there was something George could do for her if he were willing. He could receive, despatch, and deliver letters. If only she could get in touch with him, she could – through him – get in touch with Geoffrey.

The whole world changed for her. The sun was setting and chill little winds had begun to stir the lily-pads, giving a depressing air to the scene, but to Maud it seemed as if all Nature smiled. With the egotism of love, she did not perceive that what she proposed to ask George to do was practically to fulfil the humble role of the hollow tree in which lovers dump letters, to be extracted later; she did not consider George's feelings at all. He had offered to help her, and this was his job. The world is full of Georges whose task it is to hang about in the background and make themselves unobtrusively useful.

She had reached this conclusion when Albert, who had taken a short cut the more rapidly to accomplish his errand, burst upon her dramatically from the heart of a rhododendron thicket.

'M'lady! Gentleman give me this to give yer!'

Maud read the note. It was brief, and to the point.

I am staying near the castle at a cottage they call 'the one down by Platt's'. It is a rather new red-brick place. You can easily find it. I shall be waiting there if you want me.

It was signed 'The Man in the Cab'.

'Do you know a cottage called "the one down by Platt's", Albert?' asked Maud.

'Yes, m'lady. It's down by Platt's farm. I see a chicken killed there Wednesday week. Do you know, m'lady, after a chicken's 'ead is cut orf, it goes running licketty-split?'

Maud shivered slightly. Albert's fresh young enthusiasms frequently jarred upon her.

'I find a friend of mine is staying there. I want you to take a note to him from me.'

'Very good, m'lady.'

'And, Albert – '

'Yes, m'lady?'

'Perhaps it would be as well if you said nothing about this to any of your friends.'

In Lord Marshmoreton's study a council of three was sitting in debate. The subject under discussion was that other note which George had written and so ill-advisedly entrusted to one whom he had taken for a guileless gardener. The council consisted of Lord Marshmoreton, looking rather shamefaced, his son Percy looking swollen and serious, and Lady Caroline Byng, looking like a tragedy queen.

'This,' Lord Belpher was saying in a determined voice, 'settles it. From now on Maud must not be allowed out of our sight.'

Lord Marshmoreton spoke.

'I rather wish,' he said regretfully, 'I hadn't spoken about the note. I only mentioned it because I thought you might think it amusing.'

'Amusing!' Lady Caroline's voice shook the furniture.

'Amusing that the fellow should have handed me of all people a letter for Maud,' explained her brother. 'I don't want to get Maud into trouble.'

'You are criminally weak,' said Lady Caroline severely. 'I really honestly believe that you were capable of giving the note to that poor, misguided girl, and saying nothing about it.' She flushed. 'The insolence of the man, coming here and settling down at the very gates of the castle! If it was anybody but this man Platt who was giving him shelter I should insist on his being turned out. But that man Platt would be only too glad to know that he is causing us annoyance.'

'Quite!' said Lord Belpher.

'You must go to this man as soon as possible,' continued Lady Caroline, fixing her brother with a commanding stare, 'and do your best to make him see how abominable his behaviour is.'

'Oh, I couldn't!' pleaded the earl. 'I don't know the fellow. He'd throw me out.'

'Nonsense. Go at the very earliest opportunity.'

'Oh, all right, all right, all right. Well, I think I'll be slipping out to the rose-garden again now. There's a clear hour before dinner.'

There was a tap at the door. Alice Faraday entered bearing papers, a smile of sweet helpfulness on her pretty face.

'I hoped I should find you here, Lord Marshmoreton. You promised to go over these notes with me, the ones about the Essex branch – '

The hunted peer looked as if he were about to dive through the window.

'Some other time, some other time. I – I have important matters – '

'Oh, if you're busy – '

'Of course, Lord Marshmoreton will be delighted to work on your notes, Miss Faraday,' said Lady Caroline crisply. 'Take this chair. We are just going.'

Lord Marshmoreton gave one wistful glance through the open window. Then he sat down with a sigh, and felt for his reading-glasses.

10

Your true golfer is a man who, knowing that life is short and perfection hard to attain, neglects no opportunity of practising his chosen sport, allowing neither wind nor weather nor any external influence to keep him from it. There is a story, with an excellent moral lesson, of a golfer whose wife had determined to leave him for ever. 'Will nothing alter your decision?' he says. 'Will nothing induce you to stay? Well, then, while you're packing, I think I'll go out on the lawn and rub up my putting a bit.' George Bevan was of this turn of mind. He might be in love; romance might have sealed him for her own; but that was no reason for blinding himself to the fact that his long game was bound to suffer if he neglected to keep himself up to the mark. His first act on arriving at Belpher village had been to ascertain whether there was a links in the neighbourhood; and thither, on the morning after his visit to the castle and the delivery of the two notes, he repaired.

At the hour of the day which he had selected the club-house was empty, and he had just resigned himself to a solitary game, when, with a whirr and a rattle, a grey racing-car drove up, and from it emerged the same long young man whom, a couple of days earlier, he had seen wriggle out from underneath the same machine. It was Reggie Byng's habit also not to allow anything, even love, to interfere with golf; and not even the prospect of hanging about the castle grounds in the hope of catching a glimpse of Alice Faraday and exchanging timorous words with her had been enough to keep him from the links.

Reggie surveyed George with a friendly eye. He had a dim recollection of having seen him before somewhere at some time or other, and Reggie had the pleasing disposition which caused him to rank anybody whom he had seen somewhere at some time or other as a bosom friend.

'Hullo! Hullo! Hullo!' he observed.

'Good morning,' said George.

'Waiting for somebody?'

'No.'

'How about it, then? Shall we stagger forth?'

'Delighted.'

George found himself speculating upon Reggie. He was unable to place him. That he was a friend of Maud he knew, and guessed that he was also a resident of the castle. He would have liked to question Reggie, to probe him, to collect from him inside information as to the progress of events within the castle walls; but it is a peculiarity of golf, as of love, that it temporarily changes the natures of its victims; and Reggie, a confirmed babbler off the links, became while in action a stern, silent, intent person, his whole being centred on the game. With the exception of a casual remark of a technical nature when he met George on the various tees, and an occasional expletive when things went wrong with his ball, he eschewed conversation. It was not till the end of the round that he became himself again.

'If I'd known you were such hot stuff,' he declared generously, as George holed his eighteenth putt from a distance of ten feet, 'I'd have got you to give me a stroke or two.'

'I was on my game today,' said George modestly. 'Sometimes I slice as if I were cutting bread and can't putt to hit a haystack.'

'Let me know when one of those times comes along, and I'll take you on again. I don't know when I've seen anything fruitier than the way you got out of the bunker at the fifteenth. It reminded me of a match I saw between – ' Reggie became technical. At the end of his observations he climbed into the grey car.

'Can I drop you anywhere?'

'Thanks,' said George. 'If it's not taking you out your way.'

'I'm staying at Belpher Castle.'

'I live quite near there. Perhaps you'd care to come in and have a drink on your way?'

'A ripe scheme,' agreed Reggie.

Ten minutes in the grey car ate up the distance between the links and George's cottage. Reggie Byng passed these minutes, in the intervals of eluding carts and foiling the apparently suicidal intentions of some stray fowls, in jerky conversation on the subject of his iron-shots, with which he expressed a deep satisfaction.

'Topping little place! Absolutely!' was the verdict he pronounced on the exterior of the cottage as he followed George in. 'I've often thought it would be a rather sound scheme to settle down in this sort of shanty and keep chickens and grow a honey-coloured beard, and have soup and jelly brought to you by the vicar's wife and so forth. Nothing to worry you then. Do you live all alone here?'

George was busy squirting seltzer into his guest's glass.

'Yes. Mrs Platt comes in and cooks for me. The farmer's wife next door.'

An exclamation from the other caused him to look up. Reggie Byng was staring at him, wide-eyed.

'Great Scott! Mrs Platt! Then you're the Chappie?'

George found himself unequal to the intellectual pressure of the conversation.

'The Chappie?'

'The Chappie there's all the row about. The mater was telling me only this morning that you lived here.'

'Is there a row about me?'

'Is there what!' Reggie's manner became solicitous. 'I say, my dear old sportsman, I don't want to be the bearer of bad tidings and what not, if you know what I mean, but *didn't* you know there was a certain amount of angry passion rising and so forth because of you? At the castle, I mean. I don't want to seem to be discussing your private affairs, and all that sort of thing, but what I mean is . . . Well, you don't expect you can come charging in the way you have without touching the family on the raw a bit. The daughter of the house falls in love with you; the son of the house languishes in chokey because he has a row with you in Piccadilly; and on top of all that you come here and camp out at the castle gates! Naturally the family are a bit peeved. Only natural, eh? I mean to say, what?'

George listened to this address in bewilderment. Maud in love with him! It sounded incredible. That he should love her after their one meeting was a different thing altogether. That was perfectly natural and in order. But that he should have had the incredible luck to win her affection. The thing struck him as grotesque and ridiculous.

'In love with me?' he cried. 'What on earth do you mean?'

Reggie's bewilderment equalled his own.

'Well, dash it all, old top, it surely isn't news to you? She must have told you. Why, she told *me*!'

'Told *you*? Am I going mad?'

'Absolutely! I mean absolutely not! Look here.' Reggie hesitated. The subject was delicate. But, once started, it might as well be proceeded with to some conclusion. A fellow couldn't go on talking about his iron-shots after this just as if nothing had happened. This was the time for the laying down of cards, the opening of hearts. 'I say, you know,' he went on, feeling his way, 'you'll probably think it deuced rummy of me talking like this. Perfect stranger and what not. Don't even know each other's names.'

'Mine's Bevan, if that'll be any help.'

'Thanks very much, old chap. Great help! Mine's Byng. Reggie Byng. Well, as we're all pals here and the meeting's tiled and so forth, I'll start by saying that the mater is most deucedly set on my marrying Lady Maud. Been pals all our lives, you know. Children together, and all that sort of rot. Now there's nobody I think a more corking sportsman than Maud, if you know what I mean, but – this is where the catch comes in – I'm most frightfully in love with somebody else. Hopeless, and all that sort of thing, but still there it is. And all the while the mater behind me with a bradawl, sicking me on to propose to Maud who wouldn't have me if I were the only fellow on earth. You can't imagine, my dear old chap, what a relief it was to both of us when she told me the other day that she was in love with you, and wouldn't dream of looking at anybody else. I tell you, I went singing about the place.'

George felt inclined to imitate his excellent example. A burst of song was the only adequate expression of the mood of heavenly happiness which this young man's revelations had brought upon him. The whole world seemed different. Wings seemed to sprout from Reggie's shapely shoulders. The air was filled with soft music. Even the wallpaper seemed moderately attractive.

He mixed himself a second whisky and soda. It was the next best thing to singing.

'I see,' he said. It was difficult to say anything. Reggie was regarding him enviously.

'I wish I knew how the deuce fellows set about making a girl fall in love with them. Other chappies seem to do it, but I can't even start. She seems to sort of gaze through me, don't you know. She kind of looks at me as if I were more to be pitied than censured, but as if she thought I really ought to do something about it. Of course, she's a devilish brainy girl, and I'm a fearful chump. Makes it kind of hopeless, what?'

George, in his new-found happiness, found a pleasure in encouraging a less lucky mortal.

'Not a bit. What you ought to do is to – '

'Yes?' said Reggie eagerly.

George shook his head.

'No, I don't know,' he said.

'Nor do I, dash it!' said Reggie.

George pondered.

'It seems to me it's purely a question of luck. Either you're lucky or you're not. Look at me, for instance. What is there about me to make a wonderful girl love me?'

'Nothing! I see what you mean. At least, what I mean to say is – '

'No. You were right the first time. It's all a question of luck. There's nothing anyone can do.'

'I hang about a good deal and get in her way,' said Reggie. 'She's always tripping over me. I thought that might help a bit.'

'It might, of course.'

'But on the other hand, when we do meet, I can't think of anything to say.'

'That's bad.'

'Deuced funny thing. I'm not what you'd call a silent sort of chappie by nature. But, when I'm with her – I don't know. It's rum!' He drained his glass and rose. 'Well, I suppose I may as well be staggering. Don't get up. Have another game one of these days, what?'

'Splendid. Any time you like.'

'Well, so long.'

'Good-bye.'

George gave himself up to glowing thoughts. For the first time in his life he seemed to be vividly aware of his own existence. It was as if he were some newly created thing. Everything around him and everything he did had taken on a strange and novel interest. He seemed to notice the ticking of the clock for the first time. When he raised his glass the action had a curious air of newness. All his senses were oddly alert. He could even –

'How would it be', inquired Reggie, appearing in the doorway like part of a conjuring trick, 'if I gave her a flower or two every now and then? Just thought of it as I was starting the car. She's fond of flowers.'

'Fine!' said George heartily. He had not heard a word. The alertness of sense which had come to him was accompanied by a strange inability to attend to other people's speech. This would no doubt pass, but meanwhile it made him a poor listener.

'Well, it's worth trying,' said Reggie. 'I'll give it a whirl. Toodleoo!'

'Good-bye.'

'Pip-pip!'

Reggie withdrew, and presently came the noise of the car starting. George returned to his thoughts.

Time, as we understand it, ceases to exist for a man in such circumstances. Whether it was a minute later or several hours, George did not know; but presently he was aware of a small boy standing beside him – a golden-haired boy with blue eyes, who wore the uniform of a page. He came out of his trance. This, he recognized, was the boy to whom he had given the note for Maud. He was different from any other intruder. He meant something in George's scheme of things.

''Ullo!' said the youth.

'Hullo, Alphonso!' said George.

'My name's not Alphonso.'

'Well, you be very careful or it soon may be.'

'Got a note for yer. From Lidy Mord.'

'You'll find some cake and ginger-ale in the kitchen,' said the grateful George. 'Give it a trial.'

'Not 'arf!' said the stripling.

11

George opened the letter with trembling and reverent fingers.

Dear Mr Bevan,
Thank you ever so much for your note, which Albert gave me. How very, very kind . . .

'Hey, mister!'

George looked up testily. The boy Albert had reappeared.

'What's the matter? Can't you find the cake?'

'I've found the kike,' rejoined Albert, adducing proof of the statement in the shape of a massive slice, from which he took a substantial bite to assist thought. 'But I can't find the ginger-ile.'

George waved him away. This interruption at such a moment was annoying.

'Look for it, child, look for it! Sniff after it! Bay on its trail! It's somewhere about.'

''Wri'!' mumbled Albert through the cake. He flicked a crumb off his cheek with a tongue which would have excited the friendly interest of an ant-eater. 'I like ginger-ile.'

'Well, go and bathe in it.'

''Wri'!'

George returned to his letter.

Dear Mr Bevan,
Thank you ever so much for your note, which

Albert gave me. How very, very kind of you to come here like this and to say . . .

'Hey, mister!'

'Good Heavens!' George glared. 'What's the matter now? Haven't you found that ginger-ale yet?'

'I've found the ginger-ile right enough, but I can't find the thing.'

'The thing? What thing?'

'The thing. The thing wot you open ginger-ile with.'

'Oh, you mean the thing? It's in the middle drawer of the dresser. Use your eyes, my boy!'

''Wri'!'

George gave an overwrought sigh and began the letter again.

Dear Mr Bevan,

Thank you ever so much for your note, which Albert gave me. How very, very kind of you to come here like this and to say that you would help me. And how clever of you to find me after I was so secretive that day in the cab! You really can help me, if you are willing. It's too long to explain in a note, but I am in great trouble, and there is nobody except you to help me. I will explain everything when I see you. The difficulty will be to slip away from home. They are watching me every moment, I'm afraid. But I will try my hardest to see you very soon.

Yours sincerely,
Maud Marsh

Just for a moment it must be confessed, the tone of the letter damped George. He could not have said just what he had expected, but certainly Reggie's revelations had prepared him for something rather warmer, something more in the style in which a girl would write to the man she loved. The next moment, however, he saw how foolish any such expectation had been. How on earth could any reasonable man expect a girl to let herself go at this stage of the proceedings? It was for him to make the first move. Naturally she wasn't going to reveal her feelings until he had revealed his.

George raised the letter to his lips and kissed it vigorously.

'Hey, mister!'

George started guiltily. The blush of shame overspread his cheeks. The room seemed to echo with the sound of that fatuous kiss.

'Kitty, Kitty, Kitty!' he called, snapping his fingers, and repeating the incriminating noise. 'I was just calling my cat,' he explained with dignity. 'You didn't see her in there, did you?'

Albert's blue eyes met his in a derisive stare. The lid of the left one fluttered. It was but too plain that Albert was not convinced.

'A little black cat with white shirt-front,' babbled George perseveringly. 'She's usually either here or there, or – or somewhere. Kitty, Kitty, Kitty!'

The cupid's bow of Albert's mouth parted. He uttered one word.

'Swank!'

There was a tense silence. What Albert was thinking one cannot say. The thoughts of Youth are long, long thoughts. What George was thinking was that the late King Herod had been unjustly blamed for a policy which had been both statesmanlike and in the interests of the public. He was blaming the mawkish sentimentality of the modern legal system which ranks the evisceration and secret burial of small boys as a crime.

'What do you mean?'

'You know what I mean.'

'I've a good mind to – '

Albert waved a deprecating hand.

'It's all right, mister. I'm yer friend.'

'You are, are you? Well, don't let it about. I've got a reputation to keep up.'

'I'm yer friend, I tell you. I can help yer. I *want* to help yer!'

George's views on infanticide underwent a slight modification. After all, he felt, much must be excused to Youth. Youth thinks it funny to see a man kissing a letter. It is not funny, of course; it is beautiful; but it's no good arguing the point. Let Youth have its snigger, provided, after it has finished sniggering, it intends to buckle to and be of practical assistance. Albert, as an ally, was not to be despised. George did not know what Albert's duties as a page-boy were, but they seemed to be of a nature that gave him plenty of leisure and freedom; and a friendly resident of the castle with leisure and freedom was just what he needed.

'That's very good of you,' he said, twisting his reluctant features into a fairly benevolent smile.

'I can *'elp*!' persisted Albert. 'Got a cigaroot?'

'Do you smoke, child?'

'When I get 'old of a cigaroot I do.'

'I'm sorry I can't oblige you. I don't smoke cigarettes.'

'Then I'll 'ave to 'ave one of my own,' said Albert moodily.

He reached into the mysteries of his pocket and produced a piece of string, a knife, the wishbone of a fowl, two marbles, a crushed cigarette, and a match. Replacing the string, the knife, the wishbone, and the marbles, he ignited the match against the tightest part of his person and lit the cigarette.

'I can help yer. I know the ropes.'

'And smoke them,' said George, wincing.

'Pardon?'

'Nothing.'

Albert took an enjoyable whiff.

'I know all about yer.'

'You do?'

'You and Lidy Mord.'

'Oh, you do, do you?'

'I was listening at the key-'ole while the row was goin' on.'

'There was a row, was there?'

A faint smile of retrospective enjoyment lit up Albert's face.

'An orful row! Shoutin' and yellin' and cussin' all over the shop. About you and Lidy Mord.'

'And you drank it in, eh?'

'Pardon?'

'I say, you listened?'

'Not 'arf I listened. Seeing I'd just drawn you in the sweepstike, of course, I listened – not 'arf!'

George did not follow him here.

'The sweepstike? What's a sweepstike?'

'Why, a thing you puts names in 'ats and draw 'em and the one that gets the winning name wins the money.'

'Oh, you mean a sweepstake!'

'That's wot I said – a sweepstike.'

George was still puzzled.

'But I don't understand. How do you mean you drew me in a sweepstike – I mean a sweepstake? What sweepstake?'

'Down in the servants' 'all. Keggs, the butler, started it. I 'eard 'im say he always 'ad one every place 'e was in as a butler – leastways, whenever there was any dorters of the 'ouse. There's always a chance, when there's a 'ouse-party, of one of the dorters of the 'ouse gettin' married to one of the gents in the party, so Keggs 'e puts all of the gents' names in an 'at, and you pay five shillings for a chance, and the one that draws the winning name gets the money. And if the dorter of the 'ouse don't get married that time, the money's put away and added to the pool for the next 'ouse-party.'

George gasped. This revelation of life below stairs in

the stately homes of England took his breath away. Then astonishment gave way to indignation.

'Do you mean to tell me that you – you worms – made Lady Maud the – the prize of a sweepstake!'

Albert was hurt.

'Who're yer calling worms?'

George perceived the need of diplomacy. After all much depended on this child's goodwill.

'I was referring to the butler – what's his name – Keggs.'

''E ain't a worm. 'E's a serpint.' Albert drew at his cigarette. His brow darkened. ''E does the drawing, Keggs does, and I'd like to know 'ow it is 'e always manages to cop the fav'rit!'

Albert chuckled.

'But this time I done him proper. 'E didn't want me in the thing at all. Said I was too young. Tried to do the drawin' without me. "Clip that boy one side of the 'ead!" 'e says, "and turn 'im out!" 'e says. I says, "Yus, you will!" I says. "And wot price me goin' to 'is lordship and blowing the gaff?" 'E says, "Oh, orl right!" 'e says. "'Ave it yer own way!" 'e says. "Where's yer five shillings?" 'e says. "'Ere yer are!" I says. "Oh, very well," 'e says. "But you'll 'ave to draw last," 'e says, "bein' the youngest." Well, they started drawing the names, and of course Keggs 'as to draw Mr Byng.'

'Oh, he drew Mr Byng, did he?'

'Yus. And everyone knew Reggie was the fav'rit. Smiled all over his fat face, the old serpint did! And when it come to my turn, 'e says to me, "Sorry, Elbert!" 'e says, "but there ain't no more names. They've give out!" "Oh, they 'ave, 'ave they?" I says, "Well, wot's the matter with giving a fellow a sporting chance?" I says. "'Ow do you mean?" 'e says. "Why, write me out a ticket marked 'Mr X'," I says. "Then, if 'er lidyship marries anyone not in the 'ouse-party, I cop!" "Orl right," 'e says, "but you know the conditions of this 'ere sweep. Nothin' don't count only wot tikes plice during the two weeks of the 'ouse-party," 'e says. "Orl right," I says. "Write me ticket. It's a fair sportin' venture." So 'e writes me out me ticket, with "Mr X" on it, and I says to them all, I says, "I'd like to 'ave witnesses," I says, "to this 'ere thing. Do all you gents agree that if anyone not in the 'ouse-party and 'oo's name ain't on one of the other tickets marries 'er lidyship, I get the pool?" I says. They all says that's right, and then I says to 'em all straight out, I says, "I 'appen to know," I says, "that 'er lidyship is in love with a gent that's not in the party at all. An American gent," I says. They wouldn't believe it at first, but, when Keggs 'ad put two and two together, and thought of one or two things that 'ad 'appened, 'e turned as white as a sheet and said it was a swindle and wanted the drawin' done over again, but the others says "No," they says, "it's quite fair," they says, and one of 'em offered me ten bob slap out for my ticket. But I stuck to it, I did. And that,' concluded Albert throwing the cigarette into the fireplace just in time to prevent a scorched finger, 'that's why I'm going to 'elp yer!'

There is probably no attitude of mind harder for the average man to maintain than that of aloof disapproval. George was an average man, and during the degrading recital just concluded he had found himself slipping. At first he had been revolted, then, in spite of himself, amused, and now, when all the facts were before him, he could induce his mind to think of nothing else than his good fortune in securing as an ally one who appeared to combine a precocious intelligence with a helpful lack of scruple. War is war, and love is love, and in each the practical man inclines to demand from his fellow-workers the punch rather than a lofty soul. A page-boy replete with the finer feelings would have been useless in this crisis. Albert, who seemed on the evidence of a short but sufficient acquaintance, to be a lad who would not recognize the finer feelings if they were handed to him on a plate with watercress round them, promised to be invaluable. Something in his manner told George that the child was bursting with schemes for his benefit.

'Have some more cake, Albert,' he said ingratiatingly.

The boy shook his head.

'Do,' urged George. 'Just a little slice.'

'There ain't no little slice,' replied Albert with regret. 'I've ate it all.' He sighed and resumed. 'I gotta scheme!'

'Fine! What is it?'

Albert knitted his brows.

'It's like this. You want to see 'er lidyship, but you can't come to the castle, and she can't come to you – not with 'er fat brother dogging of 'er footsteps. That's it, ain't it? Or am I a liar?'

George hastened to reassure him.

'That is exactly it. What's the answer?'

'I'll tell yer wot you can do. There's the big ball tonight 'cos of its bein' 'Is Nibs' comin'-of-age tomorrow. All the county'll be 'ere.'

'You think I could slip in and be taken for a guest?'

Albert snorted contempt.

'No, I don't think nothin' of the kind, not bein' a fat-head.' George apologized. 'But wot you could do's this. I 'eard Keggs torkin to the 'ouse-keeper about 'avin' to get in a lot of temp'y waiters to 'elp out for the night – '

George reached forward and patted Albert on the head.

'Don't mess my 'air, now,' warned that youth coldly.

'Albert, you're one of the great thinkers of the age. I could get into the castle as a waiter, and you could tell Lady Maud I was there, and we could arrange a meeting. Machiavelli couldn't have thought of anything smoother.'

'Mac Who?'

'One of your ancestors. Great schemer in his day. But, one moment.'

'Now what?'

'How am I to get engaged? How do I get the job?'

'That's orl right. I'll tell the 'ousekeeper you're my

cousin – been a waiter in America at the best restaurongs – 'ome for a 'oliday, but'll come in for one night to oblige. They'll pay yer a quid.'

'I'll hand it over to you.'

'Just', said Albert approvingly, 'wot I was goin' to suggest myself.'

'Then I'll leave all the arrangements to you.'

'You'd better, if you don't want to mike a mess of everything. All you've got to do is to come to the servants' entrance at eight sharp tonight and say you're my cousin.'

'That's an awful thing to ask anyone to say.'

'Pardon?'

'Nothing!' said George.

12

The great ball in honour of Lord Belpher's coming-of-age was at its height. The reporter of the *Belpher Intelligencer and Farmers' Guide*, who was present in his official capacity, and had been allowed by butler Keggs to take a peep at the scene through a side-door, justly observed in his account of the proceedings next day that the '*tout ensemble* was fairylike', and described the company as 'a galaxy of fair women and brave men'. The floor was crowded with all that was best and noblest in the county; so that a half-brick, hurled at any given moment, must infallibly have spilt blue blood. Peers stepped on the toes of knights; honourables bumped into the spines of baronets. Probably the only titled person in the whole of the surrounding country who was not playing his part in the glittering scene was Lord Marshmoreton; who, on discovering that his private study had been converted into a cloakroom, had retired to bed with a pipe and a copy of *Roses Red and Roses White*, by Emily Ann Mackintosh (Popgood, Crooly & Co.), which he was to discover – after he was between the sheets, and it was too late to repair the error – was not, as he had supposed, a treatise on his favourite hobby, but a novel of stearine sentimentality dealing with the adventures of a pure young English girl and an artist named Claude.

George, from the shaded seclusion of a gallery, looked down upon the brilliant throng with impatience. It seemed to him that he had been doing this all his life. The novelty of the experience had long since ceased to divert him. It was all just like the second act of an old-fashioned musical comedy (Act Two: The Ballroom, Grantchester Towers: One Week Later) – a resemblance which was heightened for him by the fact that the band had more than once played dead and buried melodies of his own composition, of which he had wearied a full eighteen months back.

A complete absence of obstacles had attended his intrusion into the castle. A brief interview with a motherly old lady, whom even Albert seemed to treat with respect, and who, it appeared was Mrs Digby, the housekeeper; followed by an even briefer encounter with Keggs (fussy and irritable with responsibility, and, even while talking to George, carrying on two other conversations on topics of the moment), and he was past the censors and free for one night only to add his presence to the chosen inside the walls of Belpher. His duties were to stand in this gallery, and with the assistance of one of the maids to minister to the comfort of such of the dancers as should use it as a sitting-out place. None had so far made their appearance, the superior attractions of the main floor having exercised a great appeal; and for the past hour George had been alone with the maid and his thoughts. The maid, having asked George if he knew her cousin Frank, who had been in America nearly a year, and having received a reply in the negative, seemed to be disappointed in him, and to lose interest, and had not spoken for twenty minutes.

George scanned the approaches to the balcony for a sight of Albert as the shipwrecked mariner scans the horizon for the passing sail. It was inevitable, he supposed, this waiting. It would be difficult for Maud to slip away even for a moment on such a night.

'I say, laddie, would you mind getting me a lemonade?'

George was gazing over the balcony when the voice spoke behind him, and the muscles of his back stiffened as he recognized its genial note. This was one of the things he had prepared himself for, but, now that it had happened, he felt a wave of stage-fright such as he had only once experienced before in his life – on the occasion when he had been young enough and inexperienced enough to take a curtain-call on a first night. Reggie Byng was friendly, and would not wilfully betray him; but Reggie was also a babbler, who could not be trusted to keep things to himself. It was necessary, he perceived, to take a strong line from the start, and convince Reggie that any likeness which the latter might suppose that he detected between his companion of that afternoon and the waiter of tonight existed only in his heated imagination.

As George turned, Reggie's pleasant face, pink with healthful exercise and Lord Marshmoreton's finest Bollinger, lost most of its colour. His eyes and mouth opened wider. The fact is Reggie was shaken. All through the earlier part of the evening he had been sedulously priming himself with stimulants with a view to amassing enough nerve to propose to Alice Faraday: and, now that he had drawn her away from the throng to this secluded nook and was about to put his fortune to the test, a horrible fear swept over him that he had overdone it. He was having optical illusions.

'Good God!'

'Sir?'

Reggie loosened his collar, and pulled himself together.

'Would you mind taking a glass of lemonade to the lady in blue sitting on the settee over there by the statue,' he said carefully.

He brightened up a little.

'Pretty good that! Not absolutely a test sentence, perhaps, like "Truly rural" or "The intricacies of the British Constitution". But nevertheless no mean feat.'

'I say!' he continued, after a pause.

'Sir?'

'You haven't ever seen me before by any chance, if you know what I mean, have you?'

'No, sir.'

'You haven't a brother, or anything of that shape or order have you, no?'

'No, sir. I have often wished I had. I ought to have spoken to father about it. Father could never deny me anything.'

Reggie blinked. His misgiving returned. Either his ears, like his eyes, were playing him tricks, or else this waiter-chappie was talking pure drivel.

'What's that?'

'Sir?'

'What did you say?'

'I said, "No, sir, I have no brother".'

'Didn't you say something else?'

'No, sir.'

'What?'

'No, sir.'

Reggie's worst suspicions were confirmed.

'Good God!' he muttered. 'Then I *am*!'

Miss Faraday, when he joined her on the settee, wanted an explanation.

'What were you talking to that man about, Mr Byng? You seemed to be having a very interesting conversation.'

'I was asking him if he had a brother.'

Miss Faraday glanced quickly at him. She had had a feeling for some time during the evening that his manner had been strange.

'A brother? What made you ask him that?'

'He – I mean – that is to say – what I mean is, he looked the sort of chap who might have a brother. Lots of those fellows have!'

Alice Faraday's face took on a motherly look. She was fonder of Reggie than that love-sick youth supposed, and by sheer accident he had stumbled on the right road to her consideration. Alice Faraday was one of those girls whose dream it is to be a ministering angel to some chosen man, to be a good influence to him and raise him to an appreciation of nobler things. Hitherto, Reggie's personality had seemed to her agreeable, but negative. A positive vice like over-indulgence in alcohol altered him completely. It gave him a significance.

'I told him to get you a lemonade,' said Reggie. 'He seems to be taking his time about it. Hi!'

George approached deferentially.

'Sir?'

'Where's that lemonade?'

'Lemonade, sir?'

'Didn't I ask you to bring this lady a glass of lemonade?'

'I did not understand you to do so, sir.'

'But, Great Scott! What *were* we chatting about, then?'

'You were telling me a diverting story about an Irishman who landed in New York looking for work, sir. You would like a glass of lemonade, sir? Very good, sir.'

Alice placed a hand gently on Reggie's arm.

'Don't you think you had better lie down for a little and rest, Mr Byng? I'm sure it would do you good.'

The solicitous note in her voice made Reggie quiver like a jelly. He had never known her speak like that before. For a moment he was inclined to lay bare his soul; but his nerve was broken. He did not want her to mistake the outpouring of a strong man's heart for the irresponsible ravings of a too hearty diner. It was one of Life's ironies. Here he was for the first time all keyed up to go right ahead, and he couldn't do it.

'It's the heat of the room,' said Alice. 'Shall we go and sit outside on the terrace? Never mind about the lemonade. I'm not really thirsty.'

Reggie followed her like a lamb. The prospect of the cool night air was grateful.

'That', murmured George, as he watched them depart, 'ought to hold *you* for a while!'

He perceived Albert hastening towards him.

13

Albert was in a hurry. He skimmed over the carpet like a water-beetle.

'Quick!' he said.

He cast a glance at the maid, George's co-worker. She was reading a novelette with her back turned.

'Tell 'er you'll be back in five minutes,' said Albert, jerking a thumb.

'Unnecessary. She won't notice my absence. Ever since she discovered that I had never met her cousin Frank in America, I have meant nothing in her life.'

'Then come on.'

'Where?'

'I'll show you.'

That it was not the nearest and most direct route which they took to the trysting-place George became aware after he had followed his young guide through doors and up stairs and down stairs and had at last come to a halt in a room to which the sound of the music penetrated but faintly. He recognized the room. He had been in it before. It was the same room where he and Billie Dore had listened to Keggs telling the story of Lord Leonard and his leap. That window there, he remembered now, opened on to the very balcony from which the historic Leonard had done his spectacular dive. That it should be the scene of this other secret meeting struck George as appropriate. The coincidence appealed to him.

Albert vanished. George took a deep breath. Now that the moment had arrived for which he had waited so long he was aware of a return of that feeling of stage-fright which had come upon him when he heard Reggie Byng's voice. This sort of thing, it must be remembered, was not in George's usual line. His had been a quiet and uneventful life, and the only exciting thing which, in his recollection, had ever happened to him, previous to the dramatic entry of Lady Maud into his taxi-cab that day in Piccadilly, had occurred at college nearly ten years before, when a festive room-mate – no doubt with the best motives – had placed a Mexican horned toad in his bed on the night of the Yale football game.

A light footstep sounded outside, and the room whirled round George in a manner which, if it had happened to Reggie Byng, would have caused that injudicious drinker to abandon the habits of a lifetime. When the furniture had returned to its place and the rug had ceased to spin, Maud was standing before him.

Nothing is harder to remember than a once-seen face. It had caused George a good deal of distress and inconvenience that, try as he might, he could not conjure up anything more than a vague vision of what the only girl in the world really looked like. He had carried away with him from their meeting in the cab only a confused recollection of eyes that shone and a mouth that curved in a smile; and the brief moment in which he was able to refresh his memory, when he found her in the lane with Reggie Byng and the broken-down car, had not been enough to add definiteness. The consequence was that Maud came upon him now with the stunning effect of beauty seen for the first time. He gasped. In that dazzling ball-dress, with the flush of dancing on her cheeks and the light of dancing in her eyes, she was so much more wonderful than any picture of her which memory had been able to produce for his inspection that it was as if he had never seen her before.

Even her brother Percy, a stern critic where his nearest and dearest were concerned, had admitted on meeting her in the drawing-room before dinner that that particular dress suited Maud. It was a shimmering dream-thing of rose-leaves and moonbeams. That, at least, was how it struck George; a dressmaker would have found a longer and less romantic description for it. But that does not matter. Whoever wishes for a cold and technical catalogue of the stuffs which went to make up the picture that deprived George of speech may consult the files of the *Belpher Intelligencer and Farmers' Guide*, and read the report of the editor's wife, who 'does' the dresses for the *Intelligencer* under the pen-name of 'Birdie Bright-Eye'. As far as George was concerned, the thing was made of rose-leaves and moonbeams.

George, as I say, was deprived of speech. That any girl could possibly look so beautiful was enough to paralyse his faculties; but that this ethereal being straight from Fairyland could have stooped to love him – him – an earthy brute who wore sock-suspenders and drank coffee for breakfast . . . that was what robbed George of the power to articulate. He could do nothing but look at her.

From the Hills of Fairyland soft music came. Or, if we must be exact, Maud spoke.

'I couldn't get away before!' Then she stopped short and darted to the door listening. 'Was that somebody coming? I had to cut a dance with Mr Plummer to get here, and I'm so afraid he may . . .'

He had. A moment later it was only too evident that this was precisely what Mr Plummer had done. There was a footstep on the stairs, a heavy footstep this time, and from outside the voice of the pursuer made itself heard.

'Oh, there you are, Lady Maud! I was looking for you. This is our dance.'

George did not know who Mr Plummer was. He did not want to know. His only thought regarding Mr Plummer was a passionate realization of the superfluity of his existence. It is the presence on the globe of these Plummers that delays the coming of the Millennium.

His stunned mind leaped into sudden activity. He must

not be found here, that was certain. Waiters who ramble at large about a feudal castle and are discovered in conversation with the daughter of the house excite comment. And, conversely, daughters of the house who talk in secluded rooms with waiters also find explanations necessary. He must withdraw. He must withdraw quickly. And, as a gesture from Maud indicated, the withdrawal must be effected through the french window opening on the balcony. Estimating the distance that separated him from the approaching Plummer at three stairs – the voice had come from below – and a landing, the space of time allotted to him by a hustling Fate for disappearing was some four seconds. Inside two and a half, the french window had opened and closed, and George was out under the stars, with the cool winds of the night playing on his heated forehead.

He had now time for meditation. There are few situations which provide more scope for meditation than that of the man penned up on a small balcony a considerable distance from the ground, with his only avenue of retreat cut off behind him. So George meditated. First, he mused on Plummer. He thought some hard thoughts about Plummer. Then he brooded on the unkindness of a fortune which had granted him the opportunity of this meeting with Maud, only to snatch it away almost before it had begun. He wondered how long the late Lord Leonard had been permitted to talk on that occasion before he, too, had had to retire through these same windows. There was no doubt about one thing. Lovers who chose that room for their interviews seemed to have very little luck.

It had not occurred to George at first that there could be any further disadvantage attached to his position other than the obvious drawbacks which had already come to his notice. He was now to perceive that he had been mistaken. A voice was speaking in the room he had left, a plainly audible voice, deep and throaty; and within a minute George had become aware that he was to suffer the additional discomfort of being obliged to listen to a fellow man – one could call Plummer that by stretching the facts a little – proposing marriage. The gruesomeness of the situation became intensified. Of all moments when a man – and justice compelled George to admit that Plummer was technically human – of all moments when a man may by all the laws of decency demand to be alone without an audience of his own sex, the chiefest is the moment when he is asking a girl to marry him. George's was a sensitive nature, and he writhed at the thought of playing the eavesdropper at such a time.

He looked frantically about him for a means of escape. Plummer had now reached the stage of saying at great length that he was not worthy of Maud. He said it over and over again in different ways. George was in hearty agreement with him, but he did not want to hear it. He wanted to get away. But how? Lord Leonard on a similar occasion had leaped. Some might argue therefore on the principle that what man has done, man can do, that George should have imitated him. But men differ. There was a man attached to a circus who used to dive off the roof of Madison Square Garden on to a sloping board, strike it with his chest, turn a couple of somersaults, reach the ground, bow six times, and go off to lunch. That sort of thing is a gift. Some of us have it, some have not. George had not. Painful as it was to hear Plummer floundering through his proposal of marriage, instinct told him that it would be far more painful to hurl himself out into mid-air on the sporting chance of having his downward progress arrested by the branches of the big tree that had upheld Lord Leonard. No, there seemed nothing for it but to remain where he was.

Inside the room Plummer was now saying how much the marriage would please his mother.

'Psst!'

George looked about him. It seemed to him that he had heard a voice. He listened. No. Except for the barking of a distant dog, the faint wailing of a waltz, the rustle of a roosting bird, and the sound of Plummer saying that if her refusal was due to anything she might have heard about that breach-of-promise case of his a couple of years ago he would like to state that he was more sinned against than sinning and that the girl had absolutely misunderstood him, all was still.

'Psst! Hey, mister!'

It *was* a voice. It came from above. Was it an angel's voice? Not altogether. It was Albert's. The boy was leaning out of a window some six feet higher up the castle wall. George, his eyes by now grown used to the darkness, perceived that the stripling gesticulated as one having some message to impart. Then, glancing to one side, he saw what looked like some kind of a rope swayed against the wall. He reached for it. The thing was not a rope: it was a knotted sheet.

From above came Albert's hoarse whisper.

'Look alive!'

This was precisely what George wanted to do for at least another fifty years or so; and it seemed to him as he stood there in the starlight, gingerly fingering this flimsy linen thing, that if he were to suspend his hundred and eighty pounds of bone and sinew at the end of it over the black gulf outside the balcony he would look alive for about five seconds, and after that goodness only knew how he would look. He knew all about knotted sheets. He had read a hundred stories in which heroes, heroines, low comedy friends, and even villains did all sorts of reckless things with their assistance. There was not much comfort to be derived from that. It was one thing to read about people doing silly things like that, quite another to do them yourself. He gave Albert's sheet a tentative shake. In all his experience he thought he had never come across anything so supremely unstable. (One calls it

Albert's sheet for the sake of convenience. It was really Reggie Byng's sheet. And when Reggie got to his room in the small hours of the morning and found the thing a mass of knots he jumped to the conclusion – being a simple-hearted young man – that his bosom friend Jack Ferris, who had come up from London to see Lord Belpher through the trying experience of a coming-of-age party, had done it as a practical joke, and went and poured a jug of water over Jack's bed. That is Life. Just one long succession of misunderstandings and rash acts and what not. Absolutely!)

Albert was becoming impatient. He was in the position of a great general who thinks out some wonderful piece of strategy and can't get his army to carry it out. Many boys, seeing Plummer enter the room below and listening at the keyhole and realizing that George must have hidden somewhere and deducing that he must be out on the balcony, would have been baffled as to how to proceed. Not so Albert. To dash up to Reggie Byng's room and strip his sheet off the bed and tie it to the bed-post and fashion a series of knots in it and lower it out of the window took Albert about three minutes. His part in the business had been performed without a hitch. And now George, who had nothing in the world to do but the childish task of climbing up the sheet, was jeopardizing the success of the whole scheme by delay. Albert gave the sheet an irritable jerk.

It was the worst thing he could have done. George had almost made up his mind to take a chance when the sheet was snatched from his grasp as if it had been some live thing deliberately eluding his clutch. The thought of what would have happened had this occurred when he was in mid-air caused him to break out in a cold perspiration. He retired a pace and perched himself on the rail of the balcony.

'Psst!' said Albert.

'It's no good saying, "Psst!"' rejoined George in an

annoyed undertone. '*I* could say "Psst!" Any fool could say "Psst!"' Albert, he considered, in leaning out of the window and saying 'Psst!' was merely touching the fringe of the subject.

It is probable that he would have remained seated on the balcony rail regarding the sheet with cold aversion, indefinitely, had not his hand been forced by the man Plummer. Plummer, during these last minutes, had shot his bolt. He had said everything that a man could say, much of it twice over; and now he was through. All was ended. The verdict was in. No wedding-bells for Plummer.

'I think,' said Plummer gloomily, and the words smote on George's ear like a knell, 'I think I'd like a little air.'

George leaped from his rail like a hunted grasshopper. If Plummer was looking for air, it meant that he was going to come out on the balcony. There was only one thing to be done. It probably meant the abrupt conclusion of a promising career, but he could hesitate no longer.

George grasped the sheet – it felt like a rope of cobwebs – and swung himself out.

Maud looked out on to the balcony. Her heart which had stood still when the rejected one opened the window and stepped forth to commune with the soothing stars, beat again. There was no one there, only emptiness and Plummer.

'This,' said Plummer sombrely, gazing over the rail into the darkness, 'is the place where that fellow what's-his-name jumped off in the reign of thingummy, isn't it?'

Maud understood now, and a thrill of the purest admiration for George's heroism swept over her. So rather than compromise her, he had done Leonard's leap! How splendid of him! If George, now sitting on Reggie Byng's bed taking a rueful census of the bits of skin remaining on his hands and knees after his climb, could read her thoughts, he would have felt well rewarded for his abrasions.

'I've a jolly good mind,' said Plummer, 'to do it myself!' He uttered a short, mirthless laugh. 'Well, anyway,' he said recklessly, 'I'll jolly well go downstairs and have a brandy-and-soda!'

Albert finished untying the sheet from the bedpost, and stuffed it under the pillow.

'And now,' said Albert, 'for a quiet smoke in the scullery.'

These massive minds require their moments of relaxation.

14

George's idea was to get home. Quick. There was no possible chance of a second meeting with Maud that night. They had met and had been whirled asunder. No use to struggle with Fate. Best to give in and hope that another time Fate would be kinder. What George wanted now was to be away from all the gay glitter and the fairylike *tout ensemble* and the galaxy of fair women and brave men, safe in his own easy-chair, where nothing could happen to him. A nice sense of duty would no doubt have taken him back to his post in order fully to earn the sovereign which had been paid to him for his services as temporary waiter; but the voice of Duty called to him in vain. If the British aristocracy desired refreshments let them get them for themselves – *and* like it! He was through.

But if George had for the time being done with the British aristocracy, the British aristocracy had not done with him. Hardly had he reached the hall when he encountered the one member of the order whom he would most gladly have avoided.

Lord Belpher was not in genial mood. Late hours always made his head ache, and he was not a dancing man; so that he was by now fully as weary of the fairylike *tout ensemble* as was George. But, being the centre and cause of the night's proceedings, he was compelled to be present to the finish. He was in the position of captains who must be last to leave their ships, and of boys who stand on burning decks whence all but they had fled. He had spent several hours shaking hands with total strangers and receiving with a frozen smile their felicitations on the attainment of his majority, and he could not have been called upon to meet a larger horde of relations than had surged round him that night if he had been a rabbit. The Belpher connexion was wide, straggling over most of England; and first cousins, second cousins, and even third and fourth cousins had debouched from practically every county on the map and marched upon the home of their ancestors. The effort of having to be civil to all of these had told upon Percy. Like the heroine of his sister Maud's favourite poem he was 'aweary, aweary', and he wanted a drink. He regarded George's appearance as exceedingly opportune.

'Get me a small bottle of champagne, and bring it to the library.'

'Yes, sir.'

The two words sound innocent enough, but, wishing as he did to efface himself and avoid publicity, they were the most unfortunate which George could have chosen. If he had merely bowed acquiescence and departed, it is probable that Lord Belpher would not have taken a second look at him. Percy was in no condition to subject everyone he met to a minute scrutiny. But, when you have been addressed for an entire lifetime as 'your lordship', it startles you when a waiter calls you 'Sir'. Lord Belpher gave George a glance in which reproof and pain were nicely mingled – emotions quickly supplanted by amazement. A gurgle escaped him.

'Stop!' he cried as George turned away.

Percy was rattled. The crisis found him in two minds. On the one hand, he would have been prepared to take oath that this man before him was the man who had knocked off his hat in Piccadilly. The likeness had struck him like a blow the moment he had taken a good look at the fellow. On the other hand, there is nothing which is more likely to lead one astray than a resemblance. He had never forgotten the horror and humiliation of the occasion, which had happened in his fourteenth year, when a motherly woman at Paddington Station had called him 'dearie' and publicly embraced him, on the erroneous supposition that he was her nephew Philip. He must proceed cautiously. A brawl with an innocent waiter, coming on the heels of that infernal episode with the policeman, would give people the impression that assailing the lower orders had become a hobby of his.

'Sir?' said George politely.

His brazen front shook Lord Belpher's confidence.

'I haven't seen you before here, have I?' was all he could find to say.

'No, sir,' replied George smoothly. 'I am only temporarily attached to the castle staff.'

'Where do you come from?'

'America, sir.'

Lord Belpher started. 'America!'

'Yes, sir. I am in England on a vacation. My cousin, Albert, is page-boy at the castle, and he told me there were a few vacancies for extra help tonight, so I applied and was given the job.'

Lord Belpher frowned perplexedly. It all sounded entirely plausible. And, what was satisfactory, the statement could be checked by application to Keggs, the butler. And yet there was a lingering doubt. However, there seemed nothing to be gained by continuing the conversation.

'I see,' he said at last. 'Well, bring that champagne to the library as quick as you can.'

'Very good, sir.'

Lord Belpher remained where he stood, brooding. Reason told him he ought to be satisfied, but he was not satisfied. It would have been different had he not known that this fellow with whom Maud had become entangled was in the neighbourhood. And if that scoundrel had had the audacity to come and take a cottage at the castle gates, why not the audacity to invade the castle itself?

The appearance of one of the footmen, on his way

through the hall with a tray, gave him the opportunity for further investigation.

'Send Keggs to me!'

'Very good, your lordship.'

An interval and the butler arrived. Unlike Lord Belpher late hours were no hardship to Keggs. He was essentially a night-blooming flower. His brow was as free from wrinkles as his shirt-front. He bore himself with the conscious dignity of one who, while he would have freely admitted he did not actually own the castle, was nevertheless aware that he was one of its most conspicuous ornaments.

'You wished to see me, your lordship?'

'Yes. Keggs, there are a number of outside men helping here tonight, aren't there?'

'Indubitably, your lordship. The unprecedented scale of the entertainment necessitated the engagement of a certain number of supernumeraries,' replied Keggs with an easy fluency which Reggie Byng, now cooling his head on the lower terrace, would have bitterly envied. 'In the circumstances, such an arrangement was inevitable.'

'You engaged all these men yourself?'

'In a manner of speaking, your lordship, and for all practical purposes, yes. Mrs Digby, the 'ousekeeper, conducted the actual negotiations in many cases, but the arrangement was in no instance considered complete until I had passed each applicant.'

'Do you know anything of an American who says he is the cousin of the page-boy?'

'The boy Albert *did* introduce a nominee whom he stated to be 'is cousin 'ome from New York on a visit and anxious to oblige. I trust he 'as given no dissatisfaction, your lordship? He seemed a respectable young man.'

'No, no, not at all. I merely wished to know if you knew him. One can't be too careful.'

'No, indeed, your lordship.'

'That's all, then.'

'Thank you, your lordship.'

Lord Belpher was satisfied. He was also relieved. He felt that prudence and a steady head had kept him from making himself ridiculous. When George presently returned with the life-saving fluid, he thanked him and turned his thoughts to other things.

But, if the young master was satisfied, Keggs was not. Upon Keggs a bright light had shone. There were few men, he flattered himself, who could more readily put two and two together and bring the sum to a correct answer. Keggs knew of the strange American gentleman who had taken up his abode at the cottage down by Platt's farm. His looks, his habits, and his motives for coming there had formed food for discussion throughout one meal in the servants' hall; a stranger whose abstention from brush and palette showed him to be no artist being an object of interest. And while the solution put forward by a romantic lady's-maid, a great reader of novelettes, that the young man had come there to cure himself of some unhappy passion by communing with nature, had been scoffed at by the company, Keggs had not been so sure that there might not be something in it. Later events had deepened his suspicion, which now, after this interview with Lord Belpher, had become certainty.

The extreme fishiness of Albert's sudden production of a cousin from America was so manifest that only his preoccupation at the moment when he met the young man could have prevented him seeing it before. His knowledge of Albert told him that, if one so versed as that youth in the art of Swank had really possessed a cousin in America, he would long ago have been boring the servants' hall with fictions about the man's wealth and importance. For Albert not to lie about a thing, practically proved that thing non-existent. Such was the simple creed of Keggs.

He accosted a passing fellow-servitor.

'Seen young blighted Albert anywhere, Freddy?'

It was in this shameful manner that that mastermind was habitually referred to below stairs.

'Seen 'im going into the scullery not 'arf a minute ago,' replied Freddy.

'Thanks.'

'So long,' said Freddy.

'Be good!' returned Keggs, whose mode of speech among those of his own world differed substantially from that which he considered it became him to employ when conversing with the titled.

The fall of great men is but too often due to the failure of their miserable bodies to give the necessary support to their great brains. There are some, for example, who say that Napoleon would have won the battle of Waterloo if he had not had dyspepsia. Not otherwise was it with Albert on that present occasion. The arrival of Keggs found him at a disadvantage. He had been imprudent enough, on leaving George, to endeavour to smoke a cigar, purloined from the box which stood hospitably open on a table in the hall. But for this, who knows with what cunning counter-attacks he might have foiled the butler's onslaught? As it was, the battle was a walk-over for the enemy.

'I've been looking for you, young blighted Albert!' said Keggs coldly.

Albert turned a green but defiant face to the foe.

'Go and boil yer 'ead!' he advised.

'Never mind about *my* 'ead. If I was to do my duty to you, I'd give you a clip side of *your* 'ead, that's what I'd do.'

'And then bury it in the woods,' added Albert, wincing as the consequences of his rash act swept through his small form like some nauseous tidal wave. He shut his eyes. It upset him to see Keggs shimmering like that. A shimmering butler is an awful sight.

Keggs laughed a hard laugh. 'You and your cousins from America!'

'What about my cousins from America?'

'Yes, what about them? That's just what Lord Belpher and me have been asking ourselves.'

'I don't know wot you're talking about.'

'You soon will, young blighted Albert! Who sneaked that American fellow into the 'ouse to meet Lady Maud?'

'I never!'

'Think I didn't see through your little game? Why, I knew from the first.'

'Yes, you did! Then why did you let him into the place?'

Keggs snorted triumphantly. 'There! You admit it! It was that feller!'

Too late Albert saw his false move – a move which, in a normal state of health, he would have scorned to make. Just as Napoleon, minus a stomach-ache, would have scorned the blunder that sent his Cuirassiers plunging to destruction in the sunken road.

'I don't know what you're torkin' about,' he said weakly.

'Well,' said Keggs, 'I haven't time to stand 'ere chatting with you. I must be going back to 'is lordship, to tell 'im of the 'orrid trick you played on him.'

A second spasm shook Albert to the core of his being. The double assault was too much for him. Betrayed by the body, the spirit yielded.

'You wouldn't do that, Mr Keggs!'

There was a white flag in every syllable.

'I would if I did my duty.'

'But you don't care about that,' urged Albert ingratiatingly.

'I'll have to think it over,' mused Keggs. 'I don't want to be 'ard on a young boy.' He struggled silently with himself. 'Ruinin' 'is prospecks!'

An inspiration seemed to come to him.

'All right, young blighted Albert,' he said briskly. 'I'll go against my better nature this once and chance it. And now, young feller me lad, you just 'and over that ticket of yours! You know what I'm alloodin' to! That ticket you 'ad at the sweep, the one with "Mr X" on it.'

Albert's indomitable spirit triumphed for a moment over his stricken body.

'That's likely, ain't it!'

Keggs sighed – the sigh of a good man who has done his best to help a fellow-being and has been baffled by the other's perversity.

'Just as you please,' he said sorrowfully. 'But I *did* 'ope I shouldn't 'ave to go to 'is lordship and tell 'im 'ow you've deceived him.'

Albert capitulated. ''Ere yer are!' a piece of paper changed hands. 'It's men like you wot lead to 'arf the crime in the country!'

'Much obliged, me lad.'

'You'd walk a mile in the snow, *you* would,' continued Albert pursuing his train of thought, 'to rob a starving beggar of a ha'penny.'

'Who's robbing anyone? Don't you talk so quick, young man. I'm doing the right thing by you. You can 'ave my ticket, marked "Reggie Byng". It's a fair exchange, and no one the worse!'

'Fat lot of good that is!'

'That's as it may be. Anyhow, there it is.' Keggs prepared to withdraw. 'You're too young to 'ave all that money, Albert. You wouldn't know what to do with it. It wouldn't make you 'appy. There's other things in the world besides winning sweepstakes. And, properly speaking, you ought never to have been allowed to draw at all, being so young.'

Albert groaned hollowly. 'When you've finished torkin', I wish you'd kindly have the goodness to leave me alone. I'm not meself.'

'That,' said Keggs cordially, 'is a bit of luck for you, my boy. Accept my 'eartiest felicitations!'

Defeat is the test of the great man. Your true general is not he who rides to triumph on the tide of an easy victory, but the one who, when crushed to earth, can bend himself to the task of planning methods of rising again. Such a one was Albert, the page-boy. Observe Albert in his attic bedroom scarcely more than an hour later. His body has practically ceased to trouble him, and his soaring spirit has come into its own again. With the exception of a now very occasional spasm, his physical anguish has passed, and he is thinking, thinking hard. On the chest of drawers is a grubby envelope, addressed in an ill-formed hand to:

R. BYNG, ESQ.

On a sheet of paper, soon to be placed in the envelope, are written in the same hand these words:

Do not dispare! Remember! Fante hart never won fair lady. I shall watch your futur progres with considurable interest.

Your Well-Wisher.

The last sentence is not original. Albert's Sunday-school teacher said it to Albert on the occasion of his taking up his duties at the castle, and it stuck in his memory. Fortunately, for it expressed exactly what Albert wished to say. From now on Reggie Byng's progress with Lady Maud Marsh was to be the thing nearest to Albert's heart.

And George meanwhile? Little knowing how Fate has changed in a flash an ally into an opponent he is standing at the edge of the shrubbery near the castle gate. The night is very beautiful; the barked spots on his hands and knees are hurting much less now; and he is full of long, sweet thoughts. He has just discovered the extraordinary resemblance, which had not struck him as he was climbing up the knotted sheet, between his own position and that of the hero of Tennyson's *Maud*, a poem to which he has always been particularly addicted – and never more so than during the days since he learned the name of the only possible girl. When he has not been playing golf, Tennyson's *Maud* has been his constant companion.

Queen rose of the rosebud garden of girls
    Come hither, the dances are done,
In glass of satin and glimmer of pearls.
    Queen lily and rose in one;
Shine out, little head, sunning over with curls,
    To the flowers, and be their sun.

The music from the ballroom flows out to him through the motionless air. The smell of sweet earth and growing things is everywhere.

Come into the garden, Maud,
    For the black bat, night, hath flown,
Come into the garden, Maud,
    I am here at the gate alone;
And the woodbine spices are wafted abroad,
    And the musk of the rose is blown.

He draws a deep breath, misled young man. The night is very beautiful. It is near to the dawn now and in the bushes live things are beginning to stir and whisper.

'Maud!'

Surely she can hear him?

'Maud!'

The silver stars looked down dispassionately. This sort of thing had no novelty for them.

15

Lord Belpher's twenty-first birthday dawned brightly, heralded in by much twittering of sparrows in the ivy outside his bedroom. These Percy did not hear, for he was sound asleep and had had a late night. The first sound that was able to penetrate his heavy slumber and rouse him to a realization that his birthday had arrived was the piercing cry of Reggie Byng on his way to the bathroom across the corridor. It was Reggie's disturbing custom to urge himself on to a cold bath with encouraging yells; and the noise of this performance, followed by violent splashing and a series of sharp howls as the sponge played upon the Byng spine, made sleep an impossibility within a radius of many yards. Percy sat up in bed, and cursed Reggie silently. He discovered that he had a headache.

Presently the door flew open, and the vocalist entered in person, clad in a pink bathrobe and very tousled and rosy from the tub.

'Many happy returns of the day, Boots, old thing!'

Reggie burst rollickingly into song.

'I'm twenty-one today!
Twenty-one today!
I've got the key of the door!
Never been twenty-one before!
And father says I can do what I like!
So shout Hip-hip-hooray!
I'm a jolly good fellow,
Twenty-one today.'

Lord Belpher scowled morosely.

'I wish you wouldn't make that infernal noise!'

'What infernal noise?'

'That singing!'

'My God! This man has wounded me!' said Reggie.

'I've a headache.'

'I thought you would have, laddie, when I saw you getting away with the liquid last night. An X-ray photograph of your liver would show something that looked like a crumpled oak-leaf studded with hob-nails. You ought to take more exercise, dear heart. Except for sloshing that policeman, you haven't done anything athletic for years.'

'I wish you wouldn't harp on that affair!'

Reggie sat down on the bed.

'Between ourselves, old man,' he said confidentially, 'I also – I myself – Reginald Byng, in person – was perhaps a shade polluted during the evening. I give you my honest word that just after dinner I saw three versions of your uncle, the bishop, standing in a row side by side. I tell you, laddie, that for a moment I thought I had strayed into a Bishop's Beano at Exeter Hall or the Athenaeum or wherever it is those chappies collect in gangs. Then the three bishops sort of congealed into one bishop, a trifle blurred about the outlines, and I felt relieved. But what convinced me that I had emptied a flagon or so too many was a rather rummy thing that occurred later on. Have you ever happened, during one of these feasts of reason and flows of soul, when you were bubbling over with *joie-de-vivre* – have you ever happened to *see* things? What I mean to say is, I had a deuced odd experience last night. I could have sworn that one of the waiter-chappies was that fellow who knocked off your hat in Piccadilly.'

Lord Belpher, who had sunk back on to the pillows at Reggie's entrance and had been listening to his task with only intermittent attention, shot up in bed.

'What!'

'Absolutely! My mistake, of course, but there it was. The fellow might have been his double.'

'But you've never seen the man.'

'Oh yes, I have. I forgot to tell you. I met him on the links yesterday. I'd gone out there alone, rather expecting to have a round with the pro, but, finding this lad there, I suggested that we might go round together. We did eighteen holes, and he licked the boots off me. Very hot stuff he was. And after the game he took me off to his cottage and gave me a drink. He lives at the cottage next door to Platt's farm, so, you see, it was the identical chappie. We got extremely matey. Like brothers. Absolutely! So you can understand what a shock it gave me when I found what I took to be the same man serving bracers to the multitude the same evening. One of those nasty jars that cause a fellow's head to swim a bit, don't you know, and make him lose confidence in himself.'

Lord Belpher did not reply. His brain was whirling. So he had been right after all!

'You know,' pursued Reggie seriously, 'I think you are making the bloomer of a lifetime over this hat-swatting chappie. You've misjudged him. He's a first-rate sort. Take it from me! Nobody could have got out of the bunker at the fifteenth hole better than he did. If you'll take my advice, you'll conciliate the feller. A really first-class golfer is what you need in the family. Besides, even leaving out of the question the fact that he can do things with a niblick that I didn't think anybody except the pro could do, he's a corking good sort. A stout fellow in every respect. I took to the chappie. He's all right. Grab him, Boots, before he gets away. That's my tip to you. You'll never regret it! From first to last this lad didn't foozle a single drive, and his approach-putting has to be seen to be believed. Well, got to dress, I suppose. Mustn't waste life's springtime sitting here talking to you. Toodle-oo, laddie! We shall meet anon!'

Lord Belpher leaped from his bed. He was feeling worse

than ever now, and a glance into the mirror told him that he looked rather worse than he felt. Late nights and insufficient sleep, added to the need of a shave, always made him look like something that should have been swept up and taken away to the ash-bin. And as for his physical condition, talking to Reggie Byng never tended to make you feel better when you had a headache. Reggie's manner was not soothing, and on this particular morning his choice of a topic had been unusually irritating. Lord Belpher told himself that he could not understand Reggie. He had never been able to make his mind quite clear as to the exact relations between the latter and his sister Maud, but he had always been under the impression that, if they were not actually engaged, they were on the verge of becoming so; and it was maddening to have to listen to Reggie advocating the claims of a rival as if he had no personal interest in the affair at all. Percy felt for his complaisant friend something of the annoyance which a householder feels for the watch-dog whom he finds fraternizing with the burglar. Why, Reggie, more than anyone else, ought to be foaming with rage at the insolence of this American fellow in coming down to Belpher and planting himself at the castle gates. Instead of which, on his own showing, he appeared to have adopted an attitude towards him which would have excited remark if adopted by David towards Jonathan. He seemed to spend all his spare time frolicking with the man on the golf-links and hobnobbing with him in his house.

Lord Belpher was thoroughly upset. It was impossible to prove it or to do anything about it now, but he was convinced that the fellow had wormed his way into the castle in the guise of a waiter. He had probably met Maud and plotted further meetings with her. This thing was becoming unendurable.

One thing was certain. The family honour was in his hands. Anything that was to be done to keep Maud away from the intruder must be done by himself. Reggie was hopeless: he was capable, as far as Percy could see, of escorting Maud to the fellow's door in his own car and leaving her on the threshold with his blessing. As for Lord Marshmoreton, roses and the family history took up so much of his time that he could not be counted on for anything but moral support. He, Percy, must do the active work.

He had just come to this decision, when, approaching the window and gazing down into the grounds, he perceived his sister Maud walking rapidly – and, so it seemed to him, with a furtive air – down the east drive. And it was to the east that Platt's farm and the cottage next door to it lay.

At the moment of this discovery, Percy was in a costume ill adapted for the taking of country walks. Reggie's remarks about his liver had struck home, and it had been his intention, by way of a corrective to his headache and a general feeling of swollen ill health, to do a little work before his bath with a pair of Indian clubs. He had arrayed himself for this purpose in an old sweater, a pair of grey flannel trousers, and patent leather evening shoes. It was not the garb he would have chosen himself for a ramble, but time was flying: even to put on a pair of boots is a matter of minutes: and in another moment or two Maud would be out of sight. Percy ran downstairs, snatched up a soft shooting-hat, which proved, too late, to belong to a person with a head two sizes smaller than his own; and raced out into the grounds. He was just in time to see Maud disappearing round the corner of the drive.

Lord Belpher had never belonged to that virile class of the community which considers running a pleasure and a pastime. At Oxford, on those occasions when the members of his college had turned out on raw afternoons to trot along the river-bank encouraging the college eight with yelling and the swinging of police-rattles, Percy had always stayed prudently in his rooms with tea and buttered toast, thereby avoiding who knows what colds and coughs. When he ran, he ran reluctantly and with a definite object in view, such as the catching of a train. He was consequently not in the best of condition, and the sharp sprint which was imperative at this juncture if he was to keep his sister in view left him spent and panting. But he had the reward of reaching the gates of the drive not many seconds after Maud, and of seeing her walking – more slowly now – down the road that led to Platt's. This confirmation of his suspicions enabled him momentarily to forget the blister which was forming on the heel of his left foot. He set out after her at a good pace.

The road, after the habit of country roads, wound and twisted. The quarry was frequently out of sight. And Percy's anxiety was such that, every time Maud vanished, he broke into a gallop. Another hundred yards, and the blister no longer consented to be ignored. It cried for attention like a little child, and was rapidly insinuating itself into a position in the scheme of things where it threatened to become the centre of the world. By the time the third bend in the road was reached, it seemed to Percy that this blister had become the one great Fact in an unreal nightmare-like universe. He hobbled painfully: and when he stopped suddenly and darted back into the shelter of the hedge his foot seemed aflame. The only reason why the blister on his left heel did not at this juncture attract his entire attention was that he had become aware that there was another of equal proportions forming on his right heel.

Percy had stopped and sought cover in the hedge because, as he rounded the bend in the road, he perceived, before he had time to check his gallop, that Maud had also stopped. She was standing in the middle of the road, looking over her shoulder, not ten yards away. Had she seen him? It was a point that time alone could solve. No! She walked on again. She had not seen him. Lord

Belpher, by means of a notable triumph of mind over matter, forgot the blisters and hurried after her.

They had now reached that point in the road where three choices offer themselves to the wayfarer. By going straight on he may win through to the village of Moresby-in-the-Vale, a charming little place with a Norman church; by turning to the left he may visit the equally seductive hamlet of Little Weeting; by turning to the right off the main road and going down a leafy lane he may find himself at the door of Platt's farm. When Maud, reaching the cross-roads, suddenly swung down the one to the left, Lord Belpher was for the moment completely baffled. Reason reasserted its way the next minute, telling him that this was but a ruse. Whether or no she had caught sight of him, there was no doubt that Maud intended to shake off any possible pursuit by taking this speciously innocent turning and making a detour. She could have no possible motive in going to Little Weeting. He had never been to Little Weeting in his life, and there was no reason to suppose that Maud had either.

The sign-post informed him – a statement strenuously denied by the twin-blisters – that the distance to Little Weeting was one and a half miles. Lord Belpher's view of it was that it was nearer fifty. He dragged himself along wearily. It was simpler now to keep Maud in sight, for the road ran straight: but, there being a catch in everything in this world, the process was also messier. In order to avoid being seen, it was necessary for Percy to leave the road and tramp along in the deep ditch which ran parallel to it. There is nothing half-hearted about these ditches which accompany English country roads. They know they are intended to be ditches, not mere furrows, and they behave as such. The one that sheltered Lord Belpher was so deep that only his head and neck protruded above the level of the road, and so dirty that a bare twenty yards of travel was sufficient to coat him with mud. Rain, once fallen, is reluctant to leave the

English ditch. It nestles inside it for weeks, forming a rich, oatmeal-like substance which has to be stirred to be believed. Percy stirred it. He churned it. He ploughed and sloshed through it. The mud stuck to him like a brother.

Nevertheless, being a determined young man, he did not give in. Once he lost a shoe, but a little searching recovered that. On another occasion, a passing dog, seeing things going on in the ditch which in his opinion should not have been going on – he was a high-strung dog, unused to coming upon heads moving along the road without bodies attached – accompanied Percy for over a quarter of a mile, causing exquisite discomfort by making sudden runs at his face. A well-aimed stone settled this little misunderstanding, and Percy proceeded on his journey alone. He had Maud well in view when, to his surprise, she left the road and turned into the gate of a house which stood not far from the church.

Lord Belpher regained the road, and remained there, a puzzled man. A dreadful thought came to him that he might have had all this trouble and anguish for no reason. This house bore the unmistakable stamp of a vicarage. Maud could have no reason that was not innocent for going there. Had he gone through all this, merely to see his sister paying a visit to a clergyman? Too late it occurred to him that she might quite easily be on visiting terms with the clergy of Little Weeting. He had forgotten that he had been away at Oxford for many weeks, a period of time in which Maud, finding life in the country weigh upon her, might easily have interested herself charitably in the life of this village. He paused irresolutely. He was baffled.

Maud, meanwhile, had rung the bell. Ever since, looking over her shoulder, she had perceived her brother Percy dodging about in the background, her active young mind had been busying itself with schemes for throwing him off the trail. She must see George that morning. She could not wait another day before establishing communication between herself and Geoffrey. But it was not till she reached Little Weeting that there occurred to her any plan that promised success.

A trim maid opened the door.

'Is the vicar in?'

'No, miss. He went out half an hour back.'

Maud was as baffled for the moment as her brother Percy, now leaning against the vicarage wall in a state of advanced exhaustion.

'Oh, dear!' she said.

The maid was sympathetic.

'Mr Ferguson, the curate, miss, he's here, if he would do.'

Maud brightened.

'He would do splendidly. Will you ask him if I can see him for a moment?'

'Very well, miss. What name, please?'

'He won't know my name. Will you please tell him that a lady wishes to see him?'

'Yes, miss. Won't you step in?'

The front door closed behind Maud. She followed the maid into the drawing-room. Presently a young small curate entered. He had a willing, benevolent face. He looked alert and helpful.

'You wished to see me?'

'I am so sorry to trouble you,' said Maud, rocking the young man in his tracks with a smile of dazzling brilliancy – ('No trouble, I assure you,' said the curate dizzily) ' – but there is a man following me!'

The curate clicked his tongue indignantly.

'A rough sort of a tramp kind of man. He has been following me for miles, and I'm frightened.'

'Brute!'

'I think he's outside now. I can't think what he wants. Would you – would you mind being kind enough to go and send him away?'

The eyes that had settled George's fate for all eternity flashed upon the curate, who blinked. He squared his shoulders and drew himself up. He was perfectly willing to die for her.

'If you will wait here,' he said, 'I will go and send him about his business. It is disgraceful that the public highways should be rendered unsafe in this manner.'

'Thank you ever so much,' said Maud gratefully. 'I can't help thinking the poor fellow *may* be a little crazy. It seems so odd of him to follow me all that way. Walking in the ditch too!'

'Walking in the ditch!'

'Yes. He walked most of the way in the ditch at the side of the road. He seemed to prefer it. I can't think why.'

Lord Belpher, leaning against the wall and trying to decide whether his right or left foot hurt him the more excruciatingly, became aware that a curate was standing before him, regarding him through a pair of gold-rimmed pince-nez with a disapproving and hostile expression. Lord Belpher returned his gaze. Neither was favourably impressed by the other. Percy thought he had seen nicer-looking curates, and the curate thought he had seen more prepossessing tramps.

'Come, come!' said the curate. 'This won't do, my man!'

A few hours earlier Lord Belpher had been startled when addressed by George as 'sir'. To be called 'my man' took his breath away completely.

The gift of seeing ourselves as others see us is, as the poet indicates, vouchsafed to few men. Lord Belpher, not being one of these fortunates, had not the slightest conception how intensely revolting his personal appearance was at that moment. The red-rimmed eyes, the growth of stubble on the cheeks, and the thick coating of mud which had resulted from his rambles in the ditch combined to render him a horrifying object.

'How dare you follow that young lady? I've a good mind to give you in charge!'

Percy was outraged.

'I'm her brother!' He was about to substantiate the statement by giving his name, but stopped himself. He had had enough of letting his name come out on occasions like the present. When the policeman had arrested him in the Haymarket, his first act had been to thunder his identity at the man: and the policeman, without saying in so many words that he disbelieved him, had hinted scepticism by replying that he himself was the king of Brixton. 'I'm her brother!' he repeated thickly.

The curate's disapproval deepened. In a sense, we are all brothers; but that did not prevent him from considering that this mud-stained derelict had made an impudent and abominable mis-statement of fact. Not unnaturally he came to the conclusion that he had to do with a victim of the Demon Rum.

'You ought to be ashamed of yourself,' he said severely. 'Sad piece of human wreckage as you are, you speak like an educated man. Have you no self-respect? Do you never search your heart and shudder at the horrible degradation which you have brought on yourself by sheer weakness of will?'

He raised his voice. The subject of Temperance was one very near to the curate's heart. The vicar himself had complimented him only yesterday on the good his sermons against the drink evil were doing in the village, and the landlord of the Three Pigeons down the road had on several occasions spoken bitter things about blighters who came taking the living away from honest folks.

'It is easy enough to stop if you will but use a little resolution. You say to yourself, "Just one won't hurt me!" Perhaps not. But can you be content with just one? Ah! No, my man, there is no middle way for such as you. It must be all or nothing. Stop it now – *now*, while you still retain some semblance of humanity. Soon it will be too late! Kill that craving! Stifle it! Strangle it! Make up your mind now – *now*, that not another drop of the accursed stuff shall pass your lips. . . .'

The curate paused. He perceived that enthusiasm was leading him away from the main issue. 'A little perseverance,' he concluded rapidly, 'and you will soon find that cocoa gives you exactly the same pleasure. And now will you please be getting along. You have frightened the young lady, and she cannot continue her walk unless I assure her that you have gone away.'

Fatigue, pain, and the annoyance of having to listen to this man's well-meant but ill-judged utterances had combined to induce in Percy a condition bordering on hysteria. He stamped his foot, and uttered a howl as the blister warned him with a sharp twinge that this sort of behaviour could not be permitted.

'Stop talking!' he bellowed. 'Stop talking like an idiot! I'm going to stay here till that girl comes out, if I have to wait all day!'

The curate regarded Percy thoughtfully. Percy was no Hercules: but, then, neither was the curate. And in any case, though no Hercules, Percy was undeniably an ugly-looking brute. Strategy, rather than force, seemed to the curate to be indicated. He paused a while, as one who weighs pros and cons, then spoke briskly, with the air of the man who has decided to yield a point with a good grace.

'Dear, dear!' he said. 'That won't do! You say you are this young lady's brother?'

'Yes, I do!'

'Then perhaps you had better come with me into the house and we will speak to her.'

'All right.'

'Follow me.'

Percy followed him. Down the trim gravel walk they passed, and up the neat stone steps. Maud, peeping through the curtains, thought herself the victim of a monstrous betrayal or equally monstrous blunder. But she did not know the Rev. Cyril Ferguson. No general, adroitly leading the enemy on by strategic retreat, ever had a situation more thoroughly in hand. Passing with his companion through the open door, he crossed the hall to another door, discreetly closed.

'Wait in here,' he said. Lord Belpher moved unsuspectingly forward. A hand pressed sharply against the small of his back. Behind him a door slammed and a key clicked. He was trapped. Groping in Egyptian darkness, his hands met a coat, then a hat, then an umbrella. Then he stumbled over a golf-club and fell against a wall. It was too dark to see anything, but his sense of touch told him all he needed to know. He had been added to the vicar's collection of odds and ends in the closet reserved for that purpose.

He groped his way to the door and kicked it. He did not repeat the performance. His feet were in no shape for kicking things.

Percy's gallant soul abandoned the struggle. With a feeble oath, he sat down on a box containing croquet implements, and gave himself up to thought.

'You'll be quite safe now,' the curate was saying in the adjoining room, not without a touch of complacent self-approval such as becomes the victor in a battle of wits. 'I have locked him in the cupboard. He will be quite happy there.' An incorrect statement this. 'You may now continue your walk in perfect safety.'

'Thank you ever so much,' said Maud. 'But I do hope he won't be violent when you let him out.'

'I shall not let him out,' replied the curate, who, though brave, was not rash. 'I shall depute the task to a worthy fellow named Willis, in whom I shall have every confidence. He – he is, in fact, our local blacksmith!'

And so it came about that when, after a vigil that seemed to last for a lifetime, Percy heard the key turn in the lock and burst forth seeking whom he might devour, he experienced an almost instant quieting of his excited nervous system. Confronting him was a vast man whose muscles, like those of that other and more celebrated village blacksmith, were plainly as strong as iron bands.

This man eyed Percy with a chilly eye.

'Well,' he said. 'What's troublin' *you*?'

Percy gulped. The man's mere appearance was a sedative.

'Er – nothing!' he replied. 'Nothing!'

'There better hadn't be!' said the man darkly. 'Mr Ferguson give me this to give to you. Take it!'

Percy took it. It was a shilling.

'And this.'

The second gift was a small paper pamphlet. It was entitled 'Now's the Time!' and seemed to be a story of some kind. At any rate, Percy's eyes, before they began to swim in a manner that prevented steady reading, caught the words 'Job Roberts had always been a hard-drinking man, but one day, as he was coming out of the bar-parlour . . .' He was about to hurl it from him, when he met the other's eye and desisted. Rarely had Lord Belpher encountered a man with a more speaking eye.

'And now you get along,' said the man. 'You pop off. And I'm going to watch you do it, too. And, if I find you sneakin' off to the Three Pigeons . . .'

His pause was more eloquent than his speech and nearly as eloquent as his eye. Lord Belpher tucked the tract into his sweater, pocketed the shilling, and left the house. For nearly a mile down the well-remembered highway he was aware of a Presence in his rear, but he continued on his way without a glance behind.

Like one that on a lonely road
    Doth walk in fear and dread;
And, having once looked back, walks on
    And turns no more his head!

Because he knows a frightful fiend
  Doth close behind him tread!

Maud made her way across the fields to the cottage down by Platt's. Her heart was as light as the breeze that ruffled the green hedges. Gaily she tripped towards the cottage door. Her hand was just raised to knock, when from within came the sound of a well-known voice.

She had reached her goal, but her father had anticipated her. Lord Marshmoreton had selected the same moment as herself for paying a call upon George Bevan.

Maud tiptoed away, and hurried back to the castle. Never before had she so clearly realized what a handicap an adhesive family can be to a young girl.

16

At the moment of Lord Marshmoreton's arrival, George was reading a letter from Billie Dore, which had come by that morning's post. It dealt mainly with the vicissitudes experienced by Miss Dore's friend, Miss Sinclair, in her relations with the man Spenser Gray. Spenser Gray, it seemed, had been behaving oddly. Ardent towards Miss Sinclair almost to an embarrassing point in the early stages of their acquaintance, he had suddenly cooled; at a recent lunch had behaved with a strange aloofness; and now, at this writing, had vanished altogether, leaving nothing behind him but an abrupt note to the effect that he had been compelled to go abroad and that, much as it was to be regretted, he and she would probably never meet again.

'And if,' wrote Miss Dore, justifiably annoyed, 'after saying all those things to the poor kid and telling her she was the only thing in sight, he thinks he can just slide off with a "Good-bye! Good luck! and God bless you!" he's got another guess coming. And that's not all. He hasn't gone abroad! I saw him in Piccadilly this afternoon. He saw me, too, and what do you think he did? Ducked down a side-street, if you please. He must have run like a rabbit, at that, because, when I got there, he was nowhere to be seen. I tell you, George, there's something funny about all this.'

Having been made once or twice before the confidant of the tempestuous romances of Billie's friends, which always seemed to go wrong somewhere in the middle and to die a natural death before arriving at any definite point, George was not particularly interested, except in so far as the letter afforded rather comforting evidence that he was not the only person in the world who was having trouble of the kind. He skimmed through the rest of it, and had just finished when there was a sharp rap at the front door.

'Come in!' called George.

There entered a sturdy little man of middle age whom at first sight George could not place. And yet he had the impression that he had seen him before. Then he recognized him as the gardener to whom he had given the note for Maud that day at the castle. The alteration in the man's costume was what had momentarily baffled George. When they had met in the rose-garden, the other had been arrayed in untidy gardening clothes. Now, presumably in his Sunday suit, it was amusing to observe how almost dapper he had become. Really, you might have passed him in the lane and taken him for some neighbouring squire.

George's heart raced. Your lover is ever optimistic, and he could conceive of no errand that could have brought this man to his cottage unless he was charged with the delivery of a note from Maud. He spared a moment from his happiness to congratulate himself on having picked such an admirable go-between. Here evidently, was one of those trusty old retainers you read about, faithful, willing, discreet, ready to do anything for 'the little missy' (bless her heart!). Probably he had danced Maud on his knee in her infancy, and with a dog-like affection had watched her at her childish sports. George beamed at the honest fellow, and felt in his pocket to make sure that a suitable tip lay safely therein.

'Good morning,' he said.

'Good morning,' replied the man.

A purist might have said he spoke gruffly and without geniality. But that is the beauty of these old retainers. They make a point of deliberately trying to deceive strangers as to the goldenness of their hearts by adopting a forbidding manner. And 'Good morning!' Not 'Good morning, *sir*!' Sturdy independence, you observe, as befits a free man. George closed the door carefully. He glanced into the kitchen. Mrs Platt was not there. All was well.

'You have brought a note from Lady Maud?'

The honest fellow's rather dour expression seemed to grow a shade bleaker.

'If you are alluding to Lady Maud Marsh, my daughter,' he replied frostily, 'I have not!'

For the past few days George had been no stranger to shocks, and had indeed come almost to regard them as part of the normal everyday life; but this latest one had a stumbling effect.

'I beg your pardon?' he said.

'So you ought to,' replied the earl.

George swallowed once or twice to relieve a curious dryness of the mouth.

'Are you Lord Marshmoreton?'

'I am.'

'Good Lord!'

'You seem surprised.'

'It's nothing!' muttered George. 'At least, you – I mean to say . . . It's only that there's a curious resemblance between you and one of your gardeners at the castle. I – I daresay you have noticed it yourself.'

'My hobby is gardening.'

Light broke upon George. 'Then was it really you – ?'

'It was!'

George sat down. 'This opens up a new line of thought!' he said.

Lord Marshmoreton remained standing. He shook his head sternly.

'It won't do, Mr . . . I have never heard your name.'

'Bevan,' replied George, rather relieved at being able to remember it in the midst of his mental turmoil.

'It won't do, Mr Bevan. It must stop. I allude to this absurd entanglement between yourself and my daughter. It must stop at once.'

It seemed to George that such an entanglement could hardly be said to have begun, but he did not say so.

Lord Marshmoreton resumed his remarks. Lady Caroline had sent him to the cottage to be stern, and his firm resolve to be stern lent his style of speech something of the measured solemnity and careful phrasing of his occasional orations in the House of Lords.

'I have no wish to be unduly hard upon the indiscretions of Youth. Youth is the period of Romance, when the heart rules the head. I myself was once a young man.'

'Well, you're practically that now,' said George.

'Eh?' cried Lord Marshmoreton, forgetting the thread of his discourse in the shock of pleased surprise.

'You don't look a day over forty.'

'Oh, come, come, my boy! . . . I mean, Mr Bevan.'

'You don't honestly.'

'I'm forty-eight.'

'The Prime of Life.'

'And you don't think I look it?'

'You certainly don't.'

'Well, well, well! By the way, have you tobacco, my boy? I came without my pouch.'

'Just at your elbow. Pretty good stuff. I bought it in the village.'

'The same I smoke myself.'

'Quite a coincidence.'

'Distinctly.'

'Match?'

'Thank you, I have one.'

George filled his own pipe. The thing was becoming a love-feast.

'What was I saying?' said Lord Marshmoreton, blowing a comfortable cloud. 'Oh, yes!' He removed his pipe from his mouth with a touch of embarrassment. 'Yes, yes, to be sure!'

There was an awkward silence.

'You must see for yourself,' said the earl, 'how impossible it is.'

George shook his head.

'I may be slow at grasping a thing, but I'm bound to say I can't see that.'

Lord Marshmoreton recalled some of the things his sister had told him to say. 'For one thing, what do we know of you? You are a perfect stranger.'

'Well, we're all getting acquainted pretty quick, don't you think? I met your son in Piccadilly and had a long talk with him, and now you are paying me a neighbourly visit.'

'This was not intended to be a social call.'

'But it has become one.'

'And then, that is one point I wish to make, you know. Ours is an old family, I would like to remind you that there were Marshmoretons in Belpher before the War of the Roses.'

'There were Bevans in Brooklyn before the B.R.T.'

'I beg your pardon?'

'I was only pointing out that I can trace my ancestry a long way. You have to trace things a long way in Brooklyn, if you want to find them.'

'I have never heard of Brooklyn.'

'You've heard of New York?'

'Certainly.'

'New York's one of the outlying suburbs.'

Lord Marshmoreton relit his pipe. He had a feeling that they were wandering from the point.

'It is quite impossible.'

'I can't see it.'

'Maud is so young.'

'Your daughter could be nothing else.'

'Too young to know her own mind,' pursued Lord

Marshmoreton, resolutely crushing down a flutter of pleasure. There was no doubt that this singularly agreeable man was making things very difficult for him. It was disarming to discover that he was really capital company – the best, indeed, that the earl could remember to have discovered in the more recent period of his rather lonely life. 'At present, of course, she fancies that she is very much in love with you . . . It is absurd!'

'You needn't tell me that,' said George. Really, it was only the fact that people seemed to go out of their way to call at his cottage and tell him that Maud loved him that kept him from feeling his cause perfectly hopeless. 'It's incredible. It's a miracle.'

'You are a romantic young man, and you no doubt for the moment suppose that you are in love with her.'

'No!' George was not going to allow a remark like that to pass unchallenged. 'You are wrong there. As far as I am concerned, there is no question of its being momentary or supposititious or anything of that kind. I *am* in love with your daughter. I was from the first moment I saw her. I always shall be. She is the only girl in the world!'

'Stuff and nonsense!'

'Not at all. Absolute, cold fact.'

'You have known her so little time.'

'Long enough.'

Lord Marshmoreton sighed. 'You are upsetting things terribly.'

'Things are upsetting *me* terribly.'

'You are causing a great deal of trouble and annoyance.'

'So did Romeo.'

'Eh?'

'I said – so did Romeo.'

'I don't know anything about Romeo.'

'As far as love is concerned, I begin where he left off.'

'I wish I could persuade you to be sensible.'

'That's just what I think I am.'

'I wish I could get you to see my point of view.'

'I do see your point of view. But dimly. You see, my own takes up such a lot of the foreground.'

There was a pause.

'Then I am afraid,' Lord Marshmoreton, 'that we must leave matters as they stand.'

'Until they can be altered for the better.'

'We will say no more about it now.'

'Very well.'

'But I must ask you to understand clearly that I shall have to do everything in my power to stop what I look on as an unfortunate entanglement.'

'I understand.'

'Very well.'

Lord Marshmoreton coughed. George looked at him with some surprise. He had supposed the interview to be at an end, but the other made no move to go. There seemed to be something on the earl's mind.

'There is – ah – just one other thing,' said Lord Marshmoreton. He coughed again. He felt embarrassed. 'Just – just one other thing,' he repeated.

The reason for Lord Marshmoreton's visit to George had been twofold. In the first place, Lady Caroline had told him to go. That would have been reason enough. But what made the visit imperative was an unfortunate accident of which he had only that morning been made aware.

It will be remembered that Billie Dore had told George that the gardener with whom she had become so friendly had taken her name and address with a view later on to send her some of his roses. The scrap of paper on which this information had been written was now lost. Lord Marshmoreton had been hunting for it since breakfast without avail.

Billie Dore had made a decided impression upon Lord Marshmoreton. She belonged to a type which he had never before encountered, and it was one which he had found more than agreeable. Her knowledge of roses and the proper feeling which she manifested towards rose-growing as a life-work consolidated the earl's liking for her. Never, in his memory, had he come across so sensible and charming a girl; and he had looked forward with a singular intensity to meeting her again. And now some too zealous housemaid, tidying up after the irritating manner of her species, had destroyed the only clue to her identity.

It was not for some time after this discovery that hope dawned again for Lord Marshmoreton. Only after he had given up the search for the missing paper as fruitless did he recall that it was in George's company that Billie had first come into his life. Between her, then, and himself, George was the only link.

It was primarily for the purpose of getting Billie's name and address from George that he had come to the cottage. And now that the moment had arrived for touching upon the subject, he felt a little embarrassed.

'When you visited the castle,' he said, 'when you visited the castle . . .'

'Last Thursday,' said George helpfully.

'Exactly. When you visited the castle last Thursday, there was a young lady with you.'

Not realizing that the subject had been changed, George was under the impression that the other had shifted his front and was about to attack him from another angle. He countered what seemed to him an insinuation stoutly.

'We merely happened to meet at the castle. She came there quite independently of me.'

Lord Marshmoreton looked alarmed. 'You didn't know her?' he said anxiously.

'Certainly I knew her. She is an old friend of mine. But if you are hinting . . .'

'Not at all,' rejoined the earl, profoundly relieved. 'Not at all. I ask merely because this young lady, with whom

I had some conversation, was good enough to give me her name and address. She, too, happened to mistake me for a gardener.'

'It's those corduroy trousers,' murmured George in extenuation.

'I have unfortunately lost them.'

'You can always get another pair.'

'Eh?'

'I say you can always get another pair of corduroy trousers.'

'I have not lost my trousers. I have lost the young lady's name and address.'

'Oh!'

'I promised to send her some roses. She will be expecting them.'

'That's odd. I was just reading a letter from her when you came in. That must be what she's referring to when she says, "If you see dadda, the old dear, tell him not to forget my roses." I read it three times and couldn't make any sense out of it. Are you dadda?'

The earl smirked. 'She *did* address me in the course of our conversation as dadda.'

'Then the message is for you.'

'A very quaint and charming girl. What is her name? And where can I find her?'

'Her name's Billie Dore.'

'Billie?'

'Billie.'

'Billie!' said Lord Marshmoreton softly. 'I had better write it down. And her address?'

'I don't know her private address. But you could always reach her at the Regal Theatre.'

'Ah! She is on the stage?'

'Yes. She's in my piece, "Follow the Girl".'

'Indeed! Are you a playwright, Mr Bevan?'

'Good Lord, no!' said George, shocked. 'I'm a composer.'

'Very interesting. And you met Miss Dore through her being in this play of yours?'

'Oh, no. I knew her before she went on the stage. She was a stenographer in a music-publisher's office when we first met.'

'Good gracious! Was she really a stenographer?'

'Yes. Why?'

'Oh – ah – nothing, nothing. Something just happened to come to my mind.'

What happened to come into Lord Marshmoreton's mind was a fleeting vision of Billie installed in Miss Alice Faraday's place as his secretary. With such a helper it would be a pleasure to work on that infernal Family History which was now such a bitter toil. But the day-dream passed. He knew perfectly well that he had not the courage to dismiss Alice. In the hands of that calm-eyed girl he was as putty. She exercised over him the hypnotic spell a lion-tamer exercises over his little playmates.

'We have been pals for years,' said George. 'Billie is one of the best fellows in the world.'

'A charming girl.'

'She would give her last nickel to anyone that asked for it.'

'Delightful!'

'And as straight as a string. No one ever said a word against Billie.'

'No?'

'She may go out to lunch and supper and all that kind of thing, but there's nothing to that.'

'Nothing!' agreed the earl warmly. 'Girls must eat!'

'They do. You ought to see them.'

'A little harmless relaxation after the fatigue of the day!'

'Exactly. Nothing more.'

Lord Marshmoreton felt more drawn than ever to this sensible young man – sensible, at least, on all points but one. It was a pity they could not see eye to eye on what was and what was not suitable in the matter of the love-affairs of the aristocracy.

'So you are a composer, Mr Bevan?' he said affably.

'Yes.'

Lord Marshmoreton gave a little sigh. 'It's a long time since I went to see a musical performance. More than twenty years. When I was up at Oxford, and for some years afterwards, I was a great theatre-goer. Never used to miss a first night at the Gaiety. Those were the days of Nellie Farren and Kate Vaughan. Florence St John, too. How excellent she was in *Faust Up to Date*! But we missed Nellie Farren. Meyer Lutz was the Gaiety composer then. But a good deal of water has flowed under the bridge since those days. I don't suppose you have ever heard of Meyer Lutz?'

'I don't think I have.'

'Johnnie Toole was playing a piece called *Partners*. Not a good play. And the *Yeoman of the Guard* had just been produced at the Savoy. That makes it seem a long time ago, doesn't it? Well, I mustn't take up all your time. Good-bye, Mr Bevan. I am glad to have had the opportunity of this little talk. The Regal Theatre, I think you said, is where your piece is playing? I shall probably be going to London shortly. I hope to see it.' Lord Marshmoreton rose. 'As regards the other matter, there is no hope of inducing you to see the matter in the right light?'

'We seem to disagree as to which is the right light.'

'Then there is nothing more to be said. I will be perfectly frank with you, Mr Bevan. I like you . . .'

'The feeling is quite mutual.'

'But I don't want you as a son-in-law. And, dammit,' exploded Lord Marshmoreton, 'I won't have you as a son-in-law! Good God! do you think that you can harry and assault my son Percy in the heart of Piccadilly and generally make yourself a damned nuisance and then settle down here without an invitation at my very gates and expect to be welcomed into the bosom of the family? If I were a young man . . .'

'I thought we had agreed that you were a young man.'

'Don't interrupt me!'

'I only said . . .'

'I heard what you said. Flattery!'

'Nothing of the kind. Truth.'

Lord Marshmoreton melted. He smiled. 'Young idiot!'

'We agree there all right.'

Lord Marshmoreton hesitated. Then with a rush he unbosomed himself, and made his own position on the matter clear.

'I know what you'll be saying to yourself the moment my back is turned. You'll be calling me a stage heavy father and an old snob and a number of other things. Don't interrupt me, dammit! You *will*, I tell you! And you'll be wrong. *I* don't think the Marshmoretons are fenced off from the rest of the world by some sort of divinity. My sister does. Percy does. But Percy's an ass! If ever you find yourself thinking differently from my son Percy, on any subject, congratulate yourself. You'll be right.'

'But . . .'

'I know what you're going to say. Let me finish. If I were the only person concerned, I wouldn't stand in Maud's way, whoever she wanted to marry, provided he was a good fellow and likely to make her happy. But I'm not. There's my sister Caroline. There's a whole crowd of silly, cackling fools – my sisters – my sons-in-law – all the whole pack of them! If I didn't oppose Maud in this damned infatuation she's got for you – if I stood by and let her marry you – what do you think would happen to me? – I'd never have a moment's peace! The whole gabbling pack of them would be at me, saying I was to blame. There would be arguments, discussions, family councils! I hate arguments! I loathe discussions! Family councils make me sick! I'm a peaceable man, and I like a quiet life! And, damme, I'm going to have it. So there's the thing for you in letters of one syllable. I don't object to you personally, but I'm not going to have you bothering me like this. I'll admit freely that, since I have made your acquaintance, I have altered the unfavourable opinion I had formed of you from – from hearsay . . .'

'Exactly the same with me,' said George. 'You ought never to believe what people tell you. Everyone told me your middle name was Nero, and that . . .'

'Don't interrupt me!'

'I wasn't. I was just pointing out . . .'

'Be quiet! I say I have changed my opinion of you to a great extent. I mention this unofficially, as a matter that has no bearing on the main issue; for, as regards any idea you may have of inducing me to agree to your marrying my daughter, let me tell you that I am unalterably opposed to any such thing!'

'Don't say that.'

'What the devil do you mean – don't say that! I *do* say that! It is out of the question. Do you understand? Very well, then. Good morning.'

The door closed. Lord Marshmoreton walked away feeling that he had been commendably stern. George filled his pipe and sat smoking thoughtfully. He wondered what Maud was doing at that moment.

Maud at that moment was greeting her brother with a bright smile, as he limped downstairs after a belated shave and change of costume.

'Oh, Percy, dear,' she was saying, 'I had quite an adventure this morning. An awful tramp followed me for miles! Such a horrible-looking brute. I was so frightened that I had to ask a curate in the next village to drive him away. I did wish I had had you there to protect me. Why don't you come out with me sometimes when I take a country walk? It really isn't safe for me to be alone!'

17

The gift of hiding private emotion and keeping up appearances before strangers is not, as many suppose, entirely a product of our modern civilization. Centuries before we were born or thought of there was a widely press-agented boy in Sparta who even went so far as to let a fox gnaw his tender young stomach without permitting the discomfort inseparable from such a proceeding to interfere with either his facial expression or his flow of small talk. Historians have handed it down that, even in the later stages of the meal, the polite lad continued to be the life and soul of the party. But, while this feat may be said to have established a record never subsequently lowered, there is no doubt that almost every day in modern times men and women are performing similar and scarcely less impressive miracles of self-restraint. Of all the qualities which belong exclusively to Man and are not shared by the lower animals, this surely is the one which marks him off most sharply from the beasts of the field.

Animals care nothing about keeping up appearances. Observe Bertram the Bull when things are not going just as he could wish. He stamps. He snorts. He paws the ground. He throws back his head and bellows. He is upset, and he doesn't care who knows it. Instances could be readily multiplied. Deposit a charge of shot in some outlying section of Thomas the Tiger, and note the effect. Irritate Wilfred the Wasp, or stand behind Maud the Mule and prod her with a pin. There is not an animal on the list who has even a rudimentary sense of the social amenities; and it is this more than anything else which should make us proud that we are human beings on a loftier plane of development.

In the days which followed Lord Marshmoreton's visit to George at the cottage, not a few of the occupants of Belpher Castle had their mettle sternly tested in this respect; and it is a pleasure to be able to record that not one of them failed to come through the ordeal with success. The general public, as represented by the uncles, cousins, and aunts who had descended on the place to help Lord Belpher celebrate his coming-of-age, had not a notion that turmoil lurked behind the smooth fronts of at least half a dozen of those whom they met in the course of the daily round.

Lord Belpher, for example, though he limped rather painfully, showed nothing of the baffled fury which was reducing his weight at the rate of ounces a day. His uncle Francis, the Bishop, when he tackled him in the garden on the subject of Intemperance – for Uncle Francis, like thousands of others, had taken it for granted, on reading the report of the encounter with the policeman and Percy's subsequent arrest, that the affair had been the result of a drunken outburst – had no inkling of the volcanic emotions that seethed in his nephew's bosom. He came away from the interview, feeling that the boy had listened attentively and with a becoming regret, and that there was hope for him after all, provided that he fought the impulse. He little knew that, but for the conventions (which frown on the practice of murdering bishops), Percy would gladly have strangled him with his bare hands and jumped upon the remains.

Lord Belpher's case, inasmuch as he took himself extremely seriously and was not one of those who can extract humour even from their own misfortunes, was perhaps the hardest which comes under our notice; but his sister Maud was also experiencing mental disquietude of no mean order. Everything had gone wrong with Maud. Barely a mile separated her from George, that essential link in her chain of communication with Geoffrey Raymond; but so thickly did it bristle with obstacles and dangers that it might have been a mile of No Man's Land. Twice, since the occasion when the discovery of Lord Marshmoreton at the cottage had caused her to abandon her purpose of going in and explaining everything to George, had she attempted to make the journey; and each time some trifling, maddening accident had brought about failure. Once, just as she was starting, her aunt Augusta had insisted on joining her for what she described as 'a nice long walk'; and the second time, when she was within a bare hundred yards of her objective, some sort of a cousin popped out from nowhere and forced his loathsome company on her.

Foiled in this fashion, she had fallen back in desperation on her second line of attack. She had written a note to George, explaining the whole situation in good, clear phrases and begging him as a man of proved chivalry to help her. It had taken up much of one afternoon, this note, for it was not easy to write; and it had resulted in nothing. She had given it to Albert to deliver and Albert had returned empty-handed.

'The gentleman said there was no answer, m'lady!'

'No answer! But there must be an answer!'

'No answer, m'lady. Those was his very words,' stoutly maintained the black-souled boy, who had destroyed the letter within two minutes after it had been handed to him. He had not even bothered to read it. A deep, dangerous, dastardly stripling this, who fought to win and only to win. The ticket marked 'R. Byng' was in his pocket, and in his ruthless heart a firm resolve that R. Byng and no other should have the benefit of his assistance.

Maud could not understand it. That is to say, she resolutely kept herself from accepting the only explanation of the episode that seemed possible. In black and white she had asked George to go to London and see

Geoffrey and arrange for the passage – through himself as a sort of clearing-house – of letters between Geoffrey and herself. She had felt from the first that such a request should be made by her in person and not through the medium of writing, but surely it was incredible that a man like George, who had been through so much for her and whose only reason for being in the neighbourhood was to help her, could have coldly refused without even a word. And yet what else was she to think? Now, more than ever, she felt alone in a hostile world.

Yet, to her guests she was bright and entertaining. Not one of them had a suspicion that her life was not one of pure sunshine.

Albert, I am happy to say, was thoroughly miserable. The little brute was suffering torments. He was showering anonymous advice to the Lovelorn on Reggie Byng – excellent stuff, culled from the pages of weekly papers, of which there was a pile in the housekeeper's room, the property of a sentimental lady's maid – and nothing seemed to come of it. Every day, sometimes twice and thrice a day, he would leave on Reggie's dressing-table significant notes similar in tone to the one which he had placed there on the night of the ball; but, for all the effect they appeared to exercise on their recipient, they might have been blank pages.

The choicest quotations from the words of such established writers as 'Aunt Charlotte' of *Forget-Me-Not* and 'Doctor Cupid', the heart-expert of *Home Chat*, expended themselves fruitlessly on Reggie. As far as Albert could ascertain – and he was one of those boys who ascertain practically everything within a radius of miles – Reggie positively avoided Maud's society. And this after reading 'Doctor Cupid's' invaluable tip about 'Seeking her company on all occasions' and the dictum of 'Aunt Charlotte' to the effect that 'Many a wooer has won his lady by being persistent' – Albert spelled it 'persistuent' but the effect is the same – 'and rendering himself indispensable by constant little attentions'. So far from rendering himself indispensable to Maud by constant little attentions, Reggie, to the disgust of his backer and supporter, seemed to spend most of his time with Alice Faraday. On three separate occasions had Albert been revolted by the sight of his protégé in close association with the Faraday girl – once in a boat on the lake and twice in his grey car. It was enough to break a boy's heart; and it completely spoiled Albert's appetite – a phenomenon attributed, I am glad to say, in the Servants' Hall to reaction from recent excesses. The moment when Keggs, the butler, called him a greedy little pig and hoped it would be a lesson to him not to stuff himself at all hours with stolen cakes was a bitter moment for Albert.

It is a relief to turn from the contemplation of these tortured souls to the pleasanter picture presented by Lord Marshmoreton. Here, undeniably, we have a man without a secret sorrow, a man at peace with this best of all possible worlds. Since his visit to George a second youth seems to have come upon Lord Marshmoreton. He works in his rose-garden with a new vim, whistling or even singing to himself stray gay snatches of melodies popular in the eighties.

Hear him now as he toils. He has a long garden implement in his hand, and he is sending up the death-rate in slug circles with a devastating rapidity.

'Ta-ra-ra boom-de-ay;
Ta-ra-ra BOOM – '

And the *boom* is a death-knell. As it rings softly out on the pleasant spring air, another stout slug has made the Great Change.

It is peculiar, this gaiety. It gives one to think Others have noticed it. His lordship's valet amongst them.

'I give you my honest word, Mr Keggs,' says the valet,

awed, 'this very morning I 'eard the old devil a-singing in 'is barth! Chirruping away like a blooming linnet!'

'Lor!' says Keggs, properly impressed.

'And only last night 'e gave me 'arf a box of cigars and said I was a good, faithful feller! I tell you, there's somethin' happened to the old buster – you mark my words!'

18

Over this complex situation the mind of Keggs, the butler, played like a searchlight. Keggs was a man of discernment and sagacity. He had instinct and reasoning power. Instinct told him that Maud, all unsuspecting the change that had taken place in Albert's attitude toward her romance, would have continued to use the boy as a link between herself and George: and reason, added to an intimate knowledge of Albert, enabled him to see that the latter must inevitably have betrayed her trust. He was prepared to bet a hundred pounds that Albert had been given letters to deliver and had destroyed them. So much was clear to Keggs. It only remained to settle on some plan of action which would re-establish the broken connexion. Keggs did not conceal a tender heart beneath a rugged exterior: he did not mourn over the picture of two loving fellow human beings separated by a misunderstanding; but he did want to win that sweepstake.

His position, of course, was delicate. He could not go to Maud and beg her to confide in him. Maud would not understand his motives, and might leap to the not unjustifiable conclusion that he had been at the sherry. No! Men were easier to handle than women. As soon as his duties would permit – and in the present crowded condition of the house they were arduous – he set out for George's cottage.

'I trust I do not disturb or interrupt you, sir,' he said, beaming in the doorway like a benevolent high priest. He had doffed his professional manner of austere disapproval, as was his custom in moments of leisure.

'Not at all,' replied George, puzzled. 'Was there anything . . .?'

'There was, sir.'

'Come along in and sit down.'

'I would not take the liberty, if it is all the same to you, sir. I would prefer to remain standing.'

There was a moment of uncomfortable silence. Uncomfortable, that is to say, on the part of George, who was wondering if the butler remembered having engaged him as a waiter only a few nights back. Keggs himself was at his ease. Few things ruffled this man.

'Fine day,' said George.

'Extremely, sir, but for the rain.'

'Oh, is it raining?'

'Sharp downpour, sir.'

'Good for the crops,' said George.

'So one would be disposed to imagine, sir.'

Silence fell again. The rain dripped from the eaves.

'If I might speak freely, sir . . .?' said Keggs.

'Sure. Shoot!'

'I beg your pardon, sir?'

'I mean, yes. Go ahead!'

The butler cleared his throat.

'Might I begin by remarking that your little affair of the 'eart, if I may use the expression, is no secret in the Servants' 'All? I 'ave no wish to seem to be taking a liberty or presuming, but I should like to intimate that the Servants' 'All is aware of the facts.'

'You don't have to tell me that,' said George coldly. 'I know all about the sweepstake.'

A flicker of embarrassment passed over the butler's large, smooth face – passed, and was gone.

'I did not know that you 'ad been apprised of that little matter, sir. But you will doubtless understand and appreciate our point of view. A little sporting flutter – nothing more – designed to halleviate the monotony of life in the country.'

'Oh, don't apologize,' said George, and was reminded of a point which had exercised him a little from time to time since his vigil on the balcony. 'By the way, if it isn't giving away secrets, who drew Plummer?'

'Sir?'

'Which of you drew a man named Plummer in the sweep?'

'I rather fancy, sir,' Keggs' brow wrinkled in thought, 'I rather fancy it was one of the visiting gentlemen's gentlemen. I gave the point but slight attention at the time. I did not fancy Mr Plummer's chances. It seemed to me that Mr Plummer was a negligible quantity.'

'Your knowledge of form was sound. Plummer's out!'

'Indeed, sir! An amiable young gentleman, but lacking in many of the essential qualities. Perhaps he struck you that way, sir?'

'I never met him. Nearly, but not quite!'

'It entered my mind that you might possibly have encountered Mr Plummer on the night of the ball, sir.'

'Ah, I was wondering if you remembered me!'

'I remember you perfectly, sir, and it was the fact that we had already met in what one might almost term a social way that emboldened me to come 'ere today and offer you my services as a hintermediary, should you feel disposed to avail yourself of them.'

George was puzzled.

'Your services?'

'Precisely, sir. I fancy I am in a position to lend you what might be termed an 'elping 'and.'

'But that's remarkably altruistic of you, isn't it?'

'Sir?'

'I say that is very generous of you. Aren't you forgetting that you drew Mr Byng?'

The butler smiled indulgently.

'You are not quite abreast of the progress of events, sir. Since the original drawing of names, there 'as been a trifling hadjustment. The boy Albert now 'as Mr Byng and I 'ave you, sir. A little amicable arrangement informally conducted in the scullery on the night of the ball.'

'Amicable?'

'On my part, entirely so.'

George began to understand certain things that had been perplexing to him.

'Then all this while . . .?'

'Precisely, sir. All this while 'er ladyship, under the impression that the boy Albert was devoted to 'er cause, has no doubt been placing a misguided confidence in 'im . . . The little blighter!' said Keggs, abandoning for a moment his company manners and permitting vehemence to take the place of polish. 'I beg your pardon for the expression, sir,' he added gracefully. 'It escaped me inadvertently.'

'You think that Lady Maud gave Albert a letter to give to me, and that he destroyed it?'

'Such, I should imagine, must undoubtedly have been the case. The boy 'as no scruples, no scruples whatsoever.'

'Good Lord!'

'I appreciate your consternation, sir.'

'That must be exactly what has happened.'

'To my way of thinking there is no doubt of it. It was for that reason that I ventured to come 'ere. In the 'ope that I might be hinstrumental in arranging a meeting.'

The strong distaste which George had had for plotting with this overfed menial began to wane. It might be undignified, he told himself, but it was undeniably practical. And, after all, a man who has plotted with page-boys has little dignity to lose by plotting with butlers. He brightened up. If it meant seeing Maud again he was prepared to waive the decencies.

'What do you suggest?' he said.

'It being a rainy evening and everyone indoors playing games and what not,' – Keggs was amiably tolerant of the recreations of the aristocracy – 'you would experience little chance of a hinterruption, were you to proceed to the lane outside the heast entrance of the castle grounds and wait there. You will find in the field at the roadside a small disused barn only a short way from the gates, where you would be sheltered from the rain. In the meantime, I would hinform 'er ladyship of your movements, and no doubt it would be possible for 'er to slip off.'

'It sounds all right.'

'It *is* all right, sir. The chances of a hinterruption may be said to be reduced to a minimum. Shall we say in one hour's time?'

'Very well.'

'Then I will wish you good evening, sir. Thank you, sir. I am glad to 'ave been of assistance.'

He withdrew as he had come, with a large impressiveness. The room seemed very empty without him. George, with trembling fingers, began to put on a pair of thick boots.

For some minutes after he had set foot outside the door of the cottage, George was inclined to revile the weather for having played him false. On this evening of all evenings, he felt, the elements should, so to speak, have rallied round and done their bit. The air should have been soft and clear and scented: there should have been an afterglow of sunset in the sky to light him on his way. Instead, the air was full of that peculiar smell of hopeless dampness which comes at the end of a wet English day. The sky was leaden. The rain hissed down in a steady flow, whispering of mud and desolation, making a dreary morass of the lane through which he tramped. A curious sense of foreboding came upon George. It was as if some voice of the night had murmured maliciously in his ear a hint of troubles to come. He felt oddly nervous, as he entered the barn.

The barn was both dark and dismal. In one of the dark

corners an intermittent dripping betrayed the presence of a gap in its ancient roof. A rat scurried across the floor. The dripping stopped and began again. George struck a match and looked at his watch. He was early. Another ten minutes must elapse before he could hope for her arrival. He sat down on a broken wagon which lay on its side against one of the walls.

Depression returned. It was impossible to fight against it in this beast of a barn. The place was like a sepulchre. No one but a fool of a butler would have suggested it as a trysting-place. He wondered irritably why places like this were allowed to get into this condition. If people wanted a barn earnestly enough to take the trouble of building one, why was it not worth while to keep the thing in proper repair? Waste and futility! That was what it was. That was what everything was, if you came down to it. Sitting here, for instance, was a futile waste of time. She wouldn't come. There were a dozen reasons why she should not come. So what was the use of his courting rheumatism by waiting in this morgue of dead agricultural ambitions? None whatever – George went on waiting.

And what an awful place to expect her to come to, if by some miracle she did come – where she would be stifled by the smell of mouldy hay, damped by raindrops and – reflected George gloomily as there was another scurry and scutter along the unseen floor – gnawed by rats. You could not expect a delicately nurtured girl, accustomed to all the comforts of a home, to be bright and sunny with a platoon of rats crawling all over her . . .

The grey oblong that was the doorway suddenly darkened.

'Mr Bevan!'

George sprang up. At the sound of her voice every nerve in his body danced in mad exhilaration. He was another man. Depression fell from him like a garment. He perceived that he had misjudged all sorts of things.

The evening, for instance, was a splendid evening – not one of those awful dry, baking evenings which make you feel you can't breathe, but pleasantly moist and full of a delightfully musical patter of rain. And the barn! He had been all wrong about the barn. It was a great little place, comfortable, airy, and cheerful. What could be more invigorating than that smell of hay? Even the rats, he felt, must be pretty decent rats, when you came to know them.

'I'm here!'

Maud advanced quickly. His eyes had grown accustomed to the murk, and he could see her dimly. The smell of her damp raincoat came to him like a breath of ozone. He could even see her eyes shining in the darkness, so close was she to him.

'I hope you've not been waiting long?'

George's heart was thundering against his ribs. He could scarcely speak. He contrived to emit a No.

'I didn't think at first I could get away. I had to . . .' She broke off with a cry. The rat, fond of exercise like all rats, had made another of its excitable sprints across the floor.

A hand clutched nervously at George's arm, found it, and held it. And at the touch the last small fragment of George's self-control fled from him. The world became vague and unreal. There remained of it but one solid fact – the fact that Maud was in his arms and that he was saying a number of things very rapidly in a voice that seemed to belong to somebody he had never met before.

19

With a shock of dismay so abrupt and overwhelming that it was like a physical injury, George became aware that something was wrong. Even as he gripped her, Maud had stiffened with a sharp cry; and now she was struggling, trying to wrench herself free. She broke away from him. He could hear her breathing hard.

'You – you – ' She gulped.

'Maud!'

'How dare you!'

There was a pause that seemed to George to stretch on and on endlessly. The rain pattered on the leafy roof. Somewhere in the distance a dog howled dismally. The darkness pressed down like a blanket, stifling thought.

'Good night, Mr Bevan.' Her voice was ice. 'I didn't think you were – that kind of man.'

She was moving toward the door; and, as she reached it, George's stupor left him. He came back to life with a jerk, shaking from head to foot. All his varied emotions had become one emotion – a cold fury.

'Stop!'

Maud stopped. Her chin was tilted, and she was wasting a baleful glare on the darkness.

'Well, what is it?'

Her tone increased George's wrath. The injustice of it made him dizzy. At that moment he hated her. He was the injured party. It was he, not she, that had been deceived and made a fool of.

'I want to say something before you go.'

'I think we had better say no more about it!'

By the exercise of supreme self-control George kept

himself from speaking until he could choose milder words than those that rushed to his lips.

'I think we will!' he said between his teeth.

Maud's anger became tinged with surprise. Now that the first shock of the wretched episode was over, the calmer half of her mind was endeavouring to soothe the infuriated half by urging that George's behaviour had been but a momentary lapse, and that a man may lose his head for one wild instant, and yet remain fundamentally a gentleman and a friend. She had begun to remind herself that this man had helped her once in trouble, and only a day or two before had actually risked his life to save her from embarrassment. When she heard him call to her to stop, she supposed that his better feelings had reasserted themselves; and she had prepared herself to receive with dignity a broken, stammered apology. But the voice that had just spoken with a crisp, biting intensity was not the voice of remorse. It was a very angry man, not a penitent one, who was commanding – not begging – her to stop and listen to him.

'Well?' she said again, more coldly this time. She was quite unable to understand this attitude of his. She was the injured party. It was she, not he who had trusted and been betrayed.

'I should like to explain.'

'Please do not apologize.'

George ground his teeth in the gloom.

'I haven't the slightest intention of apologizing. I said I would like to explain. When I have finished explaining, you can go.'

'I shall go when I please,' flared Maud.

This man was intolerable.

'There is nothing to be afraid of. There will be no repetition of the – incident.'

Maud was outraged by this monstrous misinterpretation of her words.

'I am not afraid!'

'Then, perhaps, you will be kind enough to listen. I won't detain you long. My explanation is quite simple. I have been made a fool of. I seem to be in the position of the tinker in the play whom everybody conspired to delude into the belief that he was a king. First a friend of yours, Mr Byng, came to me and told me that you had confided to him that you loved me.'

Maud gasped. Either this man was mad, or Reggie Byng was. She chose the politer solution.

'Reggie Byng must have lost his senses.'

'So I supposed. At least, I imagined that he must be mistaken. But a man in love is an optimistic fool, of course, and I had loved you ever since you got into my cab that morning . . .'

'What!'

'So after a while,' proceeded George, ignoring the interruption, 'I almost persuaded myself that miracles could still happen, and that what Byng said was true. And when your father called on me and told me the very same thing I was convinced. It seemed incredible, but I had to believe it. Now it seems that, for some inscrutable reason, both Byng and your father were making a fool of me. That's all. Good night.'

Maud's reply was the last which George or any man would have expected. There was a moment's silence, and then she burst into a peal of laughter. It was the laughter of overstrained nerves, but to George's ears it had the ring of genuine amusement.

'I'm glad you find my story entertaining,' he said dryly. He was convinced now that he loathed this girl, and that all he desired was to see her go out of his life for ever. 'Later, no doubt, the funny side of it will hit me. Just at present my sense of humour is rather dormant.'

Maud gave a little cry.

'I'm sorry! I'm so sorry, Mr Bevan. It wasn't that. It wasn't that at all. Oh, I am so sorry. I don't know why I laughed. It certainly wasn't because I thought it funny.

It's tragic. There's been a dreadful mistake!'

'I noticed that,' said George bitterly. The darkness began to afflict his nerves. 'I wish to God we had some light.'

The glare of a pocket-torch smote upon him.

'I brought it to see my way back with,' said Maud in a curious, small voice. 'It's very dark across the fields. I didn't light it before, because I was afraid somebody might see.'

She came towards him, holding the torch over her head. The beam showed her face, troubled and sympathetic, and at the sight all George's resentment left him. There were mysteries here beyond his unravelling, but of one thing he was certain: this girl was not to blame. She was a thoroughbred, as straight as a wand. She was pure gold.

'I came here to tell you everything,' she said. She placed the torch on the wagon-wheel so that its ray fell in a pool of light on the ground between them. 'I'll do it now. Only – only it isn't so easy now. Mr Bevan, there's a man – there's a man that father and Reggie Byng mistook – they thought . . . You see, they knew it was you that I was with that day in the cab, and so they naturally thought, when you came down here, that you were the man I had gone to meet that day – the man I – I – '

'The man you love.'

'Yes,' said Maud in a small voice; and there was silence again.

George could feel nothing but sympathy. It mastered every other emotion in him, even the grey despair that had come with her words. He could feel all that she was feeling.

'Tell me all about it,' he said.

'I met him in Wales last year.' Maud's voice was a whisper. 'The family found out, and I was hurried back here, and have been here ever since. That day when I met you I had managed to slip away from home. I had found out that he was in London, and I was going to meet him. Then I saw Percy, and got into your cab. It's all been a horrible mistake. I'm sorry.'

'I see,' said George thoughtfully. 'I see.'

His heart ached like a living wound. She had told so little, and he could guess so much. This unknown man who had triumphed seemed to sneer scornfully at him from the shadows.

'I'm sorry,' said Maud again.

'You mustn't feel like that. How can I help you? That's the point. What is it you want me to do?'

'But I can't ask you now.'

'Of course you can. Why not?'

'Why – oh, I couldn't!'

George managed to laugh. It was a laugh that did not sound convincing even to himself, but it served.

'That's morbid,' he said. 'Be sensible. You need help, and I may be able to give it. Surely a man isn't barred for ever from doing you a service just because he happens to love you? Suppose you were drowning and Mr Plummer was the only swimmer within call, wouldn't you let him rescue you?'

'Mr Plummer? What do you mean?'

'You've not forgotten that I was a reluctant ear-witness to his recent proposal of marriage?'

Maud uttered an exclamation.

'I never asked! How terrible of me. Were you much hurt?'

'Hurt?' George could not follow her.

'That night. When you were on the balcony, and – '

'Oh!' George understood. 'Oh, no, hardly at all. A few scratches. I scraped my hands a little.'

'It was a wonderful thing to do,' said Maud, her admiration glowing for a man who could treat such a leap so lightly. She had always had a private theory that Lord Leonard, after performing the same feat, had bragged about it for the rest of his life.

'No, no, nothing,' said George, who had since wondered why he had ever made such a to-do about climbing up a perfectly stout sheet.

'It was splendid!'

George blushed.

'We are wandering from the main theme,' he said. 'I want to help you. I came here at enormous expense to help you. How can I do it?'

Maud hesitated.

'I think you may be offended at my asking such a thing.'

'You needn't.'

'You see, the whole trouble is that I can't get in touch with Geoffrey. He's in London, and I'm here. And any chance I might have of getting to London vanished that day I met you, when Percy saw me in Piccadilly.'

'How did your people find out it was you?'

'They asked me – straight out.'

'And you owned up?'

'I had to. I couldn't tell them a direct lie.'

George thrilled. This was the girl he had had doubts of.

'So then it was worse than ever,' continued Maud. 'I daren't risk writing to Geoffrey and having the letter intercepted. I was wondering – I had the idea almost as soon as I found that you had come here – '

'You want me to take a letter from you and see that it reaches him. And then he can write back to my address, and I can smuggle the letter to you?'

'That's exactly what I do want. But I almost didn't like to ask.'

'Why not? I'll be delighted to do it.'

'I'm so grateful.'

'Why, it's nothing. I thought you were going to ask me to look in on your brother and smash another of his hats.'

Maud laughed delightedly. The whole tension of the situation had been eased for her. More and more she found herself liking George. Yet, deep down in her, she realized with a pang that for him there had been no easing of the situation. She was sad for George. The Plummers of this world she had consigned to what they declared would be perpetual sorrow with scarcely a twinge of regret. But George was different.

'Poor Percy!' she said. 'I don't suppose he'll ever get over it. He will have other hats, but it won't be the same.' She came back to the subject nearest her heart. 'Mr Bevan, I wonder if you would do just a little more for me?'

'If it isn't criminal. Or, for that matter, if it is.'

'Could you go to Geoffrey, and see him, and tell him all about me and – and come back and tell me how he looks, and what he said and – and so on?'

'Certainly. What is his name, and where do I find him?'

'I never told you. How stupid of me. His name is Geoffrey Raymond, and he lives with his uncle, Mr Wilbur Raymond, at 11a, Belgrave Square.'

'I'll go to him tomorrow.'

'Thank you ever so much.'

George got up. The movement seemed to put him in touch with the outer world. He noticed that the rain had stopped, and that stars had climbed into the oblong of the doorway. He had an impression that he had been in the barn a very long time; and confirmed this with a glance at his watch, though the watch, he felt, understated the facts by the length of several centuries. He was abstaining from too close an examination of his emotions from a prudent feeling that he was going to suffer soon enough without assistance from himself.

'I think you had better be going back,' he said. 'It's rather late. They may be missing you.'

Maud laughed happily.

'I don't mind now what they do. But I suppose dinners must be dressed for, whatever happens.' They moved together to the door. 'What a lovely night after all! I never thought the rain would stop in this world. It's like when you're unhappy and think it's going on for ever.'

'Yes,' said George.

Maud held out her hand.

'Good night, Mr Bevan.'

'Good night.'

He wondered if there would be any allusion to the earlier passages of their interview. There was none. Maud was of the class whose education consists mainly of a training in the delicate ignoring of delicate situations.

'Then you will go and see Geoffrey?'

'Tomorrow.'

'Thank you ever so much.'

'Not at all.'

George admired her. The little touch of formality which she had contrived to impart to the conversation struck just the right note, created just the atmosphere which would enable them to part without weighing too heavily on the deeper aspect of that parting.

'You're a real friend, Mr Bevan.'

'Watch me prove it.'

'Well, I must rush, I suppose. Good night!'

'Good night!'

She moved off quickly across the field. Darkness covered her. The dog in the distance had begun to howl again. He had his troubles, too.

20

Trouble sharpens the vision. In our moments of distress we can see clearly that what is wrong with this world of ours is the fact that Misery loves company and seldom gets it. Toothache is an unpleasant ailment; but, if toothache were a natural condition of life, if all mankind were afflicted with toothache at birth, we should not notice it. It is the freedom from aching teeth of all those with whom we come in contact that emphasizes the agony. And, as with toothache, so with trouble. Until our private affairs go wrong, we never realize how bubbling over with happiness the bulk of mankind seems to be. Our aching heart is apparently nothing but a desert island in an ocean of joy.

George, waking next morning with a heavy heart, made this discovery before the day was an hour old. The sun was shining, and birds sang merrily, but this did not disturb him. Nature is ever callous to human woes, laughing while we weep; and we grow to take her callousness for granted. What jarred upon George was the infernal cheerfulness of his fellow men. They seemed to be doing it on purpose – triumphing over him – glorying in the fact, that, however Fate might have shattered him, they were all right.

People were happy who had never been happy before. Mrs Platt, for instance. A grey, depressed woman of middle age, she had seemed hitherto to have few pleasures beyond breaking dishes and relating the symptoms of sick neighbours who were not expected to live through the week. She now sang. George could hear her as she prepared his breakfast in the kitchen. At first he had had a hope that she was moaning with pain; but this was dispelled when he had finished his toilet and proceeded downstairs. The sounds she emitted suggested anguish, but the words, when he was able to distinguish them, told another story. Incredible as it might seem, on this particular morning Mrs Platt had elected to be light-hearted. What she was singing sounded like a dirge, but actually it was 'Stop your tickling, Jock!' And, later, when she brought George his coffee and eggs, she spent a full ten minutes prattling as he tried to read his paper, pointing out to him a number of merry murders and sprightly suicides which otherwise he might have missed. The woman went out of her way to show him that for her, if not for less fortunate people, God this morning was in his heaven and all was right in the world.

Two tramps of supernatural exuberance called at the cottage shortly after breakfast to ask George, whom they had never even consulted about their marriages, to help support their wives and children. Nothing could have been more care-free and debonair than the demeanour of these men.

And then Reggie Byng arrived in his grey racing car, more cheerful than any of them.

Fate could not have mocked George more subtly. A sorrow's crown of sorrow is remembering happier things, and the sight of Reggie in that room reminded him that on the last occasion when they had talked together across this same table it was he who had been in a Fool's Paradise and Reggie who had borne a weight of care. Reggie this morning was brighter than the shining sun and gayer than the carolling birds.

'Hullo-ullo-ullo-ullo-ullo-ullo-ul-Lo! Topping morning, isn't it!' observed Reggie. 'The sunshine! The birds! The absolute what-do-you-call-it of everything and so forth, and all that sort of thing, if you know what I mean! I feel like a two-year-old!'

George, who felt older than this by some ninety-eight

years, groaned in spirit. This was more than man was meant to bear.

'I say,' continued Reggie, absently reaching out for a slice of bread and smearing it with marmalade, 'this business of marriage, now, and all that species of rot! What I mean to say is, what about it? Not a bad scheme, taking it by and large? Or don't you think so?'

George writhed. The knife twisted in the wound. Surely it was bad enough to see a happy man eating bread and marmalade without having to listen to him talking about marriage.

'Well, anyhow, be that as it may,' said Reggie, biting jovially and speaking in a thick but joyous voice. 'I'm getting married today, and chance it. This morning, this very morning, I leap off the dock!'

George was startled out of his despondency.

'What!'

'Absolutely, laddie!'

George remembered the conventions.

'I congratulate you.'

'Thanks, old man. And not without reason. I'm the luckiest fellow alive. I hardly knew I *was* alive till now.'

'Isn't this rather sudden?'

Reggie looked a trifle furtive. His manner became that of a conspirator.

'I should jolly well say it *is* sudden! It's got to be sudden. Dashed sudden and deuced secret! If the mater were to hear of it, there's no doubt whatever she would form a flying wedge and bust up the proceedings with no uncertain voice. You see, laddie, it's Miss Faraday I'm marrying, and the mater – dear old soul – has other ideas for Reginald. Life's a rummy thing, isn't it! What I mean to say is, it's rummy, don't you know, and all that.'

'Very,' agreed George.

'Who'd have thought, a week ago, that I'd be sitting in this jolly old chair asking you to be my best man? Why, a week ago I didn't know you, and, if anybody had told me Alice Faraday was going to marry me, I'd have given one of those hollow, mirthless laughs.'

'Do you want me to be your best man?'

'Absolutely, if you don't mind. You see,' said Reggie confidentially, 'it's like this. I've got lots of pals, of course, buzzing about all over London and its outskirts, who'd be glad enough to rally round and join the execution-squad; but you know how it is. Their maters are all pals of my mater, and I don't want to get them into trouble for aiding and abetting my little show, if you understand what I mean. Now, you're different. You don't know the mater, so it doesn't matter to you if she rolls around and puts the Curse of the Byngs on you, and all that sort of thing. Besides, I don't know,' Reggie mused. 'Of course, this is the happiest day of my life,' he proceeded, 'and I'm not saying it isn't, but you know how it is – there's absolutely no doubt that a chappie does *not* show at his best when he's being married. What I mean to say is, he's more or less bound to look a fearful ass. And I'm perfectly certain it would put me right off my stroke if I felt that some chump like Jack Ferris or Ronnie Fitzgerald was trying not to giggle in the background. So, if you will be a sportsman and come and hold my hand till the thing's over, I shall be eternally grateful.'

'Where are you going to be married?'

'In London. Alice sneaked off there last night. It was easy, as it happened, because by a bit of luck old Marshmoreton had gone to town yesterday morning – nobody knows why: he doesn't go up to London more than a couple of times a year. She's going to meet me at the Savoy, and then the scheme was to toddle round to the nearest registrar and request the lad to unleash the marriage service. I'm whizzing up in the car, and I'm hoping to be able to persuade you to come with me. Say the word, laddie!'

George reflected. He liked Reggie, and there was no

particular reason in the world why he should not give him aid and comfort in this crisis. True, in his present frame of mind, it would be torture to witness a wedding ceremony; but he ought not to let that stand in the way of helping a friend.

'All right,' he said.

'Stout fellow! I don't know how to thank you. It isn't putting you out or upsetting your plans, I hope, or anything on those lines?'

'Not at all. I had to go up to London today, anyway.'

'Well, you can't get there quicker than in my car. She's a hummer. By the way, I forgot to ask. How is your little affair coming along? Everything going all right?'

'In a way,' said George. He was not equal to confiding his troubles to Reggie.

'Of course, your trouble isn't like mine was. What I mean is, Maud loves you, and all that, and all you've got to think out is a scheme for laying the jolly old family a stymie. It's a pity – almost – that yours isn't a case of having to win the girl, like me; because by Jove, laddie,' said Reggie with solemn emphasis, 'I could help you there. I've got the thing down fine. I've got the infallible dope.'

George smiled bleakly.

'You have? You're a useful fellow to have around. I wish you would tell me what it is.'

'But you don't need it.'

'No, of course not. I was forgetting.'

Reggie looked at his watch.

'We ought to be shifting in a quarter of an hour or so. I don't want to be late. It appears that there's a catch of some sort in this business of getting married. As far as I can make out, if you roll in after a certain hour, the Johnnie in charge of the proceedings gives you the miss-in baulk, and you have to turn up again next day. However, we shall be all right unless we have a breakdown, and there's not much chance of that. I've been tuning up the old car since seven this morning, and she's sound in wind and limb, absolutely. Oil – petrol – water – air – nuts – bolts – sprockets – carburetter – all present and correct. I've been looking after them like a lot of baby sisters. Well, as I was saying, I've got the dope. A week ago I was just one of the mugs – didn't know a thing about it – but now! Gaze on me, laddie! You see before you old Colonel Romeo, the Man who Knows! It all started on the night of the ball. There was the dickens of a big ball, you know, to celebrate old Boots' coming-of-age – to which, poor devil, he contributed nothing but the sunshine of his smile, never having learned to dance. On that occasion a most rummy and extraordinary thing happened. I got pickled to the eyebrows!' He laughed happily. 'I don't mean that that was a unique occurrence and so forth, because, when I was a bachelor, it was rather a habit of mine to get a trifle submerged every now and again on occasions of decent mirth and festivity. But the rummy thing that night was that I showed it. Up till then, I've been told by experts, I was a chappie in whom it was absolutely impossible to detect the symptoms. You might get a bit suspicious if you found I couldn't move, but you could never be certain. On the night of the ball, however, I suppose I had been filling the radiator a trifle too enthusiastically. You see, I had deliberately tried to shove myself more or less below the surface in order to get enough nerve to propose to Alice. I don't know what your experience has been, but mine is that proposing's a thing that simply isn't within the scope of a man who isn't moderately woozled. I've often wondered how marriages ever occur in the dry States of America. Well, as I was saying, on the night of the ball a most rummy thing happened. I thought one of the waiters was you!'

He paused impressively to allow this startling statement to sink in.

'And was he?' said George.

'Absolutely not! That was the rummy part of it. He looked as like you as your twin brother.'

'I haven't a twin brother.'

'No, I know what you mean, but what I mean to say is he looked just like your twin brother would have looked if you had had a twin brother. Well, I had a word or two with this chappie, and after a brief conversation it was borne in upon me that I was up to the gills. Alice was with me at the time, and she noticed it too. Now you'd have thought that that would have put a girl off a fellow, and all that. But no. Nobody could have been more sympathetic. And she has confided to me since that it was seeing me in my oiled condition that really turned the scale. What I mean is, she made up her mind to save me from myself. You know how some girls are. Angels absolutely! Always on the look out to pluck brands from the burning, and what not. You may take it from me that the good seed was definitely sown that night.'

'Is that your recipe, then? You would advise the would-be bridegroom to buy a case of champagne and a wedding licence and get to work? After that it would be all over except sending out the invitations?'

Reggie shook his head.

'Not at all. You need a lot more than that. That's only the start. You've got to follow up the good work, you see. That's where a number of chappies would slip up, and I'm pretty certain I should have slipped up myself, but for another singularly rummy occurrence. Have you ever had a what-do-you-call it? What's the word I want? One of those things fellows get sometimes.'

'Headaches?' hazarded George.

'No, no. Nothing like that. I don't mean anything you get – I mean something you *get*, if you know what I mean.'

'Measles?'

'Anonymous letter. That's what I was trying to say. It's a most extraordinary thing, and I can't understand even now where the deuce they came from, but just about then I started to get a whole bunch of anonymous letters from some chappie unknown who didn't sign his name.'

'What you mean is that the letters were anonymous,' said George.

'Absolutely. I used to get two or three a day sometimes. Whenever I went up to my room, I'd find another waiting for me on the dressing-table.'

'Offensive?'

'Eh?'

'Were the letters offensive? Anonymous letters usually are.'

'These weren't. Not at all, and quite the reverse. They contained a series of perfectly topping tips on how a fellow should proceed who wants to get hold of a girl.'

'It sounds as though somebody had been teaching you jujitsu by post.'

'They were great! Real red-hot stuff straight from the stable. Priceless tips like "Make yourself indispensable to her in little ways", "Study her tastes", and so on and so forth. I tell you, laddie, I pretty soon stopped worrying about who was sending them to me, and concentrated the old bean on acting on them. They worked like magic. The last one came yesterday morning, and it was a topper! It was all about how a chappie who was nervous should proceed. Technical stuff, you know, about holding her hand and telling her you're lonely and being sincere and straightforward and letting your heart dictate the rest. Have you ever asked for one card when you wanted to fill a royal flush and happened to pick out the necessary ace? I did once, when I was up at Oxford, and, by Jove, this letter gave me just the same thrill. I didn't hesitate. I just sailed in. I was cold sober, but I didn't worry about that. Something told me I couldn't lose. It was like having to hole out a three-inch putt. And – well, there you are, don't you know.' Reggie became thoughtful. 'Dash it all! I'd like to know who the fellow was who sent me those letters. I'd like to send him a wedding-present or a bit of the cake or something. Though I suppose there won't be any cake, seeing the thing's taking place at a registrar's.'

'You could buy a bun,' suggested George.

'Well, I shall never know, I suppose. And now how about trickling forth? I say, laddie, you don't object if I sing slightly from time to time during the journey? I'm so dashed happy, you know.'

'Not at all, if it's not against the traffic regulations.'

Reggie wandered aimlessly about the room in an ecstasy.

'It's a rummy thing,' he said meditatively, 'I've just remembered that, when I was at school, I used to sing a thing called the what's-its-name's wedding song. At house-suppers, don't you know, and what not. Jolly little thing. I daresay you know it. It starts "Ding dong! Ding dong!" or words to that effect, "Hurry along! For it is my wedding-morning!" I remember you had to stretch out the "mor" a bit. Deuced awkward, if you hadn't laid in enough breath. "The Yeoman's Wedding-Song". That was it. I knew it was some chappie or other's. And it went on "And the bride in something or other is doing something I can't recollect." Well, what I mean is, now it's *my* wedding-morning! Rummy, when you come to think of it, what? Well, as it's getting tolerable late, what about it? Shift ho?'

'I'm ready. Would you like me to bring some rice?'

'Thank you, laddie, no. Dashed dangerous stuff, rice! Worse than shrapnel. Got your hat? All set?'

'I'm waiting.'

'Then let the revels commence,' said Reggie. 'Ding dong! Ding dong! Hurry along! For it is my wedding-morning! And the bride – Dash it, I wish I could remember what the bride was doing!'

'Probably writing you a note to say that she's changed her mind, and it's all off.'

'Oh, my God!' exclaimed Reggie. 'Come on!'

21

Mr and Mrs Reginald Byng, seated at a table in the corner of the Regent Grill-room, gazed fondly into each other's eyes. George, seated at the same table, but feeling many miles away, watched them moodily, fighting to hold off a depression which, cured for a while by the exhilaration of the ride in Reggie's racing-car (it had beaten its previous record for the trip to London by nearly twenty minutes), now threatened to return. The gay scene, the ecstasy of Reggie, the more restrained but equally manifest happiness of his bride – these things induced melancholy in George. He had not wished to attend the wedding-lunch, but the happy pair seemed to be revolted at the idea that he should stroll off and get a bite to eat somewhere else.

'Stick by us, laddie,' Reggie had said pleadingly, 'for there is much to discuss, and we need the counsel of a man of the world. We are married all right – '

'Though it didn't seem legal in that little registrar's office,' put in Alice.

' – But that, as the blighters say in books, is but a beginning, not an end. We have now to think out the most tactful way of letting the news seep through, as it were, to the mater.'

'And Lord Marshmoreton,' said Alice. 'Don't forget he has lost his secretary.'

'*And* Lord Marshmoreton,' amended Reggie. 'And about a million other people who'll be most frightfully peeved at my doing the Wedding Glide without consulting them. Stick by us, old top. Join our simple meal. And over the old Coronas we will discuss many things.'

The arrival of a waiter with dishes broke up the silent communion between husband and wife, and lowered Reggie to a more earthly plane. He refilled the glasses from the stout bottle that nestled in the ice-bucket – ('Only this one, dear!' murmured the bride in a warning undertone, and 'All right, darling!' replied the dutiful groom) – and raised his own to his lips.

'Cheerio! Here's to us all! Maddest, merriest day of all the glad New Year and so forth. And now,' he continued, becoming sternly practical, 'about the good old sequel and aftermath, so to speak, of this little binge of ours. What's to be done. You're a brainy sort of feller, Bevan, old man, and we look to you for suggestions. How would *you* set about breaking the news to mother?'

'Write her a letter,' said George.

Reggie was profoundly impressed.

'Didn't I tell you he would have some devilish shrewd scheme?' he said enthusiastically to Alice. 'Write her a letter! What could be better? Poetry, by Gad!' His face clouded. 'But what would you say in it? That's a pretty knotty point.'

'Not at all. Be perfectly frank and straightforward. Say you are sorry to go against her wishes – '

'Wishes,' murmured Reggie, scribbling industriously on the back of the marriage licence.

' – But you know that all she wants is your happiness – '

Reggie looked doubtful.

'I'm not sure about that last bit, old thing. You don't know the mater!'

'Never mind, Reggie,' put in Alice. 'Say it, anyhow. Mr Bevan is perfectly right.'

'Right ho, darling! All right, laddie – "happiness". And then?'

'Point out in a few well-chosen sentences how charming Mrs Byng is . . .'

'*Mrs Byng*!' Reggie smiled fatuously. 'I don't think I ever heard anything that sounded so indescribably ripping. That part'll be easy enough. Besides, the mater knows Alice.'

'Lady Caroline has *seen* me at the castle,' said his bride doubtfully, 'but I shouldn't say she knows me. She has hardly spoken a dozen words to me.'

'There', said Reggie, earnestly, 'you're in luck, dear heart! The mater's a great speaker, especially in moments of excitement. I'm not looking forward to the time when she starts on me. Between ourselves, laddie, and meaning no disrespect to the dear soul, when the mater is moved and begins to talk, she uses up most of the language.'

'Outspoken, is she?'

'I should hate to meet the person who could out-speak her,' said Reggie.

George sought information on a delicate point.

'And financially? Does she exercise any authority over you in that way?'

'You mean has the mater the first call on the family doubloons?' said Reggie. 'Oh, absolutely not! You see, when I call her the mater, it's using the word in a loose sense, so to speak. She's my stepmother really. She has her own little collection of pieces of eight, and I have mine. That part's simple enough.'

'Then the whole thing is simple. I don't see what you've been worrying about.'

'Just what I keep telling him, Mr Bevan,' said Alice.

'You're a perfectly free agent. She has no hold on you of any kind.'

Reggie Byng blinked dizzily.

'Why, now you put it like that,' he exclaimed, 'I can see that I jolly well am! It's an amazing thing, you know, habit and all that. I've been so accustomed for years to jumping through hoops and shamming dead when the mater lifted a little finger, that it absolutely never occurred to me that I had a soul of my Own. I give you my honest word I never saw it till this moment.'

'And now, it's too late!'

'Eh?'

George indicated Alice with a gesture. The newly made Mrs Byng smiled.

'Mr Bevan means that now you've got to jump through hoops and sham dead when I lift a little finger!'

Reggie raised her hand to his lips, and nibbled at it gently.

'Blessums 'ittle finger! It *shall* lift it and have 'ums Reggie jumping through . . .' He broke off and tendered George a manly apology. 'Sorry, old top! Forgot myself for the moment. Shan't occur again! Have another chicken or an éclair or some soup or something!'

Over the cigars Reggie became expansive.

'Now that you've lifted the frightful weight of the mater off my mind, dear old lad,' he said, puffing luxuriously, 'I find myself surveying the future in a calmer spirit. It seems to me that the best thing to do, as regards the mater and everybody else, is simply to prolong the merry wedding-trip till Time the Great Healer has had a chance to cure the wound. Alice wants to put in a week or so in Paris . . .'

'Paris!' murmured the bride ecstatically.

'Then *I* would like to trickle southwards to the Riviera . . .'

'If you mean Monte Carlo, dear,' said his wife with gentle firmness, 'no!'

'No, no, not Monte Carlo,' said Reggie hastily, 'though it's a great place. Air – scenery – and what not! But Nice and Bordighera and Mentone and other fairly ripe resorts. You'd enjoy them. And after that . . . I had a scheme for buying back my yacht, the jolly old *Siren*, and cruising about the Mediterranean for a month or so. I sold her to a local sportsman when I was in America a couple of years ago. But I saw in the paper yesterday that the poor old buffer had died suddenly, so I suppose it would be difficult to get hold of her for the time being.' Reggie broke off with a sharp exclamation.

'My sainted aunt!'

'What's the matter?'

Both his companions were looking past him, wide-eyed. George occupied the chair that had its back to the door, and was unable to see what it was that had caused their consternation; but he deduced that someone known to both of them must have entered the restaurant; and his first thought, perhaps naturally, was that it must be Reggie's 'mater'. Reggie dived behind a menu, which he held before him like a shield, and his bride, after one quick look, had turned away so that her face was hidden. George swung around, but the newcomer, whoever he or she was, was now seated and indistinguishable from the rest of the lunchers.

'Who is it?'

Reggie laid down the menu with the air of one who after a momentary panic rallies.

'Don't know what I'm making such a fuss about,' he said stoutly. 'I keep forgetting that none of these blighters really matter in the scheme of things. I've a good mind to go over and pass the time of day.'

'Don't!' pleaded his wife. 'I feel so guilty.'

'Who is it?' asked George again. 'Your step-mother?'

'Great Scott, no!' said Reggie. 'Nothing so bad as that. It's old Marshmoreton.'

'Lord Marshmoreton!'

'Absolutely! And looking positively festive.'

'I feel so awful, Mr Bevan,' said Alice. 'You know, I left the castle without a word to anyone, and he doesn't know yet that there won't be any secretary waiting for him when he gets back.'

Reggie took another look over George's shoulder and chuckled.

'It's all right, darling. Don't worry. We can nip off secretly by the other door. He's not going to stop us. He's got a girl with him! The old boy has come to life – absolutely! He's gassing away sixteen to the dozen to a frightfully pretty girl with gold hair. If you slew the ole bean round at an angle of about forty-five, Bevan, old top, you can see her. Take a look. He won't see you. He's got his back to us.'

'Do you call her pretty?' asked Alice disparagingly.

'Now that I take a good look, precious,' replied Reggie with alacrity, 'no! Absolutely not! Not my style at all!'

His wife crumbled bread.

'I think she must know you, Reggie, dear,' she said softly. 'She's waving to you.'

'She's waving to *me*,' said George, bringing back the sunshine to Reggie's life, and causing the latter's face to lose its hunted look. 'I know her very well. Her name's Dore. Billie Dore.'

'Old man,' said Reggie, 'be a good fellow and slide over to their table and cover our retreat. I know there's nothing to be afraid of really, but I simply can't face the old boy.'

'And break the news to him that I've gone, Mr Bevan,' added Alice.

'Very well, I'll say good-bye, then.'

'Good-bye, Mr Bevan, and thank you ever so much.'

Reggie shook George's hand warmly.

'Good-bye, Bevan old thing, you're a ripper. I can't tell you how bucked up I am at the sportsmanlike way you've rallied round. I'll do the same for you one of these days. Just hold the old boy in play for a minute or two while we leg it. And, if he wants us, tell him our address till further notice is Paris. What ho! What ho! What ho! Toodle-oo, laddie, toodle-oo!'

George threaded his way across the room. Billie Dore

welcomed him with a friendly smile. The earl, who had turned to observe his progress, seemed less delighted to see him. His weather-beaten face wore an almost furtive look. He reminded George of a schoolboy who has been caught in some breach of the law.

'Fancy seeing you here, George!' said Billie. 'We're always meeting, aren't we? How did you come to separate yourself from the pigs and chickens? I thought you were never going to leave them.'

'I had to run up on business,' explained George. 'How are you, Lord Marshmoreton?'

The earl nodded briefly.

'So you're on to him, too?' said Billie. 'When did *you* get wise?'

'Lord Marshmoreton was kind enough to call on me the other morning and drop the incognito.'

'Isn't dadda the foxiest old thing!' said Billie delightedly. 'Imagine him standing there that day in the garden, kidding us along like that! I tell you, when they brought me his card last night after the first act and I went down to take a slant at this Lord Marshmoreton and found dadda hanging round the stage door, you could have knocked me over with a whisk-broom.'

'I have not stood at the stage door for twenty-five years,' said Lord Marshmoreton sadly.

'Now, it's no use your pulling that Henry W. Methuselah stuff,' said Billie affectionately. 'You can't get away with it. Anyone can see you're just a kid. Can't they, George?' She indicated the blushing earl with a wave of the hand. 'Isn't dadda the youngest thing that ever happened?'

'Exactly what I told him myself.'

Lord Marshmoreton giggled. There is no other verb that describes the sound that proceeded from him.

'I feel young,' he admitted.

'I wish some of the juveniles in the shows I've been in,' said Billie, 'were as young as you. It's getting so nowadays that one's thankful if a juvenile has teeth.' She glanced across the room. 'Your pals are walking out on you, George. The people you were lunching with,' she explained. 'They're leaving.'

'That's all right. I said good-bye to them.' He looked at Lord Marshmoreton. It seemed a suitable opportunity to break the news. 'I was lunching with Mr and Mrs Byng,' he said.

Nothing appeared to stir beneath Lord Marshmoreton's tanned forehead.

'Reggie Byng and his wife, Lord Marshmoreton,' added George.

This time he secured the earl's interest. Lord Marshmoreton started.

'What!'

'They are just off to Paris,' said George.

'Reggie Byng is not married!'

'Married this morning. I was best man.'

'Busy little creature!' interjected Billie.

'But – but – !'

'You know his wife,' said George casually. 'She was a Miss Faraday. I think she was your secretary.'

It would have been impossible to deny that Lord Marshmoreton showed emotion. His mouth opened, and he clutched the tablecloth. But just what the emotion was George was unable to say till, with a sigh that seemed to come from his innermost being, the other exclaimed 'Thank Heaven!'

George was surprised.

'You're glad?'

'Of course I'm glad!'

'It's a pity they didn't know how you were going to feel. It would have saved them a lot of anxiety. I rather gathered they supposed that the shock was apt to darken your whole life.'

'That girl,' said Lord Marshmoreton vehemently, 'was driving me crazy. Always bothering me to come and work on that damned family history. Never gave me a moment's peace . . .'

'I liked her,' said George.

'Nice enough girl,' admitted his lordship grudgingly. 'But a damned nuisance about the house; always at me to go on with the family history. As if there weren't better things to do with one's time than writing all day about my infernal fools of ancestors!'

'Isn't dadda fractious today?' said Billie reprovingly, giving the earl's hand a pat. 'Quit knocking your ancestors! You're very lucky to have ancestors. I wish I had. The Dore family seems to go back about as far as the presidency of Willard Filmore, and then it kind of gets discouraged and quite cold. Gee! I'd like to feel that my great-great-great-grandmother had helped Queen Elizabeth with the rent. I'm strong for the fine old stately families of England.'

'Stately old fiddlesticks!' snapped the earl.

'Did you see his eyes flash then, George? That's what they call aristocratic rage. It's the fine old spirit of the Marshmoretons boiling over.'

'I noticed it,' said George. 'Just like lightning.'

'It's no use trying to fool us, dadda,' said Billie. 'You know just as well as I do that it makes you feel good to think that, every time you cut yourself with your safety-razor, you bleed blue!'

'A lot of silly nonsense!' grumbled the earl.

'What is?'

'This foolery of titles and aristocracy. Silly fetish-worship! One man's as good as another . . .'

'This is the spirit of '76!' said George approvingly.

'Regular I.W.W. stuff,' agreed Billie. 'Shake hands with the President of the Bolsheviki!'

Lord Marshmoreton ignored the interruption. There was a strange look in his eyes. It was evident to George, watching him with close interest, that here was a revelation of the man's soul; that thoughts, locked away for years in the other's bosom, were crying for utterance.

'Damned silly nonsense! When I was a boy, I wanted to be an engine-driver. When I was a young man, I was a Socialist and hadn't any idea except to work for my living and make a name for myself. I was going to the colonies. Canada. The fruit farm was actually bought. Bought and paid for!' He brooded a moment on that long-lost fruit farm. 'My father was a younger son. And then my uncle must go and break his neck hunting, and the baby, poor little chap, got croup or something . . . And there I was, saddled with the title, and all my plans gone up in smoke . . . Silly nonsense! Silly nonsense!' He bit the end of a cigar. 'And you can't stand up against it,' he went on ruefully. 'It saps you. It's like some damned drug. I fought against it as long as I could, but it was no use. I'm as big a snob as any of them now. I'm afraid to do what I want to do. Always thinking of the family dignity. I haven't taken a free step for twenty-five years.'

George and Billie exchanged glances. Each had the uncomfortable feeling that they were eavesdropping and hearing things not meant to be heard. George rose.

'I must be getting along now,' he said. 'I've one or two things to do. Glad to have seen you again, Billie. Is the show going all right?'

'Fine. Making money for you right along.'

'Good-bye, Lord Marshmoreton.'

The earl nodded without speaking. It was not often now that he rebelled even in thoughts against the lot which fate had thrust upon him, and never in his life before had he done so in words. He was still in the grip of the strange discontent which had come upon him so abruptly.

There was a silence after George had gone.

'I'm glad we met George,' said Billie. 'He's a good boy.' She spoke soberly. She was conscious of a curious feeling of affection for the sturdy, weather-tanned little man opposite her. The glimpse she had been given of his inner self had somehow made him come alive for her.

'He wants to marry my daughter,' said Lord Marshmoreton.

A few moments before, Billie would undoubtedly have replied to such a statement with some jocular remark expressing disbelief that the earl could have a daughter old enough to be married. But now she felt oddly serious and unlike her usual flippant self.

'Oh?' was all she could find to say.

'She wants to marry him.'

Not for years had Billie Dore felt embarrassed, but she felt so now. She judged herself unworthy to be the recipient of these very private confidences.

'Oh?' she said again.

'He's a good fellow. I like him. I liked him the moment we met. He knew it, too. And I knew he liked me.'

A group of men and girls from a neighbouring table passed on their way to the door. One of the girls nodded to Billie. She returned the nod absently. The party moved on. Billie frowned down at the tablecloth and drew a pattern on it with a fork.

'Why don't you let George marry your daughter, Lord Marshmoreton?'

The earl drew at his cigar in silence.

'I know it's not my business,' said Billie apologetically, interpreting the silence as a rebuff.

'Because I'm the Earl of Marshmoreton.'

'I see.'

'No you don't,' snapped the earl. 'You think I mean by that that I think your friend isn't good enough to marry my daughter. You think that I'm an incurable snob. And I've no doubt he thinks so, too, though I took the trouble to explain my attitude to him when we last met. You're wrong. It isn't that at all. When I say "I'm the Earl of Marshmoreton", I mean that I'm a poor spineless fool who's afraid to do the right thing because he daren't go in the teeth of the family.'

'I don't understand. What have your family got to do with it?'

'They'd worry the life out of me. I wish you could meet my sister Caroline! That's what they've got to do with it. Girls in my daughter's unfortunate position have got to marry position or money.'

'Well, I don't know about position, but when it comes to money – why, George is the fellow that made the dollar-bill famous. He and Rockefeller have got all there is, except the little bit they have let Andy Carnegie have for car-fare.'

'What do you mean? He told me he worked for a living.'

Billie was becoming herself again. Embarrassment had fled.

'If you call it work. He's a composer.'

'I know. Writes tunes and things.'

Bille regarded him compassionately.

'And I suppose, living out in the woods the way you do, that you haven't a notion that they pay him for it.'

'Pay him? Yes, but how much? Composers were not rich men in my day.'

'I wish you wouldn't talk of "your day" as if you were Noah telling the boys down at the corner store about the good times they all had before the Flood. You're one of the Younger Set, and don't let me have to tell you again. Say, listen! You know that show you saw last night. The one where I was star, supported by a few underlings. Well, George wrote the music for that.'

'I know. He told me so.'

'Well, did he tell you that he draws three per cent of the gross receipts? You saw the house we had last night. It was a fair average house. We are playing to over fourteen thousand dollars a week. George's little bit of that is – I can't do it in my head, but it's a round four hundred dollars. That's eighty pounds of your money. And did he tell you that this same show ran over a year in New York to big business all the time, and that there are three companies on the road now? And did he mention that this is the ninth show he's done, and that seven of the others were just as big hits as this one? And did he remark in passing that he gets royalties on every copy of his music that's sold, and that at least ten of his things have sold over half a million? No, he didn't, because he isn't the sort of fellow who stands around blowing about his income. But you know it now.'

'Why, he's a rich man!'

'I don't know what you call rich, but, keeping on the safe side, I should say that George pulls down in a good year, during the season – around five thousand dollars a week.'

Lord Marshmoreton was frankly staggered.

'A thousand pounds a week! I had no idea!'

'I thought you hadn't. And, while I'm boosting George, let me tell you another thing. He's one of the whitest men that ever happened. I know him. You can take it from me, if there's anything rotten in a fellow, the show business will bring it out, and it hasn't come out in George yet, so I guess it isn't there. George is all right!'

'He has at least an excellent advocate.'

'Oh, I'm strong for George. I wish there were more like him . . . Well, if you think I've butted in on your private affairs sufficiently, I suppose I ought to be moving. We've a rehearsal this afternoon.'

'Let it go!' said Lord Marshmoreton boyishly.

'Yes, and how quick do you think they would let me go, if I did? I'm an honest working-girl, and I can't afford to lose jobs.'

Lord Marshmoreton fiddled with his cigar-butt.

'I could offer you an alternative position, if you cared to accept it.'

Billie looked at him keenly. Other men in similar circumstances had made much the same remark to her.

She was conscious of feeling a little disappointed in her new friend.

'Well?' she said dryly. 'Shoot.'

'You gathered, no doubt, from Mr Bevan's conversation, that my secretary has left me and run away and got married? Would you like to take her place?'

It was not easy to disconcert Billie Dore, but she was taken aback. She had been expecting something different.

'You're a shriek, dadda!'

'I'm perfectly serious.'

'Can you see me at a castle?'

'I can see you perfectly.' Lord Marshmoreton's rather formal manner left him. 'Do please accept, my dear child. I've got to finish this damned family history some time or other. The family expect me to. Only yesterday my sister Caroline got me in a corner and bored me for half an hour about it. And I simply can't face the prospect of getting another Alice Faraday from an agency. Charming girl, charming girl, of course, but . . . but . . . well, I'll be damned if I do it, and that's the long and short of it!'

Billie bubbled over with laughter.

'Of all the impulsive kids!' she gurgled. 'I never met anyone like you, dadda! You don't even know that I can use a typewriter.'

'I do. Mr Bevan told me you were an excellent stenographer.'

'So George has been boosting me, too, has he?' She mused. 'I must say, I'd love to come. That old place got me when I saw it that day.'

'That's settled, then,' said Lord Marshmoreton masterfully. 'Go to the theatre and tell them – tell whatever is usual in these cases. And then go home and pack, and meet me at Waterloo at six o'clock. The train leaves at six-fifteen.'

'Return of the wanderer, accompanied by dizzy

blonde! You've certainly got it all fixed, haven't you! Do you think the family will stand for me?'

'Damn the family!' said Lord Marshmoreton, stoutly.

'There's one thing,' said Billie complacently, eyeing her reflection in the mirror of her vanity-case, 'I may glitter in the fighting-top, but it *is* genuine. When I was a kid, I was a regular little tow-head.'

'I never supposed for a moment that it was anything but genuine.'

'Then you've got a fine, unsuspicious nature, dadda, and I admire you for it.'

'Six o'clock at Waterloo,' said the earl. 'I'll be waiting for you.'

Billie regarded him with affectionate admiration.

'Boys will be boys,' she said. 'All right. I'll be there.'

22

'Young blighted Albert,' said Keggs the butler, shifting his weight so that it distributed itself more comfortably over the creaking chair in which he reclined, 'let this be a lesson to you, young feller me lad.'

The day was a week after Lord Marshmoreton's visit to London, the hour six o'clock. The housekeeper's room, in which the upper servants took their meals, had emptied. Of the gay company which had just finished dinner only Keggs remained, placidly digesting. Albert, whose duty it was to wait on the upper servants, was moving to and fro, morosely collecting the plates and glasses. The boy was in no happy frame of mind. Throughout dinner the conversation at table had dealt almost exclusively with the now celebrated elopement of Reggie Byng and his bride, and few subjects could have made more painful listening to Albert.

'What's been the result and what I might call the upshot,' said Keggs, continuing his homily, 'of all your making yourself so busy and thrusting of yourself forward and meddling in the affairs of your elders and betters? The upshot and issue of it 'as been that you are out five shillings and nothing to show for it. Five shillings what you might have spent on some good book and improved your mind! And goodness knows it wants all the improving it can get, for of all the worthless, idle little messers it's ever been my misfortune to have dealings with, you are the champion. Be careful of them plates, young man, and don't breathe so hard. You 'aven't got hasthma or something, 'ave you?'

'I can't breathe now!' complained the stricken child.

'Not like a grampus you can't, and don't you forget it.'

Keggs wagged his head reprovingly. 'Well, so your Reggie Byng's gone and eloped, has he! That ought to teach you to be more careful another time 'ow you go gambling and plunging into sweepstakes. The idea of a child of your age 'aving the audacity to thrust 'isself forward like that!'

'Don't call him my Reggie Byng! *I* didn't draw 'im!'

'There's no need to go into all that again, young feller. You accepted 'im freely and without prejudice when the fair exchange was suggested, so for all practical intents and purposes he is your Reggie Byng. I 'ope you're going to send him a wedding-present.'

'Well, you ain't any better off than me, with all your 'ighway robbery!'

'My what?'

'You 'eard what I said.'

'Well, don't let me 'ear it again. The idea! If you 'ad any objections to parting with that ticket, you should have stated them clearly at the time. And what do you mean by saying I ain't any better off than you are?'

'I 'ave my reasons.'

'You *think* you 'ave, which is a very different thing. I suppose you imagine that you've put a stopper on a certain little affair by surreptitiously destroying letters entrusted to you.'

'I never!' exclaimed Albert with a convulsive start that nearly sent eleven plates dashing to destruction.

''Ow many times have I got to tell you to be careful of them plates?' said Keggs sternly. 'Who do you think you are – a juggler on the 'Alls, 'urling them about like that? Yes, I know all about that letter. You thought you was very clever, I've no doubt. But let me tell you, young blighted Albert, that only the other evening 'er ladyship and Mr Bevan 'ad a long and extended interview in spite of all your hefforts. I saw through your little game, and I proceeded and went and arranged the meeting.'

In spite of himself Albert was awed. He was oppressed by the sense of struggling with a superior intellect.

'Yes, you did!' he managed to say with the proper note of incredulity, but in his heart he was not incredulous. Dimly, Albert had begun to perceive that years must elapse before he could become capable of matching himself in battles of wits with this master-strategist.

'Yes, I certainly did!' said Keggs. 'I don't know what 'appened at the interview – not being present in person. But I've no doubt that everything proceeded satisfactorily.'

'And a fat lot of good that's going to do you, when 'e ain't allowed to come inside the 'ouse!'

A bland smile irradiated the butler's moon-like face.

'If by 'e you're alloodin' to Mr Bevan, young blighted Albert, let me tell you that it won't be long before 'e becomes a regular duly invited guest at the castle!'

'A lot of chance!'

'Would you care to 'ave another five shillings even money on it?'

Albert recoiled. He had had enough of speculation where the butler was concerned. Where that schemer was allowed to get within reach of it, hard cash melted away.

'What are you going to do?'

'Never you mind what I'm going to do. I 'ave my methods. All I 'ave to say to you is that tomorrow or the day after Mr Bevan will be seated in our dining-'all with 'is feet under our table, replying according to his personal taste and preference, when I ask 'im if 'e'll 'ave 'ock or sherry. Brush all them crumbs carefully off the tablecloth, young blighted Albert – don't shuffle your feet – breathe softly through your nose – and close the door be'ind you when you've finished!'

'Oh, go and eat coke!' said Albert bitterly. But he said it to his immortal soul, not aloud. The lad's spirit was broken.

Keggs, the processes of digestion completed, presented himself before Lord Belpher in the billiard-room. Percy was alone. The house-party, so numerous on the night of the ball and on his birthday, had melted down now to reasonable proportions. The second and third cousins had retired, flushed and gratified, to obscure dens from which they had emerged, and the castle housed only the more prominent members of the family, always harder to dislodge than the small fry. The Bishop still remained, and the Colonel. Besides these, there were perhaps half a dozen more of the closer relations: to Lord Belpher's way of thinking, half a dozen too many. He was not fond of his family.

'Might I have a word with your lordship?'

'What is it, Keggs?'

Keggs was a self-possessed man, but he found it a little hard to begin. Then he remembered that once in the misty past he had seen Lord Belpher spanked for stealing jam, he himself having acted on that occasion as prosecuting attorney; and the memory nerved him.

'I earnestly 'ope that your lordship will not think that I am taking a liberty. I 'ave been in his lordship your father's service many years now, and the family honour is, if I may be pardoned for saying so, extremely near my 'eart. I 'ave known your lordship since you were a mere boy, and . . .'

Lord Belpher had listened with growing impatience to this preamble. His temper was seldom at its best these days, and the rolling periods annoyed him.

'Yes, yes, of course,' he said. 'What is it?'

Keggs was himself now. In his opening remarks he had simply been, as it were, winding up. He was now prepared to begin.

'Your lordship will recall inquiring of me on the night of the ball as to the *bona fides* of one of the temporary waiters? The one that stated that 'e was the cousin of young bli – of the boy Albert, the page? I have been making inquiries, your lordship, and I regret to say I find that the man was an impostor. He informed me that 'e was Albert's cousin, but Albert now informs me that 'e 'as no cousin in America. I am extremely sorry that this should have occurred, your lordship, and I 'ope you will attribute it to the bustle and haste inseparable from duties such as mine on such a occasion.'

'I know the fellow was an impostor. He was probably after the spoons!'

Keggs coughed.

'If I might be allowed to take a further liberty, your lordship, might I suggest that I am aware of the man's identity and of his motive for visiting the castle.'

He waited a little apprehensively. This was the crucial point in the interview. If Lord Belpher did not now freeze him with a glance and order him from the room, the danger would be past, and he could speak freely. His light blue eyes were expressionless as they met Percy's, but inwardly he was feeling much the same sensation as he was wont to experience when the family was in town and he had managed to slip off to Kempton Park or some other race-course and put some of his savings on a horse. As he felt when the racing steeds thundered down the straight, so did he feel now.

Astonishment showed in Lord Belpher's round face. Just as it was about to be succeeded by indignation, the butler spoke again.

'I am aware, your lordship, that it is not my place to offer suggestions as to the private and intimate affairs of the family I 'ave the honour to serve, but, if your lordship would consent to overlook the liberty, I think I could be of 'elp and assistance in a matter which is causing annoyance and unpleasantness to all.'

He invigorated himself with another dip into the waters of memory. Yes. The young man before him might be Lord Belpher, son of his employer and heir to all these great estates, but once he had seen him spanked.

Perhaps Percy also remembered this. Perhaps he merely felt that Keggs was a faithful old servant and, as such, entitled to thrust himself into the family affairs. Whatever his reasons, he now definitely lowered the barrier.

'Well,' he said, with a glance at the door to make sure that there were no witnesses to an act of which the aristocrat in him disapproved, 'go on!'

Keggs breathed freely. The danger-point was past.

''Aving a natural interest, your lordship,' he said, 'we of the Servants' 'All generally manage to become respectfully aware of whatever 'appens to be transpirin' above stairs. May I say that I became acquainted at an early stage with the trouble which your lordship is unfortunately 'aving with a certain party?'

Lord Belpher, although his whole being revolted against what practically amounted to hobnobbing with a butler, perceived that he had committed himself to the discussion. It revolted him to think that these delicate family secrets were the subject of conversation in menial circles, but it was too late to do anything now. And such was the whole-heartedness with which he had declared war upon George Bevan that, at this stage in the proceedings, his chief emotion was a hope that Keggs might have something sensible to suggest.

'I think, begging your lordship's pardon for making the remark, that you are acting injudicious. I 'ave been in service a great number of years, startin' as steward's room boy and rising to my present position, and I may say I 'ave 'ad experience during those years of several cases where the daughter or son of the 'ouse contemplated a misalliance, and all but one of the cases ended disastrously, your lordship, on account of the family trying opposition. It is my experience that opposition in matters of the 'eart is useless, feedin', as it, so to speak, does the flame. Young people, your lordship, if I may be pardoned for employing the expression in the present case, are naturally romantic and if you keep 'em away from a thing they sit and pity themselves and want it all the more. And in the end you may be sure they get it. There's no way of stoppin' them. I was not on sufficiently easy terms with the late Lord Worlingham to give 'im the benefit of my experience on the occasion when the Honourable Aubrey Pershore fell in love with the young person at the Gaiety Theatre. Otherwise I could 'ave told 'im he was not acting judicious. His lordship opposed the match in every way, and the young couple ran off and got married at a registrar's. It was the same when a young man who was tutor to 'er ladyship's brother attracted Lady Evelyn Walls, the only daughter of the Earl of Ackleton. In fact, your lordship, the only entanglement of the kind that came to a satisfactory conclusion in the whole of my personal experience was the affair of Lady Catherine Duseby, Lord Bridgefield's daughter, who injudiciously became infatuated with a roller-skating instructor.'

Lord Belpher had ceased to feel distantly superior to his companion. The butler's powerful personality hypnotized him. Long ere the harangue was ended, he was as a little child drinking in the utterances of a master. He bent forward eagerly. Keggs had broken off his remarks at the most interesting point.

'What happened?' inquired Percy.

'The young man,' proceeded Keggs, 'was a young man of considerable personal attractions, 'aving large brown eyes and a athletic lissom figure, brought about by roller-skating. It was no wonder, in the opinion of the Servants' 'All, that 'er ladyship should have found 'erself fascinated by him, particularly as I myself 'ad 'eard her observe at a full luncheon-table that roller-skating was in her opinion the only thing except her toy Pomeranian that made life worth living. But when she announced that she had become engaged to this young man, there was the greatest consternation. I was not, of course, privileged to be a participant at the many councils and discussions that ensued and took place, but I was aware that such transpired with great frequency. Eventually 'is lordship took the shrewd step of assuming acquiescence and inviting the young man to visit us in Scotland. And within ten days of his arrival, your lordship, the match was broken off. He went back to 'is roller-skating, and 'er ladyship took up visiting the poor and eventually contracted an altogether suitable alliance by marrying Lord Ronald Spofforth, the second son of his Grace the Duke of Gorbals and Strathbungo.'

'How did it happen?'

'Seein' the young man in the surroundings of 'er own 'ome, 'er ladyship soon began to see that she had taken too romantic a view of 'im previous, your lordship. 'E was one of the lower middle class, what is sometimes termed the bourjoisy, and 'is 'abits were not the 'abits of the class to which 'er ladyship belonged. 'E 'ad nothing in common with the rest of the 'ouse-party, and was injudicious in 'is choice of forks. The very first night at dinner 'e took a steel knife to the ontray, and I see 'er ladyship look at him very sharp, as much as to say that scales had fallen from 'er eyes. It didn't take 'er long after that to become convinced that 'er 'eart 'ad led 'er astray.'

'Then you think – ?'

'It is not for me to presume to offer anything but the most respectful advice, your lordship, but I should most certainly advocate a similar procedure in the present instance.'

Lord Belpher reflected. Recent events had brought home to him the magnitude of the task he had assumed when he had appointed himself the watcher of his sister's movements. The affair of the curate and the village blacksmith had shaken him both physically and spiritually. His feet were still sore, and his confidence in himself had waned considerably. The thought of having to continue his espionage indefinitely was not a pleasant one. How much simpler and more effective it would be to adopt the suggestion which had been offered to him.

' – I'm not sure you aren't right, Keggs.'

'Thank you, your lordship. I feel convinced of it.'

'I will speak to my father tonight.'

'Very good, your lordship. I am glad to have been of service.'

'Young blighted Albert,' said Keggs crisply, shortly after breakfast on the following morning, 'you're to take this note to Mr Bevan at the cottage down by Platt's farm, and you're to deliver it without playing any of your monkey-tricks, and you're to wait for an answer, and you're to bring that answer back to me, too, and to Lord Marshmoreton. And I may tell you, to save you the trouble of opening it with steam from the kitchen kettle, that I 'ave already done so. It's an invitation to dine with us tonight. So now you know. Look slippy!'

Albert capitulated. For the first time in his life he felt humble. He perceived how misguided he had been ever to suppose that he could pit his pygmy wits against this smooth-faced worker of wonders.

'Crikey!' he ejaculated.

It was all that he could say.

'And there's one more thing, young feller me lad,' added Keggs earnestly, 'don't you ever grow up to be such a fat'ead as our friend Percy. Don't forget I warned you.'

23

Life is like some crazy machine that is always going either too slow or too fast. From the cradle to the grave we alternate between the Sargasso Sea and the rapids – forever either becalmed or storm-tossed. It seemed to Maud, as she looked across the dinner-table in order to make sure for the twentieth time that it really was George Bevan who sat opposite her, that, after months in which nothing whatever had happened, she was now living through a period when everything was happening at once. Life, from being a broken-down machine, had suddenly begun to race.

To the orderly routine that stretched back to the time when she had been hurried home in disgrace from Wales there had succeeded a mad whirl of events, to which the miracle of tonight had come as a fitting climax. She had not begun to dress for dinner till somewhat late, and had consequently entered the drawing-room just as Keggs was announcing that the meal was ready. She had received her first shock when the love-sick Plummer, emerging from a mixed crowd of relatives and friends, had informed her that he was to take her in. She had not expected Plummer to be there, though he lived in the neighbourhood. Plummer, at their last meeting, had stated his intention of going abroad for a bit to mend his bruised heart: and it was a little disconcerting to a sensitive girl to find her victim popping up again like this. She did not know that, as far as Plummer was concerned, the whole affair was to be considered opened again. To Plummer, analysing the girl's motives in refusing him, there had come the idea that there was Another, and that this other must be Reggie Byng. From the first he had always looked upon Reggie as his worst rival. And now Reggie had bolted with the Faraday girl, leaving Maud in excellent condition, so it seemed to Plummer, to console herself with a worthier man. Plummer knew all about the Rebound and the part it plays in the affairs of the heart. His own breach-of-promise case two years earlier had been entirely due to the fact that the refusal of the youngest Devenish girl to marry him had caused him to rebound into the dangerous society of the second girl from the O.P. end of the first row in the 'Summertime is Kissing-time' number in the Alhambra revue. He had come to the castle tonight gloomy, but not without hope.

Maud's second shock eclipsed the first entirely. No notification had been given to her either by her father or by Percy of the proposed extension of the hand of hospitality to George, and the sight of him standing there talking to her aunt Caroline made her momentarily dizzy. Life, which for several days had had all the properties now of a dream, now of a nightmare, became more unreal than ever. She could conceive no explanation of George's presence. He could not be there – that was all there was to it; yet there undoubtedly he was. Her manner, as she accompanied Plummer down the stairs, took on such a dazed sweetness that her escort felt that in coming there that night he had done the wisest act of a lifetime studded but sparsely with wise acts. It seemed to Plummer that this girl had softened towards him. Certainly something had changed her. He could not know that she was merely wondering if she was awake.

George, meanwhile, across the table, was also having a little difficulty in adjusting his faculties to the progress of events. He had given up trying to imagine why he had been invited to this dinner, and was now endeavouring to find some theory which would square with the fact of Billie Dore being at the castle. At precisely this hour Billie, by rights, should have been putting the finishing touches on her make-up in a second-floor dressing-room at the Regal. Yet there she sat, very much at her ease in this aristocratic company, so quietly and unobtrusively dressed in some black stuff that at first he had scarcely recognized her. She was talking to the Bishop . . .

The voice of Keggs at his elbow broke in on his reverie.

'Sherry or 'ock, sir?'

George could not have explained why this reminder of the butler's presence should have made him feel better, but it did. There was something solid and tranquillizing about Keggs. He had noticed it before. For the first time the sensation of having been smitten over the head with some blunt instrument began to abate. It was as if Keggs by the mere intonation of his voice had said, 'All this no doubt seems very strange and unusual to you, but feel no alarm! *I* am here!'

George began to sit up and take notice. A cloud seemed to have cleared from his brain. He found himself looking on his fellow-diners as individuals rather than as a confused mass. The prophet Daniel, after the initial embarrassment of finding himself in the society of the lions had passed away, must have experienced a somewhat similar sensation.

He began to sort these people out and label them. There had been introductions in the drawing-room, but they had left him with a bewildered sense of having heard somebody recite a page from *Burke's Peerage*. Not since that day in the free library in London, when he had dived into that fascinating volume in order to discover Maud's identity, had he undergone such a rain of titles. He now took stock, to ascertain how many of these people he could identify.

The stock-taking was an absolute failure. Of all those present the only individuals he could swear to were his own personal little playmates with whom he had sported in other surroundings. There was Lord Belpher, for instance, eyeing him with a hostility that could hardly be called veiled. There was Lord Marshmoreton at the head of the table, listening glumly to the conversation of a stout woman with a pearl necklace, but who was that woman? Was it Lady Jane Allenby or Lady Edith Wade-Beverly or Lady Patricia Fowles? And who, above all, was the pie-faced fellow with the moustache talking to Maud?

He sought assistance from the girl he had taken in to dinner. She appeared, as far as he could ascertain from a short acquaintance, to be an amiable little thing. She was small and young and fluffy, and he had caught enough of her name at the moment of introduction to gather that she was plain 'Miss' Something – a fact which seemed to him to draw them together.

'I wish you would tell me who some of these people are,' he said, as she turned from talking to the man on her other side. 'Who is the man over there?'

'Which man?'

'The one talking to Lady Maud. The fellow whose face ought to be shuffled and dealt again.'

'That's my brother.'

That held George during the soup.

'I'm sorry about your brother,' he said rallying with the fish.

'That's very sweet of you.'

'It was the light that deceived me. Now that I look again, I see that his face has great charm.'

The girl giggled. George began to feel better.

'Who are some of the others? I didn't get your name, for instance. They shot it at me so quick that it had whizzed by before I could catch it.'

'My name is Plummer.'

George was electrified. He looked across the table with more vivid interest. The amorous Plummer had been just a Voice to him till now. It was exciting to see him in the flesh.

'And who are the rest of them?'

'They are all members of the family. I thought you knew them.'

'I know Lord Marshmoreton. And Lady Maud. And, of course, Lord Belpher.' He caught Percy's eye as it surveyed him coldly from the other side of the table, and nodded cheerfully. 'Great pal of mine, Lord Belpher.'

The fluffy Miss Plummer twisted her pretty face into a grimace of disapproval.

'I don't like Percy.'

'No!'

'I think he's conceited.'

'Surely not? What could he have to be conceited about?'

'He's stiff.'

'Yes, of course, that's how he strikes people at first. The first time I met him, I thought he was an awful stiff. But you should see him in his moments of relaxation. He's one of those fellows you have to get to know. He grows on you.'

'Yes, but look at that affair with the policeman in London. Everybody in the county is talking about it.'

'Young blood!' sighed George. 'Young blood! Of course, Percy is wild.'

'He must have been intoxicated.'

'Oh, undoubtedly,' said George.

Miss Plummer glanced across the table.

'Do look at Edwin!'

'Which is Edwin?'

'My brother, I mean. Look at the way he keeps staring at Maud. Edwin's awfully in love with Maud,' she rattled on with engaging frankness. 'At least, he thinks he is. He's been in love with a different girl every season since I came out. And now that Reggie Byng has gone and married Alice Faraday, he thinks he has a chance. You heard about that, I suppose?'

'Yes, I did hear something about it.'

'Of course, Edwin's wasting his time, really. I happen

to know' – Miss Plummer sank her voice to a whisper – 'I happen to know that Maud's awfully in love with some man she met in Wales last year, but the family won't hear of it.'

'Families are like that,' agreed George.

'Nobody knows who he is, but everybody in the county knows all about it. Those things get about, you know. Of course, it's out of the question. Maud will have to marry somebody awfully rich or with a title. Her family's one of the oldest in England you know.'

'So I understand.'

'It isn't as if she were the daughter of Lord Peebles, or somebody like that.'

'Why Lord Peebles?'

'Well, what I mean to say is,' said Miss Plummer, with a silvery echo of Reggie Byng, 'he made his money in whisky.'

'That's better than spending it that way,' argued George.

Miss Plummer looked puzzled. 'I see what you mean,' she said a little vaguely. 'Lord Marshmoreton is so different.'

'Haughty nobleman stuff, eh?'

'Yes.'

'So you think this mysterious man in Wales hasn't a chance?'

'Not unless he and Maud elope like Reggie Byng and Alice. Wasn't that exciting? Who would ever have suspected that Reggie had the dash to do a thing like that? Lord Marshmoreton's new secretary is very pretty, don't you think?'

'Which is she?'

'The girl in black with the golden hair.'

'Is she Lord Marshmoreton's secretary?'

'Yes. She's an American girl. I think she's much nicer than Alice Faraday. I was talking to her before dinner. Her name is Dore. Her father was a captain in the

American army, who died without leaving her a penny. He was the younger son of a very distinguished family, but his family disowned him because he married against their wishes.'

'Something ought to be done to stop these families,' said George. 'They're always up to something.'

'So Miss Dore had to go out and earn her own living. It must have been awful for her, mustn't it, having to give up society?'

'Did she give up society?'

'Oh, yes. She used to go everywhere in New York before her father died. I think American girls are wonderful. They have so much enterprise.'

George at the moment was thinking that it was in imagination that they excelled.

'I wish I could go out and earn my living,' said Miss Plummer. 'But the family won't dream of it.'

'The family again!' said George sympathetically. 'They're a perfect curse.'

'I want to go on the stage. Are you fond of the theatre?'

'Fairly.'

'I love it. Have you seen Hubert Broadleigh in "'Twas Once in Spring"?'

'I'm afraid I haven't.'

'He's wonderful. Have you seen Cynthia Dane in "A Woman's No"?'

'I missed that one too.'

'Perhaps you prefer musical pieces? I saw an awfully good musical comedy before I left town. It's called "Follow the Girl". It's at the Regal Theatre. Have you seen it?'

'I wrote it.'

'You – what!'

'That is to say, I wrote the music.'

'But the music's lovely,' gasped little Miss Plummer, as if the fact made his claim ridiculous. 'I've been humming it ever since.'

'I can't help that. I still stick to it that I wrote it.'

'You aren't *George* Bevan!'

'I am!'

'But – ' Miss Plummer's voice almost failed here – 'But I've been dancing to your music for years! I've got about fifty of your records on the Victrola at home.'

George blushed. However successful a man may be he can never get used to Fame at close range.

'Why, that trickly thing – you know, in the second act – is the darlingest thing I ever heard. I'm mad about it.'

'Do you mean the one that goes lumty-lumty-tum, tumty-tumtu-tum?'

'No, the one that goes ta-rumty-tum-tum, ta-rumty-tum. You know! The one about Granny dancing the shimmy.'

'I'm not responsible for the words, you know,' urged George hastily. 'Those are wished on me by the lyricist.'

'I think the words are splendid. Although poor popper thinks it's improper, Granny's always doing it and nobody can stop her! I loved it.' Miss Plummer leaned forward excitedly. She was an impulsive girl. 'Lady Caroline.'

Conversation stopped. Lady Caroline turned.

'Yes, Millie?'

'Did you know that Mr Bevan was *the* Mr Bevan?'

Everybody was listening now. George huddled pinkly in his chair. He had not foreseen this bally-hooing. Shadrach, Meschach, and Abednego combined had never felt a tithe of the warmth that consumed him. He was essentially a modest young man.

'*The* Mr Bevan?' echoed Lady Caroline coldly. It was painful to her to have to recognize George's existence on the same planet as herself. To admire him, as Miss Plummer apparently expected her to do, was a loathsome task. She cast one glance, fresh from the refrigerator, at the shrinking George, and elevated her aristocratic eyebrows.

Miss Plummer was not damped. She was at the hero-worshipping age, and George shared with the Messrs Douglas Fairbanks, Francis X. Bushman, and one or two tennis champions an imposing pedestal in her Hall of Fame.

'*You* know! *George* Bevan, who wrote the music of "Follow the Girl".'

Lady Caroline showed no signs of thawing. She had not heard of 'Follow the Girl'. Her attitude suggested that, while she admitted the possibility of George having disgraced himself in the manner indicated, it was nothing to her.

'And all those other things,' pursued Miss Plummer indefatigably. 'You must have heard his music on the Victrola.'

'Why, of course!'

It was not Lady Caroline who spoke, but a man further down the table. He spoke with enthusiasm.

'Of course, by Jove!' he said. 'The Schenectady Shimmy, by Jove, and all that! Ripping!'

Everybody seemed pleased and interested. Everybody, that is to say, except Lady Caroline and Lord Belpher. Percy was feeling that he had been tricked. He cursed the imbecility of Keggs in suggesting that this man should be invited to dinner. Everything had gone wrong. George was an undoubted success. The majority of the company were solid for him. As far as exposing his unworthiness in the eyes of Maud was concerned, the dinner had been a ghastly failure. Much better to have left him to lurk in his infernal cottage. Lord Belpher drained his glass moodily. He was seriously upset.

But his discomfort at that moment was as nothing to the agony which rent his tortured soul a moment later. Lord Marshmoreton, who had been listening with growing excitement to the chorus of approval, rose from his seat. He cleared his throat. It was plain that Lord Marshmoreton had something on his mind.

'Er . . .' he said.

The clatter of conversation ceased once more – stunned, as it always is at dinner parties when one of the gathering is seen to have assumed an upright position. Lord Marshmoreton cleared his throat again. His tanned face had taken on a deeper hue, and there was a look in his eyes which seemed to suggest that he was defying something or somebody. It was the look which Ajax had in his eyes when he defied the lightning, the look which nervous husbands have when they announce their intention of going round the corner to bowl a few games with the boys. One could not say definitely that Lord Marshmoreton looked pop-eyed. On the other hand, one could not assert truthfully that he did not. At any rate, he was manifestly embarrassed. He had made up his mind to a certain course of action on the spur of the moment, taking advantage, as others have done, of the trend of popular enthusiasm: and his state of mind was nervous but resolute, like that of a soldier going over the top. He cleared his throat for the third time, took one swift glance at his sister Caroline, then gazed glassily into the emptiness above her head.

'Take this opportunity,' he said rapidly, clutching at the tablecloth for support, 'take this opportunity of announcing the engagement of my daughter Maud to Mr Bevan. And,' he concluded with a rush, pouring back into his chair, 'I should like you all to drink their health!'

There was a silence that hurt. It was broken by two sounds, occurring simultaneously in different parts of the room. One was a gasp from Lady Caroline. The other was a crash of glass.

For the first time in a long unblemished career Keggs the butler had dropped a tray.

24

Out on the terrace the night was very still. From a steel-blue sky the stars looked down as calmly as they had looked on the night of the ball, when George had waited by the shrubbery listening to the wailing of the music and thinking long thoughts. From the dark meadows by the brook came the cry of a corncrake, its harsh note softened by distance.

'What shall we do?' said Maud. She was sitting on the stone seat where Reggie Byng had sat and meditated on his love for Alice Faraday and his unfortunate habit of slicing his approach-shots. To George, as he stood beside her, she was a white blur in the darkness. He could not see her face.

'I don't know!' he said frankly.

Nor did he. Like Lady Caroline and Lord Belpher and Keggs, the butler, he had been completely overwhelmed by Lord Marshmoreton's dramatic announcement. The situation had come upon him unheralded by any warning, and had found him unequal to it.

A choking sound suddenly proceeded from the whiteness that was Maud. In the stillness it sounded like some loud noise. It jarred on George's disturbed nerves.

'Please!'

'I c-can't help it!'

'There's nothing to cry about, really! If we think long enough, we shall find some way out all right. Please don't cry.'

'I'm not crying!' The choking sound became an unmistakable ripple of mirth. 'It's so absurd! Poor father getting up like that in front of everyone! Did you see Aunt Caroline's face?'

'It haunts me still,' said George. 'I shall never forget it. Your brother didn't seem any too pleased, either.'

Maud stopped laughing.

'It's an awful position,' she said soberly. 'The announcement will be in the *Morning Post* the day after tomorrow. And then the letters of congratulation will begin to pour in. And after that the presents. And I simply can't see how we can convince them all that there has been a mistake.' Another aspect of the matter struck her. 'It's so hard on you, too.'

'Don't think about me,' urged George. 'Heaven knows I'd give the whole world if we could just let the thing go on, but there's no use discussing impossibilities.' He lowered his voice. 'There's no use, either, in my pretending that I'm not going to have a pretty bad time. But we won't discuss that. It was my own fault. I came butting in on your life of my own free will, and, whatever happens, it's been worth it to have known you and tried to be of service to you.'

'You're the best friend I've ever had.'

'I'm glad you think that.'

'The best and kindest friend any girl ever had. I wish . . .' She broke off. 'Oh, well . . .'

There was a silence. In the castle somebody had begun to play the piano. Then a man's voice began to sing.

'That's Edwin Plummer,' said Maud. 'How badly he sings.'

George laughed. Somehow the intrusion of Plummer had removed the tension. Plummer, whether designedly and as a sombre commentary on the situation or because he was the sort of man who does sing that particular song, was chanting Tosti's 'Good-bye'. He was giving to its never very cheery notes a wailing melancholy all his own. A dog in the stables began to howl in sympathy, and with the sound came a curious soothing of George's nerves. He might feel broken-hearted later, but for the moment, with this double accompaniment, it was impossible for a man with humour in his soul to dwell on the deeper emotions. Plummer and his canine duettist had brought him to earth. He felt calm and practical.

'We'd better talk the whole thing over quietly,' he said. 'There's certain to be some solution. At the worst you can always go to Lord Marshmoreton and tell him that he spoke without a sufficient grasp of his subject.'

'I *could,*' said Maud, 'but, just at present, I feel as if I'd rather do anything else in the world. You don't realize what it must have cost father to defy Aunt Caroline openly like that. Ever since I was old enough to notice anything, I've seen how she dominated him. It was Aunt Caroline who really caused all this trouble. If it had only been father, I could have coaxed him to let me marry anyone I pleased. I wish, if you possibly can, you would think of some other solution.'

'I haven't had an opportunity of telling you,' said George, 'that I called at Belgrave Square, as you asked me to do. I went there directly I had seen Reggie Byng safely married.'

'Did you see him married?'

'I was best man.'

'Dear old Reggie! I hope he will be happy.'

'He will. Don't worry about that. Well, as I was saying, I called at Belgrave Square, and found the house shut up. I couldn't get any answer to the bell, though I kept my thumb on it for minutes at a time. I think they must have gone abroad again.'

'No, it wasn't that. I had a letter from Geoffrey this morning. His uncle died of apoplexy, while they were in Manchester on a business trip.' She paused. 'He left Geoffrey all his money,' she went on. 'Every penny.'

The silence seemed to stretch out interminably. The music from the castle had ceased. The quiet of the summer night was unbroken. To George the stillness had a touch of the sinister. It was the ghastly silence of the end of the world. With a shock he realized that even now he had been permitting himself to hope, futile as he recognized the hope to be. Maud had told him she loved another man. That should have been final. And yet somehow his indomitable subconscious self had refused to accept it as final. But this news ended everything. The only obstacle that had held Maud and this man apart was removed. There was nothing to prevent them marrying. George was conscious of a vast depression. The last strand of the rope had parted, and he was drifting alone out into the ocean of desolation.

'Oh!' he said, and was surprised that his voice sounded very much the same as usual. Speech was so difficult that it seemed strange that it should show no signs of effort. 'That alters everything, doesn't it?'

'He said in his letter that he wanted me to meet him in London and – talk things over, I suppose.'

'There's nothing now to prevent your going. I mean, now that your father has made this announcement, you are free to go where you please.'

'Yes, I suppose I am.'

There was another silence.

'Everything's so difficult,' said Maud.

'In what way?'

'Oh, I don't know.'

'If you are thinking of me,' said George, 'please don't. I know exactly what you mean. You are hating the thought of hurting my feelings. I wish you would look on me as having no feelings. All I want is to see you happy. As I said just now, it's enough for me to know that I've helped you. Do be reasonable about it. The fact that our engagement has been officially announced makes no difference in our relations to each other. As far as we two are concerned, we are exactly where we were the last time we met. It's no worse for me now than it was then to know that I'm not the man you love, and that there's somebody else you loved before you ever knew of my existence. For goodness' sake, a girl like you must be used to having men tell her that they love her and having to tell them that she can't love them in return.'

'But you're so different.'

'Not a bit of it. I'm just one of the crowd.'

'I've never known anybody quite like you.'

'Well, you've never known anybody quite like Plummer, I should imagine. But the thought of his sufferings didn't break your heart.'

'I've known a million men exactly like Edwin Plummer,' said Maud emphatically. 'All the men I ever have known have been like him – quite nice and pleasant and negative. It never seemed to matter refusing them. One knew that they would be just a little bit piqued for a week or two and then wander off and fall in love with somebody else. But you're different. You . . . matter.'

'That is where we disagree. My argument is that, where your happiness is concerned, I don't matter.'

Maud rested her chin on her hand, and stared out into the velvet darkness.

'You ought to have been my brother instead of Percy,' she said at last. 'What chums we should have been! And how simple that would have made everything!'

'The best thing for you to do is to regard me as an honorary brother. That will make everything simple.'

'It's easy to talk like that . . . No, it isn't. It's horribly hard. I know exactly how difficult it is for you to talk as you have been doing – to try to make me feel better by pretending the whole trouble is just a trifle . . . It's strange . . . We have only met really for a few minutes at a time, and three weeks ago I didn't know there was such a person as you, but somehow I seem to know everything you're thinking. I've never felt like that before with any man . . . Even Geoffrey . . . He always puzzled me . . .'

She broke off. The corncrake began to call again out in the distance.

'I wish I knew what to do,' she said with a catch in her voice.

'I'll tell you in two words what to do. The whole thing is absurdly simple. You love this man and he loves you, and all that kept you apart before was the fact that he could not afford to marry you. Now that he is rich, there is no obstacle at all. I simply won't let you look on me and my feelings as an obstacle. Rule me out altogether. Your father's mistake has made the situation a little more complicated than it need have been, but that can easily be remedied. Imitate the excellent example of Reggie Byng. He was in a position where it would have been embarrassing to announce what he intended to do, so he very sensibly went quietly off and did it and left everybody to find out after it was done. I'm bound to say I never looked on Reggie as a mastermind, but, when it came to find a way out of embarrassing situations, one has to admit he had the right idea. Do what he did!'

Maud started. She half rose from the stone seat. George could hear the quick intake of her breath.

'You mean – run away?'

'Exactly. Run away!'

An automobile swung round the corner of the castle from the direction of the garage, and drew up, purring, at the steps. There was a flood of light and the sound of voices, as the great door opened. Maud rose.

'People are leaving,' she said. 'I didn't know it was so late.' She stood irresolutely. 'I suppose I ought to go in and say good-bye. But I don't think I can.'

'Stay where you are. Nobody will see you.'

More automobiles arrived. The quiet of the night was shattered by the noise of their engines. Maud sat down again.

'I suppose they will think it very odd of me not being there.'

'Never mind what people think. Reggie Byng didn't.'

Maud's foot traced circles on the dry turf.

'What a lovely night,' she said. 'There's no dew at all.'

The automobiles snorted, tooted, back-fired, and passed away. Their clamour died in the distance, leaving the night a thing of peace and magic once more. The door of the castle closed with a bang.

'I suppose I ought to be going in now,' said Maud.

'I suppose so. And I ought to be there, too, politely making my farewells. But something seems to tell me that Lady Caroline and your brother will be quite ready to dispense with the formalities. I shall go home.'

They faced each other in the darkness.

'Would you really do that?' asked Maud. 'Run away, I mean, and get married in London.'

'It's the only thing to do.'

'But . . . can one get married as quickly as that?'

'At a registrar's? Nothing simpler. You should have seen Reggie Byng's wedding. It was over before one realized it had started. A snuffy little man in a black coat with a cold in his head asked a few questions, wrote a few words, and the thing was done.'

'That sounds rather . . . dreadful.'

'Reggie didn't seem to think so.'

'Unromantic, I mean . . . prosaic.'

'You would supply the romance.'

'Of course, one ought to be sensible. It is just the same as a regular wedding.'

'In effects, absolutely.'

They moved up the terrace together. On the gravel drive by the steps they paused.

'I'll do it!' said Maud.

George had to make an effort before he could reply. For all his sane and convincing arguments, he could not check a pang at this definite acceptance of them. He had begun to appreciate now the strain under which he had been speaking.

'You must,' he said. 'Well . . . good-bye.'

There was light on the drive. He could see her face. Her eyes were troubled.

'What will you do?' she asked.

'Do?'

'I mean, are you going to stay on in your cottage?'

'No, I hardly think I could do that. I shall go back to London tomorrow, and stay at the Carlton for a few days. Then I shall sail for America. There are a couple of pieces I've got to do for the Fall. I ought to be starting on them.'

Maud looked away.

'You've got your work,' she said almost inaudibly.

George understood her.

'Yes, I've got my work.'

'I'm glad.'

She held out her hand.

'You've been very wonderful . . . Right from the beginning . . . You've been . . . oh, what's the use of me saying anything?'

'I've had my reward. I've known you. We're friends, aren't we?'

'My best friend.'

'Pals?'

'Pals!'

They shook hands.

25

'I was never so upset in my life!' said Lady Caroline.

She had been saying the same thing and many other things for the past five minutes. Until the departure of the last guest she had kept an icy command of herself and shown an unruffled front to the world. She had even contrived to smile. But now, with the final automobile whirring homewards, she had thrown off the mask. The very furniture of Lord Marshmoreton's study seemed to shrink, seared by the flame of her wrath. As for Lord Marshmoreton himself, he looked quite shrivelled.

It had not been an easy matter to bring her erring brother to bay. The hunt had been in progress full ten minutes before she and Lord Belpher finally cornered the poor wretch. His plea, through the keyhole of the locked door, that he was working on the family history and could not be disturbed, was ignored; and now he was face to face with the avengers.

'I cannot understand it,' continued Lady Caroline. 'You know that for months we have all been straining every nerve to break off this horrible entanglement, and, just as we had begun to hope that something might be done, you announce the engagement in the most public manner. I think you must be out of your mind. I can hardly believe even now that this appalling thing has happened. I am hoping that I shall wake up and find it is all a nightmare. How you can have done such a thing, I cannot understand.'

'Quite!' said Lord Belpher.

If Lady Caroline was upset, there are no words in the

language that will adequately describe the emotions of Percy.

From the very start of this lamentable episode in high life, Percy had been in the forefront of the battle. It was Percy who had had his best hat smitten from his head in the full view of all Piccadilly. It was Percy who had suffered arrest and imprisonment in the cause. It was Percy who had been crippled for days owing to his zeal in tracking Maud across country. And now all his sufferings were in vain. He had been betrayed by his own father.

There was, so the historians of the Middle West tell us, a man of Chicago named Young, who once, when his nerves were unstrung, put his mother (unseen) in the chopping-machine, and canned her and labelled her 'Tongue'. It is enough to say that the glance of disapproval which Percy cast upon his father at this juncture would have been unduly severe if cast by the Young offspring upon their parent at the moment of confession.

Lord Marshmoreton had rallied from his initial panic. The spirit of revolt began to burn again in his bosom. Once the die is cast for revolution, there can be no looking back. One must defy, not apologize. Perhaps the inherited tendencies of a line of ancestors who, whatever their shortcomings, had at least known how to treat their women folk, came to his aid. Possibly there stood by his side in this crisis ghosts of dead and buried Marshmoretons, whispering spectral encouragement in his ear – the ghosts, let us suppose, of that earl who, in the days of the seventh Henry, had stabbed his wife with a dagger to cure her tendency to lecture him at night; or of that other earl who, at a previous date in the annals of the family, had caused two aunts and a sister to be poisoned apparently from a mere whim. At any rate, Lord Marshmoreton produced from some source sufficient courage to talk back.

'Silly nonsense!' he grunted. 'Don't see what you're making all this fuss about. Maud loves the fellow. I like the fellow. Perfectly decent fellow. Nothing to make a fuss about. Why shouldn't I announce the engagement?'

'You must be mad!' cried Lady Caroline. 'Your only daughter and a man nobody knows anything about!'

'Quite!' said Percy.

Lord Marshmoreton seized his advantage with the skill of an adroit debater.

'That's where you're wrong. I know all about him. He's a very rich man. You heard the way all those people at dinner behaved when they heard his name. Very celebrated man! Makes thousands of pounds a year. Perfectly suitable match in every way.'

'It is not a suitable match,' said Lady Caroline vehemently. 'I don't care whether this Mr Bevan makes thousands of pounds a year or twopence-ha'penny. The match is not suitable. Money is not everything.'

She broke off. A knock had come on the door. The door opened, and Billie Dore came in. A kind-hearted girl, she had foreseen that Lord Marshmoreton might be glad of a change of subject at about this time.

'Would you like me to help you tonight?' she asked brightly, 'I thought I would ask if there was anything you wanted me to do.'

Lady Caroline snatched hurriedly at her aristocratic calm. She resented the interruption acutely, but her manner, when she spoke, was bland.

'Lord Marshmoreton will not require your help tonight,' she said. 'He will not be working.'

'Good night,' said Billie.

'Good night,' said Lady Caroline.

Percy scowled a valediction.

'Money,' resumed Lady Caroline, 'is immaterial. Maud is in no position to be obliged to marry a rich man. What makes the thing impossible is that Mr Bevan is nobody. He comes from nowhere. He has no social standing whatsoever.'

'Don't see it,' said Lord Marshmoreton. 'The fellow's a thoroughly decent fellow. That's all that matters.'

'How can you be so pig-headed! You are talking like an imbecile. Your secretary, Miss Dore, is a nice girl. But how would you feel if Percy were to come to you and say that he was engaged to be married to her?'

'Exactly!' said Percy. 'Quite!'

Lord Marshmoreton rose and moved to the door. He did it with a certain dignity, but there was a strange hunted expression in his eyes.

'That would be impossible,' he said.

'Precisely,' said his sister. 'I am glad that you admit it.'

Lord Marshmoreton had reached the door, and was standing holding the handle. He seemed to gather strength from its support.

'I've been meaning to tell you about that,' he said.

'About what?'

'About Miss Dore. I married her myself last Wednesday,' said Lord Marshmoreton, and disappeared like a diving duck.

26

At a quarter past four in the afternoon, two days after the memorable dinner-party at which Lord Marshmoreton had behaved with so notable a lack of judgement, Maud sat in Ye Cosy Nooke, waiting for Geoffrey Raymond. He had said in his telegram that he would meet her there at four-thirty: but eagerness had brought Maud to the tryst a quarter of an hour ahead of time: and already the sadness of her surroundings was causing her to regret this impulsiveness. Depression had settled upon her spirit. She was aware of something that resembled foreboding.

Ye Cosy Nooke, as its name will immediately suggest to those who know their London, is a tea-shop in Bond Street, conducted by distressed gentlewomen. In London, when a gentlewoman becomes distressed – which she seems to do on the slightest provocation – she collects about her two or three other distressed gentlewomen, forming a quorum, and starts a tea-shop in the West-End, which she calls Ye Oak Leaf, Ye Olde Willow-Pattern, Ye Linden-Tree, or Ye Snug Harbour, according to personal taste. There, dressed in Tyrolese, Japanese, Norwegian, or some other exotic costume, she and her associates administer refreshments of an afternoon with a proud languor calculated to knock the nonsense out of the cheeriest customer. Here you will find none of the coarse bustle and efficiency of the rival establishments of Lyons and Co., nor the glitter and gaiety of Rumpelmayer's. These places have an atmosphere of their own. They rely for their effect on an insufficiency of light, an almost total lack of ventilation, a property chocolate cake which you are not supposed to cut, and the sad aloofness of their ministering angels. It is to be doubted whether there is anything in the world more damping to the spirit than a London tea-shop of this kind, unless it be another London tea-shop of the same kind.

Maud sat and waited. Somewhere out of sight a kettle bubbled in an undertone, like a whispering pessimist. Across the room two distressed gentlewomen in fancy dress leaned against the wall. They, too, were whispering. Their expressions suggested that they looked on life as low and wished they were well out of it, like the body upstairs. One assumed that there was a body upstairs. One cannot help it at these places. One's first thought on entering is that the lady assistant will approach one and ask in a hushed voice, 'Tea or chocolate? And would you care to view the remains?'

Maud looked at her watch. It was twenty past four. She could scarcely believe that she had only been there five minutes, but the ticking of the watch assured her that it had not stopped. Her depression deepened. Why had Geoffrey told her to meet him in a cavern of gloom like this instead of at the Savoy? She would have enjoyed the Savoy. But here she seemed to have lost beyond recovery the first gay eagerness with which she had set out to meet the man she loved.

Suddenly she began to feel frightened. Some evil spirit, possibly the kettle, seemed to whisper to her that she had been foolish in coming here, to cast doubts on what she had hitherto regarded as the one rock-solid fact in the world, her love for Geoffrey. Could she have changed since those days in Wales? Life had been so confusing of late. In the vividness of recent happenings those days in Wales seemed a long way off, and she herself different from the girl of a year ago. She found herself thinking about George Bevan . . .

It was a curious fact that, the moment she began to think of George Bevan, she felt better. It was as if she had lost her way in a wilderness and had met a friend. There was something so capable, so soothing about George. And how well he had behaved at that last interview. George seemed somehow to be part of her life. She could not imagine a life in which he had no share. And he was at this moment probably packing to return to America, and she would never see him again. Something stabbed at her heart. It was as if she were realizing now for the first time that he was really going.

She tried to rid herself of the ache at her heart by thinking of Wales. She closed her eyes, and found that that helped her to remember. With her eyes shut, she could bring it all back – that rainy day, the graceful, supple figure that had come to her out of the mist, those walks over the hills . . . If only Geoffrey would come! It was the sight of him that she needed.

'There you are!'

Maud opened her eyes with a start. The voice had sounded like Geoffrey's. But it was a stranger who stood by the table. And not a particularly prepossessing stranger. In the dim light of Ye Cosy Nooke, to which her opening eyes had not yet grown accustomed, all she could see of the man was that he was remarkably stout. She stiffened defensively. This was what a girl who sat about in tea-rooms alone had to expect.

'Hope I'm not late,' said the stranger, sitting down and breathing heavily. 'I thought a little exercise would do me good, so I walked.'

Every nerve in Maud's body seemed to come to life simultaneously. She tingled from head to foot. It was Geoffrey!

He was looking over his shoulder and endeavouring by snapping his fingers to attract the attention of the nearest distressed gentlewoman: and this gave Maud time to recover from the frightful shock she had received. Her dizziness left her: and, leaving, was succeeded by a panic dismay. This couldn't be Geoffrey! It was outrageous that it should be Geoffrey! And yet it undeniably was Geoffrey. For a year she had prayed that Geoffrey might be given back to her, and the gods had heard her prayer. They had given her back Geoffrey, and with a careless generosity they had given her twice as much of him as she had expected. She had asked for the slim Apollo whom she had loved in Wales, and this colossal changeling had arrived in his stead.

We all of us have our prejudices. Maud had a prejudice against fat men. It may have been the spectacle of her brother Percy, bulging more and more every year she had known him, that had caused this kink in her character. At any rate, it existed: and she gazed in sickened silence at Geoffrey. He had turned again now, and she was enabled to get a full and complete view of him. He was not merely stout. He was gross. The slim figure which had haunted her for a year had spread into a sea of waistcoat. The keen lines of his face had disappeared altogether. His cheeks were pink jellies.

One of the distressed gentlewomen had approached with a slow disdain, and was standing by the table, brooding on the corpse upstairs. It seemed a shame to bother her.

'Tea or chocolate?' she inquired proudly.

'Tea, please,' said Maud, finding her voice.

'One tea,' sighed the mourner.

'Chocolate for me,' said Geoffrey briskly, with the air of one discoursing on a congenial topic. 'I'd like plenty of whipped cream. And please see that it's hot.'

'One chocolate.'

Geoffrey pondered. This was no light matter that occupied him.

'And bring some fancy cakes – I like the ones with icing on them – and some tea-cake and buttered toast. Please see that there's plenty of butter on it.'

Maud shivered. This man before her was a man in whose lexicon there should have been no such word as butter, a man who should have called for the police had some enemy endeavoured to thrust butter upon him.

'Well,' said Geoffrey, leaning forward, as the haughty ministrant drifted away, 'you haven't changed a bit. To look at, I mean.'

'No?' said Maud.

'You're just the same. I think I' – he squinted down at his waistcoat – 'have put on a little weight. I don't know if you notice it?'

Maud shivered again. He thought he had put on a little weight, and didn't know if she had noticed it! She was oppressed by the eternal melancholy miracle of the fat man who does not realize that he has become fat.

'It was living on the yacht that put me a little out of condition,' said Geoffrey. 'I was on the yacht nearly all the time since I saw you last. The old boy had a Japanese cook and lived pretty high. It was apoplexy that got him. We had a great time touring about. We were on the Mediterranean all last winter, mostly at Nice.'

'I should like to go to Nice,' said Maud, for something to say. She was feeling that it was not only externally that Geoffrey had changed. Or had he in reality always been like this, commonplace and prosaic, and was it merely in her imagination that he had been wonderful?

'If you ever go,' said Geoffrey, earnestly, 'don't fail to lunch at the Hôtel Côte d'Azur. They give you the most amazing selection of *hors d'œuvres* you ever saw. Crayfish as big as baby lobsters! And there's a fish – I've forgotten its name, it'll come back to me – that's just like the Florida pompano. Be careful to have it broiled, not fried. Otherwise you lose the flavour. Tell the waiter you must have it broiled, with melted butter and a little parsley and some plain boiled potatoes. It's really astonishing. It's best to stick to fish on the Continent. People can say what they like, but I maintain that the French don't really understand steaks or any sort of red meat. The veal isn't bad, though I prefer our way of serving it. Of course, what the French are real geniuses at is the omelet. I remember, when we put in at Toulon for coal, I went ashore for a stroll, and had the most delicious omelet with chicken livers beautifully cooked, at quite a small, unpretentious place near the harbour. I shall always remember it.'

The mourner returned, bearing a laden tray, from which she removed the funeral bakemeats and placed them limply on the table. Geoffrey shook his head, annoyed.

'I particularly asked for plenty of butter on my toast!' he said. 'I hate buttered toast if there isn't lots of butter. It isn't worth eating. Get me a couple of pats, will you, and I'll spread it myself. Do hurry, please, before the toast gets cold. It's no good if the toast gets cold. They don't understand tea as a meal at these places,' he said to Maud, as the mourner withdrew. 'You have to go to the country to appreciate the real thing. I remember we lay off Lyme Regis down Devonshire way, for a few days, and I went and had tea at a farmhouse there. It was quite amazing! Thick Devonshire cream and home-made jam and cakes of every kind. This sort of thing here is just a farce. I do wish that woman would make haste with that butter. It'll be too late in a minute.'

Maud sipped her tea in silence. Her heart was like lead within her. The recurrence of the butter theme as a sort of *leitmotif* in her companion's conversation was fraying her nerves till she felt she could endure little more. She cast her mind's eye back over the horrid months and had a horrid vision of Geoffrey steadily absorbing butter, day after day, week after week – ever becoming more and more of a human keg. She shuddered.

Indignation at the injustice of Fate in causing her to give her heart to a man and then changing him into another and quite different man fought with a cold terror, which grew as she realized more and more clearly the magnitude of the mistake she had made. She felt that she must escape. And yet how could she escape? She had definitely pledged herself to this man. ('Ah!' cried Geoffrey gaily, as the pats of butter arrived. 'That's more like it!' He began to smear the toast. Maud averted her eyes.) She had told him that she loved him, that he was the whole world to her, that there never would be anyone else. He had come to claim her. How could she refuse him just because he was about thirty pounds overweight?

Geoffrey finished his meal. He took out a cigarette. ('No smoking, please!' said the distressed gentlewoman.) He put the cigarette back in its case. There was a new expression in his eyes, now, a tender expression. For the first time since they had met Maud seemed to catch a far-off glimpse of the man she had loved in Wales. Butter appeared to have softened Geoffrey.

'So you couldn't wait!' he said with pathos.

Maud did not understand.

'I waited over a quarter of an hour. It was you who were late.'

'I don't mean that. I am referring to your engagement. I saw the announcement in the *Morning Post*. Well, I hope you will let me offer you my best wishes. This Mr George Bevan, whoever he is, is lucky.'

Maud had opened her mouth to explain, to say that it was all a mistake. She closed it again without speaking.

'So you couldn't wait!' proceeded Geoffrey with gentle regret. 'Well, I suppose I ought not to blame you. You are at an age when it is easy to forget. I had no right to hope that you would be proof against a few months' separation. I expected too much. But it is ironical, isn't it! There was I, thinking always of those days last summer when we were everything to each other, while you had forgotten me – Forgotten me!' sighed Geoffrey. He picked a fragment of cake absently off the tablecloth and inserted it in his mouth.

The unfairness of the attack stung Maud to speech.

She looked back over the months, thought of all she had suffered, and ached with self-pity.

'I hadn't,' she cried.

'You hadn't? But you let this other man, this George Bevan, make love to you.'

'I didn't! That was all a mistake.'

'A mistake?'

'Yes. It would take too long to explain, but . . .' She stopped. It had come to her suddenly, in a flash of clear vision, that the mistake was one which she had no desire to correct. She felt like one who, lost in a jungle, comes out after long wandering into the open air. For days she had been thinking confusedly, unable to interpret her own emotions: and now everything had abruptly become clarified. It was as if the sight of Geoffrey had been the key to a cipher. She loved George Bevan, the man she had sent out of her life for ever. She knew it now, and the shock of realization made her feel faint and helpless. And, mingled with the shock of realization, there came to her the mortification of knowing that her aunt, Lady Caroline, and her brother, Percy, had been right after all. What she had mistaken for the love of a lifetime had been, as they had so often insisted, a mere infatuation, unable to survive the spectacle of a Geoffrey who had been eating too much butter and had put on flesh.

Geoffrey swallowed his piece of cake, and bent forward.

'Aren't you engaged to this man Bevan?'

Maud avoided his eye. She was aware that the crisis had arrived, and that her whole future hung on her next words.

And then Fate came to her rescue. Before she could speak, there was an interruption.

'Pardon me,' said a voice. 'One moment!'

So intent had Maud and her companion been on their own affairs that neither of them observed the entrance of a third party. This was a young man with mouse-coloured hair and a freckled, badly shaven face which seemed undecided whether to be furtive or impudent. He had small eyes, and his costume was a blend of the flashy and the shabby. He wore a bowler hat, tilted a little rakishly to one side, and carried a small bag, which he rested on the table between them.

'Sorry to intrude, miss.' He bowed gallantly to Maud, 'but I want to have a few words with Mr Spenser Gray here.'

Maud, looking across at Geoffrey, was surprised to see that his florid face had lost much of its colour. His mouth was open, and his eyes had taken a glassy expression.

'I think you have made a mistake,' she said coldly. She disliked the young man at sight. 'This is Mr Raymond.'

Geoffrey found speech.

'Of course I'm Mr Raymond!' he cried angrily. 'What do you mean by coming and annoying us like this?'

The young man was not discomposed. He appeared to be used to being unpopular. He proceeded as though there had been no interruption. He produced a dingy card.

'Glance at that,' he said. 'Messrs Willoughby and Son, Solicitors. I'm son. The guv'nor put this little matter into my hands. I've been looking for you for days, Mr Gray, to hand you this paper.' He opened the bag like a conjurer performing a trick, and brought out a stiff document of legal aspect. 'You're a witness, miss, that I've served the papers. You know what this is, of course?' he said to Geoffrey. 'Action for breach of promise of marriage. Our client, Miss Yvonne Sinclair, of the Regal Theatre, is suing you for ten thousand pounds. And, if you ask me,' said the young man with genial candour, dropping the professional manner, 'I don't mind telling you, I think it's a walk-over! It's the best little action for breach we've handled for years.' He became professional again. 'Your lawyers will no doubt communicate with us in due course. And, if you take my advice,' he concluded, with another of his swift changes of manner, 'you'll get 'em to settle out of court, for, between me and you and the lamp-post, you haven't an earthly!'

Geoffrey had started to his feet. He was puffing with outraged innocence.

'What the devil do you mean by this?' he demanded. 'Can't you see you've made a mistake? My name is not Gray. This lady has told you that I am Geoffrey Raymond!'

'Makes it all the worse for you,' said the young man imperturbably, 'making advances to our client under an assumed name. We've got letters and witnesses and the whole bag of tricks. And how about this photo?' He dived into the bag again. 'Do you recognize that, miss?'

Maud looked at the photograph. It was unmistakably Geoffrey. And it had evidently been taken recently, for it showed the later Geoffrey, the man of substance. It was a full-length photograph and across the stout legs was written in a flowing hand the legend, 'To Babe from her little Pootles'. Maud gave a shudder and handed it back to the young man just as Geoffrey, reaching across the table, made a grab for it.

'I recognize it,' she said.

Mr Willoughby junior packed the photograph away in his bag, and turned to go.

'That's all for today, then, I think,' he said, affably.

He bowed again in his courtly way, tilted the hat a little more to the left, and having greeted one of the distressed gentlewomen who loitered limply in his path with a polite 'If *you* please, Mabel!' which drew upon him a freezing stare of which he seemed oblivious, he passed out, leaving behind him strained silence.

Maud was the first to break it.

'I think I'll be going,' she said.

The words seemed to rouse her companion from his stupor.

'Let me explain!'

'There's nothing to explain.'

'It was just a . . . it was just a passing . . . It was nothing . . . nothing.'

'Pootles!' murmured Maud.

Geoffrey followed her as she moved to the door.

'Be reasonable!' pleaded Geoffrey. 'Men aren't saints! It was nothing! . . . Are you going to end . . . everything . . . just because I lost my head?'

Maud looked at him with a smile. She was conscious of an overwhelming relief. The dim interior of Ye Cosy Nooke no longer seemed depressing. She could have kissed this unknown 'Babe' whose businesslike action had enabled her to close a regrettable chapter in her life with a clear conscience.

'But you haven't only lost your head, Geoffrey,' she said. 'You've lost your figure as well.'

She went out quickly. With a convulsive bound Geoffrey started to follow her, but was checked before he had gone a yard.

There are formalities to be observed before a patron can leave Ye Cosy Nooke.

'*If* you please!' said a distressed gentlewomanly voice.

The lady whom Mr Willoughby had addressed as Mabel – erroneously, for her name was Ernestine – was standing beside him with a slip of paper.

'Six and twopence,' said Ernestine.

For a moment this appalling statement drew the unhappy man's mind from the main issue.

'Six and twopence for a cup of chocolate and a few cakes?' he cried, aghast. 'It's robbery!'

'Six and twopence, please!' said the queen of the bandits with undisturbed calm. She had been through this sort of thing before. Ye Cosy Nooke did not get many customers; but it made the most of those it did get.

'Here!' Geoffrey produced a half-sovereign. 'I haven't time to argue!'

The distressed brigand showed no gratification. She had the air of one who is aloof from worldly things. All she wanted was rest and leisure – leisure to meditate upon the body upstairs. All flesh is as grass. We are here today and gone tomorrow. But there, beyond the grave, is peace.

'Your change?' she said.

'Damn the change!'

'You are forgetting your hat.'

'Damn my hat!'

Geoffrey dashed from the room. He heaved his body through the door. He lumbered down the stairs.

Out in Bond Street the traffic moved up and the traffic moved down. Strollers strolled upon the sidewalks.

But Maud had gone.

27

In his bedroom at the Carlton Hotel George Bevan was packing. That is to say, he had begun packing; but for the last twenty minutes he had been sitting on the side of the bed, staring into a future which became bleaker and bleaker the more he examined it. In the last two days he had been no stranger to these grey moods, and they had become harder and harder to dispel. Now, with the steamer-trunk before him gaping to receive its contents, he gave himself up whole-heartedly to gloom.

Somehow the steamer-trunk, with all that it implied of partings and voyagings, seemed to emphasize the fact that he was going out alone into an empty world. Soon he would be on board the liner, every revolution of whose engines would be taking him farther away from where his heart would always be. There were moments when the torment of this realization became almost physical.

It was incredible that three short weeks ago he had been a happy man. Lonely, perhaps, but only in a vague, impersonal way. Not lonely with this aching loneliness that tortured him now. What was there left for him? As regards any triumphs which the future might bring in connexion with his work, he was, as Mac the stage-door keeper had said, 'blarzy'. Any success he might have would be but a stale repetition of other successes which he had achieved. He would go on working of course, but –. The ringing of the telephone bell across the room jerked him back to the present. He got up with a muttered malediction. Someone calling up again from the theatre probably. They had been doing it all the time since he had announced his intention of leaving for America by Saturday's boat.

'Hullo?' he said wearily.

'Is that George?' asked a voice. It seemed familiar, but all female voices sound the same over the telephone.

'This is George,' he replied. 'Who are you?'

'Don't you know my voice?'

'I do not.'

'You'll know it quite well before long. I'm a great talker.'

'Is that Billie?'

'It is not Billie, whoever Billie may be. I am female, George.'

'So is Billie.'

'Well, you had better run through the list of your feminine friends till you reach me.'

'I haven't any feminine friends.'

'None?'

'No.'

'That's odd.'

'Why?'

'You told me in the garden two nights ago that you looked on me as a pal.'

George sat down abruptly. He felt boneless.

'Is – is that *you*?' he stammered. 'It can't be – Maud!'

'How clever of you to guess. George, I want to ask you one or two things. In the first place, are you fond of butter?'

George blinked. This was not a dream. He had just bumped his knee against the corner of the telephone table, and it still hurt most convincingly. He needed the evidence to assure himself that he was awake.

'Butter?' he queried. 'What do you mean?'

'Oh, well, if you don't even know what butter means, I expect it's all right. What is your weight, George?'

'About a hundred and eighty pounds. But I don't understand.'

'Wait a minute.' There was a silence at the other end of the wire. 'About thirteen stone,' said Maud's voice. 'I've been doing it in my head. And what was it this time last year?'

'About the same, I think. I always weigh about the same.'

'How wonderful! George!'

'Yes?'

'This is very important. Have you ever been in Florida?'

'I was there one winter.'

'Do you know a fish called the pompano?'

'Yes.'

'Tell me about it.'

'How do you mean? It's just a fish. You eat it.'

'I know. Go into details.'

'There aren't any details. You just eat it.'

The voice at the other end of the wire purred with approval.

'I never heard anything so splendid. The last man who mentioned pompano to me became absolutely lyrical about sprigs of parsley and melted butter. Well, that's that. Now, here's another very important point. How about wall-paper?'

George pressed his unoccupied hand against his forehead. This conversation was unnerving him.

'I didn't get that,' he said.

'Didn't get what?'

'I mean, I didn't quite catch what you said that time. It sounded to me like "What about wall-paper?"'

'It *was* "What about wall-paper?" Why not?'

'But,' said George weakly, 'it doesn't make any sense.'

'Oh, but it does. I mean, what about wall-paper for your den?'

'My den?'

'Your den. You must have a den. Where do you suppose

you're going to work, if you don't? Now, my idea would be some nice quiet grass-cloth. And, of course, you would have lots of pictures and books. And a photograph of me. I'll go and be taken specially. Then there would be a piano for you to work on, and two or three really comfortable chairs. And – well, that would be about all, wouldn't it?'

George pulled himself together.

'Hullo!' he said.

'Why do you say "Hullo"?'

'I forgot I was in London. I should have said "Are you there?"'

'Yes, I'm here.'

'Well, then, what does it all mean?'

'What does what mean?'

'What you've been saying – about butter and pompanos and wall-paper and my den and all that? I don't understand.'

'How stupid of you! I was asking you what sort of wall-paper you would like in your den after we were married and settled down.'

George dropped the receiver. It clashed against the side of the table. He groped for it blindly.

'Hullo!' he said.

'Don't say "Hullo!". It sounds so abrupt!'

'What did you say then?'

'I said "Don't say Hullo!"'

'No, before that! Before that! You said something about getting married.'

'Well, aren't we going to get married? Our engagement is announced in the *Morning Post*.'

'But – But – '

'George!' Maud's voice shook. 'Don't tell me you are going to jilt me!' she said tragically. 'Because, if you are, let me know in time, as I shall want to bring an action for breach of promise. I've just met such a capable young man who will look after the whole thing for me. He wears a bowler hat on the side of his head and calls waitresses "Mabel". Answer "yes" or "no". Will you marry me?'

'But – But – how about – I mean, what about – I mean how about – ?'

'Make up your mind what you do mean.'

'The other fellow!' gasped George.

A musical laugh was wafted to him over the wire.

'What about him?'

'Well, *what* about him?' said George.

'Isn't a girl allowed to change her mind?' said Maud.

George yelped excitedly. Maud gave a cry.

'Don't sing!' she said. 'You nearly made me deaf.'

'Have you changed your mind?'

'Certainly I have!'

'And you really think – You really want – I mean, you really want – You really think – '

'Don't be so incoherent!'

'Maud!'

'Well?'

'Will you marry me?'

'Of course I will.'

'Gosh!'

'What did you say?'

'I said Gosh! And listen to me, when I say Gosh, I *mean* Gosh! Where are you? I must see you. Where can we meet? I want to see you! For Heavens' sake, tell me where you are. I want to see you! Where are you? Where are you?'

'I'm downstairs.'

'Where? Here at the Carlton?'

'Here at the Carlton!'

'Alone?'

'Quite alone.'

'You won't be long!'

He hung up the receiver, and bounded across the room to where his coat hung over the back of a chair. The edge of the steamer-trunk caught his shin.

'Well,' said George to the steamer-trunk, 'and what are *you* butting in for? Who wants *you*, I should like to know!'

The P G Wodehouse Society (UK)

The P G Wodehouse Society (UK) was formed in 1997 and exists to promote the enjoyment of the works of the greatest humorist of the twentieth century.

The Society publishes a quarterly magazine, *Wooster Sauce*, which features articles, reviews, archive material and current news. It also publishes an occasional newsletter in the *By The Way* series which relates a single matter of Wodehousean interest. Members are rewarded in their second and subsequent years by receiving a specially produced text of a Wodehouse magazine story which has never been collected into one of his books.

A variety of Society events are arranged for members including regular meetings at a London club, a golf day, a cricket match, a Society dinner, and walks round Bertie Wooster's London. Meetings are also arranged in other parts of the country.

Membership enquiries

Membership of the Society is available to applicants from all parts of the world. The cost of a year's membership in 1999 was £15. Enquiries and requests for an application form should be addressed in writing to the Membership Secretary, Helen Murphy, at 16 Herbert Street, Plaistow, London E13 8BE, or write to the Editor of *Wooster Sauce*, Tony Ring, at 34 Longfield Road, Great Missenden, Bucks HP16 0EG.

You can visit their website at:
http://www.eclipse.co.uk/wodehouse

When Maud Marsh flings herself into George Bevan's cab in Piccadilly, he starts believing in damsels in distress

George traces his mysterious travelling companion to Belpher Castle, home of Lord Marshmoreton, where things become severely muddled. Maud's aunt, Lady Caroline Byng, wants Maud to marry Reggie, her step-son. Maud, meanwhile, is known to be in love with an unknown American she met in Wales. So when George turns up speaking American, a nasty case of mistaken identity breaks out. In fact the scene is set for the perfect Wodehouse comedy of errors.

PENGUIN
Fiction

ISBN 0-140-01599-X
9 780140 015997
U.K. £5.99 CAN. $11.99
U.S.A. $8.00
www.penguin.com
Cover illustration: David Hitch